For my husband — the one who helped me find my light in a world
that once felt so dark.
And for my readers — for those who have danced with their demons and survived the song.
May your fire never fade?

The first time I learned to be quiet was the night my father threw a bottle across the room. It shattered against the wall above my head, glass raining down into my hair. I didn't cry. Crying made it worse. He was drunk, like always, his voice thick with anger that never needed a reason. My mother was gone, she was always gone when he was like this, slipping out the door before the storm broke. That left me. Small. Helpless. A target he couldn't miss. I crawled under my bed, pressing my hands to my ears. My heart thudded so loud I was sure he could hear it. The floorboards shook with his footsteps, heavy and uneven, pacing back and forth as he cursed at the world, cursed at me, cursed at everything he'd lost. I learned not to move. Not to breathe too loud. To make myself invisible. That night, I swore I'd grow up strong enough that no one could ever corner me again. But the body doesn't forget. Even years later, even with my name on glass doors and men twice my age afraid of me in courtrooms, that little girl still whispers in the dark. She reminds me what it felt like to hide, to wait for the storm to pass, to pray I'd be left in one piece. And maybe that's why, when I saw him years later—the man the city feared the way I once feared my father—I didn't turn away. Because I knew what it was to live in fear. And I knew, deep down, that the most dangerous men are often the ones we can't stop ourselves from looking at twice.

Chapter 1— The Sentence of Forever

The office had gone quiet hours ago.

Thirty-two floors above the city, Vale & Associates was a skeleton of glass and marble, the hum of copiers and clipped voices long since gone. Claudia Vale sat alone in her corner office, a pool of lamplight spreading across the last of the documents on her desk. The city pressed its reflection into the darkened windows behind her, a restless giant always moving, always hungry.

Her pen scratched one final signature across a motion, the ink crisp against the paper. She capped it, slid the document into a red folder, and leaned back.

The brass plate on her drawer caught the light. State v. Dominguez.

Claudia shut the folder into place with more force than necessary. Paper was safer than sleep. Sleep brought her back under a bed, counting breaths while glass rained from a bottle her father had thrown.

That girl wasn't here anymore. Claudia Vale, Managing Partner, was.

She gathered her briefcase, locked the office behind her, and walked across the deserted lobby. Her heels clicked against the marble, each step echoing like a metronome in the silence. At the private elevator, she scanned her fob. The doors slid open with a soft sigh.

Chrome walls reflected her back to herself: high bun, white blouse, jawline sharp as the corners of her folder. Other people called her intimidating. She called it necessary.

The elevator dropped. Claudia breathed in counts of four, the ritual her therapist had once prescribed. It didn't banish the ghosts, but it made them orderly.

When the doors opened, summer heat rolled in heavy and damp. At midnight, the city had its own pulse: sirens two blocks over, a train groaning across the viaduct, laughter spilling from a corner bar. Claudia adjusted her grip on the briefcase and started toward the parking garage a block and a half away.

Her shoes tapped steadily. Shadows tested her. She let them.

Halfway down the block, the laughter cut sharper. Male voices, too loud, too casual, bouncing off the walls of the street ahead. Claudia didn't quicken her pace. Didn't cross the street. Fear made you prey. She had sworn off prey.

Still, when the laughter thinned and died, her skin prickled.

He was there.

Not leaning against a wall. Not pretending to smoke. Just standing at the center of the group like gravity itself, the rest of them orbiting without realizing why. Tattoos inked his arms, crawling from wrist to sleeve in black and green. A thin scar traced the edge of his jaw.

He didn't move, but the air bent toward him.

Claudia didn't know his name yet, but he wore it the way other men wore knives.

The first man grinned too wide, singsong in his tone. "Late night, huh, lady lawyer?"

Claudia kept her eyes forward. "Evening."

The others chuckled. But the leader, the one who didn't have to ask for attention, shifted just enough that the sidewalk narrowed near him. Not blocking her. Just making her choose.

"You work in that tower," he said. His voice was low, unhurried, like he had all the time in the world. "Vale & Associates."

Her grip on the briefcase tightened. “You like reading building directories?”

He tilted his head. “Your name’s the only one still glowing after midnight. Easy guess.”

A ripple moved through the men behind him. They were watching her the way dogs watch their leader’s eyes.

Claudia’s shoes tapped closer. “Excuse me.”

He shifted—fraction of an inch—forcing proximity. He wasn’t tall enough to tower, but his stillness was heavier than height. His eyes swept her face, then her balance on the sidewalk, then the way she carried tension on her shoulders.

“What’s your name?” he asked.

“Late.”

The corner of his mouth twitched. “Late’s not a name.”

“It is tonight.”

That earned a real smile—small, restrained, like he didn’t want the others to see it.

One of the men behind him laughed too loud, trying to fill the silence. Angelo didn’t turn his head, but the man quieted instantly.

Claudia stepped past. The air between them charged her skin.

“Busy night, Claudia,” he said.

Her heart lurched. She hadn’t told him her name.

She didn’t slow. She reached the corner, kept walking. Her car was a block away.

But when she slid into the driver's seat, phone buzzing in the console, she flipped it over.

Unknown Number: Careful, Claudia. The calendar won't miss you. Some people might.

Her pulse pounded. She typed back before she could think.

Lose this number.

The dots appeared. Disappeared. Appeared again.

Unknown Number: You are first.
The next morning, Claudia walked into the office at eight sharp, eyes on the folder she carried. She had convinced herself the message was nothing more than street theater. A warning meant to scare.

By eleven, her receptionist buzzed. "Ms. Vale? A Mr. Angelo Romano is here. Says he's a potential client. No appointment."

"Tell him we're booking three weeks out."

"He says he only needs three minutes. And he said…" A pause. "He said you already gave him two last night."

Claudia froze.

Through her glass office door, she saw him. Clean T-shirt under a gray jacket. Tattoos hidden under cuffs. Scar sharper in daylight.

Angelo.

Claudia pressed the intercom. "Send him in." The door shut behind him with a click that felt louder than it was. Claudia didn't stand. Power, she'd learned long ago, comes from stillness.

"Three minutes," she said.

Angelo sat across from her without slouching. His presence filled the office like smoke— calm, deliberate, impossible to ignore. His eyes moved over the diplomas on her wall, the framed cityscape behind her desk, the neat stack of motions waiting for court. Not impressed. Assessing.

"You did your hair differently," he said.

Claudia arched one brow. "You noticed?"

"I notice everything." He leaned forward, elbows on his knees. "Calendar still lying?"

Her pulse jumped. She forced her expression flat. "You came here to talk about my planner?"

"I came here," Angelo said evenly, "to give you two pieces of advice. First: don't use the garage tonight. Second: the Dominguez case isn't what you think."

Her grip on the pen in her hand tightened until it threatened to snap. "You're threatening me in my office. That's a poor choice."

"Not a threat." His gaze didn't waver. "A warning."

"You think I'm the type who folds under warnings?"

"I think you're the type who knows when a floorboard is about to break."

For a moment, silence stretched. Claudia hated that she couldn't hear the building's usual hum over the beat of her heart.

"You have one minute left," she said.

Angelo reached into his jacket slowly and set a card on her desk. Thick white stock, no name, just a number and a single line of text: When the calendar lies.

Claudia didn't touch it. "You like theatrics."

"I like survival." He stood, scar pulling faintly at his jaw. "Skip the garage, Claudia. That's the last time I'll repeat myself."

He left without waiting for dismissal.

The card sat on her desk like a loaded gun.

By noon, Claudia knew Angelo had been right.

From her office window she saw the flashing lights of a tow truck idling at the garage entrance, police officers jotting notes beside a sedan with its windshield smashed in. A security guard waved cars past, directing them away from the top levels.

Someone hadn't skipped the garage.

Claudia set her coffee down and stared at the scene until her chest tightened. The phrase replayed: Careful, Claudia. The calendar won't miss you.

Back at her desk, her receptionist slipped a note under the door. Chain of custody update—please confirm receipt. On the back, in faint pencil, a single word: Careful.

This time, the handwriting was familiar.

She locked her office door, picked up the phone, and called the clerk. "Who handled the
Dominguez packet yesterday?"

"Khan stamped it, I logged it," the clerk said briskly. Then her voice faltered. "And…
Romano."

Claudia's throat dried. "Angelo Romano?"

"That's what he signed. Brought in a subpoena. The deputy recognized him, so I didn't argue."

Claudia thanked her, hung up, and stared at the card still sitting on her desk. She dialed the number with steady hands.

Angelo answered on the second ring.

"You were in the clerk's office," she said. "Why?"

"Because your case isn't as clean as you think."

"Dominguez?"

"All of them." A pause. "But him first."

"Then stop talking in riddles," Claudia snapped. "Give me proof."

Silence. Then: "Rooftop. Ten minutes. No cameras."

The line went dead.

Claudia should have deleted the number. Instead, she grabbed her coat, slipped the card into her pocket, and took the stairs.

The rooftop was mostly gravel, scattered HVAC units, and a view of the river cutting silver through the city. Angelo stood near the ledge, jacket unbuttoned, hands loose at his sides. He didn't turn until she was close enough to smell faint smoke on him, though he wasn't smoking.

"You came," he said.

"I want proof, not poetry."

He studied for a long moment. "You think I'm your enemy. Maybe I am. But not tonight.
Not when someone else wants you scared."

"Scared isn't in my vocabulary."

"Sure, it is. You just call it something else."

He handed her a folded photo. Grainy security footage—warehouse exterior, timestamped. Claudia's eyes narrowed.

"The night Dominguez's alibi says he was at his cousin's," Angelo said. "Camera was
'Malfunctioning.' Except here it is. Proof he wasn't."

She looked up. "How do you have this?"

"Because I know where to look when the city pretends not to see."

"Why show me?"

Angelo stepped closer. Not touching, just near enough that the warmth of him broke through the rooftop chill. "Because you don't run when bottles break. Because you've already lived through worse."

Her breath hitched before she could stop it.

"Claudia," he said softly, her name a weight and a promise all at once, "skip the garage again tonight."

She wanted to demand answers. Wanted to push him back. Instead, for one reckless heartbeat, she let him brush his fingers against her wrist. Not a grip. Not a claim. Just steadying.

It was more dangerous than any threat.

Chapter 2— The Red Folder

The garage was too empty. Too quiet. Concrete always echoed, but tonight every sound came back larger, meaner, as if the walls wanted me to remember what silence really meant.

I walked steady, heels clicking against painted numbers 3A, 3B, 3C—each step rehearsed calm. Inside, my pulse chased itself ragged.

At my car I slid behind the wheel and slammed the door. The noise ricocheted and thinned out in the distance. My hands rested on the wheel like stone, but my chest was a drum.

He said my name.

There were explanations. The gold letters on the office door. The website. Any gossiping clerk at the courthouse. A dozen harmless ways.

But it hadn't sounded harmless when he said it. It had sounded like ownership.

The engine turned over, smoothly. Relief hummed through me. I started down the spiral ramp, eyes sharp on mirrors, when the phone buzzed against the console. I braked too hard, seatbelt cutting across my collarbone.

Unknown Number: Careful, Clara. The calendar won't miss you. Some people might.

My blood turned thin. I forced my fingers steady.

Me: Lose this number.

The dots appeared. Paused. Appeared again.

Unknown Number: You are first.

I tossed the phone onto the passenger seat like it had teeth.

Out on the street, the city was jaundiced and half-asleep, sirens a lullaby for no one. I couldn't help it—I glanced at the corner where he had stood. Empty now, but absence has weight.

By the time I reached my penthouse, the sky was bruising with the first smear of dawn. I double-locked the door, dropped my keys, and poured water into a glass. It sat untouched.

The mirror in the hallway showed me perfect—silk blouse crisp, hair pinned, mouth firm. Clara Vale, CEO. Untouchable. But when I blinked, I saw another reflection overlaid knees drawn to chest under a bed, glass raining from above, a mother slipping out the back door.

I pressed a palm to the cool mirror. Not her anymore.

The phone buzzed again.

Unknown Number: You were seven the first time you hid under a bed. The bottle didn't miss you by accident. He never missed anything by accident.

My breath caught sharp in my throat. That memory wasn't in any report. It was mine alone. The weight of it bent me for one long moment before I straightened.

I escaped from work. Routine. Evidence. Facts. The Dominguez file waited on the bench. I cracked it open, familiar pages stacked clean, comfort in order.

Until page three.

In the margin of a transcript, graphite angled across the white. A single word: Careful.

Not my handwriting. Not my paralegal's. Someone had touched what no one should. The intrusion felt physical, like breath on my neck.

I shut the file fast. My fortress had cracks.

The next morning the fortress mocked me outright. On my desk, a heavy vase overflowed with peonies—lush, almost indecent. Liza had signed for them, all cheerful oblivion.

"There wasn't a card," she chirped, sliding the delivery slip onto my desk. "But you've got an admirer."

I smiled the kind of smile I use in court when someone's about to regret opening their mouth. She blinked and retreated.

When I turned the vase, I found the message taped on the back. One-word, black ink: Curtains.

My throat tightened. He was in my walls, in my windows. He wanted me to know.

I peeled the note free and slid it into a drawer, shut it like that could contain him.

The intercom buzzed before I'd even steadied my hands. Liza's voice, nervous now. "Ms. Vale? There's a man downstairs. He doesn't have an appointment. Says he only needs three minutes. His words."

I froze.

"What's his name?"

"He said you already know it."

The girl under the bed whispered: hide.
The woman I had built said: no.

"Tell him," I said, voice steady as law, "I'll give him one minute. In the lobby. With the cameras." The night wind pulled Claudia's hair loose from its pins. She didn't move, not even when Angelo's fingers brushed her wrist again—so slight, so deliberately it could have been accidental. But nothing about him was accidental.

“Don’t mistake this for loyalty,” she said, though her voice betrayed the thrum in her chest.
“You and I are on opposite sides of the law.”

He tilted his head, eyes narrowing. “Law isn’t sides, Claudia. It’s a game. Some of us just don’t bother pretending the rules are fair.”

She should have stepped back. Instead, she let the silence hang between them until it became something alive, pulsing with all the things neither of them could afford to admit.

Finally, Claudia pulled her wrist free. “I don’t need warnings. I need evidence admissible in court. Anything else is noise.”

Angelo’s smile was quick and humorless. “Then listen to the noise carefully. Sometimes it’s louder than the verdict.”

He handed her another folded slip of paper, this one not a photo but a copy of a chain-of custody log. A courier’s name circled in dark ink.

“Khan?” she asked, recognizing her paralegal’s familiar signature.

“Not him.” Angelo tapped the circled courier. “This one. Pick up files from your office twice a week. He also runs errands for people you’d rather not meet.”

“How do you know?”

Angelo’s expression didn’t shift. “Because he works for me, too.”

The rooftop tilted beneath her feet. “You’re admitting that?”

“Not an admission. A courtesy.” His voice dropped, softer now. “I told you—this isn’t a threat. If I wanted you scared, I wouldn’t be here. I’d just let you find out the hard way.”

The paper crumpled faintly in her hand as her grip tightened. She hated the part of her body that remembered how to tremble. Hated that he seemed to notice.

“Stay away from my office,” she said, each word deliberates.

“I can’t.”

“Won’t?”

He shook his head. “Can’t. You’re standing in the middle of a storm you haven’t seen yet. If I walk away, it swallows you.”

“Or maybe you’re the storm,” Claudia shot back.

He smiled, not offended. “Maybe.”

For a long beat, neither of them moved. Then the rooftop door clanged open behind her.

“Ms. Vale?” It was her assistant, breathless, clutching a stack of files. She froze when she saw Angelo, eyes darting between them. “I—I didn’t mean to interrupt.”

Claudia folded the paper and slid it into her pocket. “You didn’t.”

But when she turned back, Angelo was already gone, the city swallowing him whole.

The next morning, Claudia called in early. She needed to see the courier’s face with her own eyes.

The man arrived just after ten, carrying a messenger bag, sweat beading at his temple despite the mild weather. Claudia’s gaze tracked every detail, the way he avoided eye contact, the ink of a serpent tattoo curling just above his collar, the slight limp in his step.

“Morning, Ms. Vale,” he muttered, sliding the day’s delivery onto her desk.

She forced her tone casual. “How long have you been working with the clerk’s office?”

“Couple years.” His smile didn’t reach his eyes. “Why?”

“Just curious.”

He shifted, fingers twitching against the strap of his bag. “Anything else?”

“No.”

He left quickly, almost too quickly. Claudia watched him go, her jaw set.

As soon as the door closed, she opened the stack of motions he’d delivered. The first two were clean. The third—Dominguez v. State—carried a faint pencil scrawl at the bottom corner. One word.

Careful.

Her chest was constricted. She dropped the file onto her desk and pressed her palms against the wood to steady herself.

Someone inside her firm was playing on both sides.

And the worst part, the part that made her stomach twist—was that Angelo Romano had been right.

That night, Claudia took the long way home again. She told herself it was strategy, which retracing her path past the street corner was due to diligence. But when she reached the cracked sidewalk under the lamppost, Angelo wasn’t there. Only the halo of light and the memory of his eyes watching her as though he’d already mapped the cracks in her armor.

She walked faster, refusing to admit disappointment.

At the garage entrance, she stopped short. A car sat on the top level, its windshield glinting under the sodium lamps—shattered, just like yesterday’s. Another warning. Another message.

Claudia exhaled slowly. Her body wanted to retreat, but her bones remembered something else: how to survive storms by standing still until they passed.

Her phone buzzed. Unknown Number.

Some storms don't pass, Claudia. Some you walk into.

She typed back, fingers steady despite the chill seeping into her skin.

Then tell me which kind you are.

This time, there were no dots. No reply. Just the night, holding its breath.

Chapter 3 — The Dominguez File

The courtroom was already humming when Claudia stepped through the heavy oak doors.

Lawyers shuffled their files at the plaintiff's table, the bailiff exchanged jokes with the clerk, and a half dozen spectators murmured like churchgoers before the sermon. Claudia's heels struck clean notes across the marble, and the sound carried enough weight that heads turned.

She liked that. Command was a performance, and she had mastered it years ago. But today, as she set her briefcase on the polished oak table, the echo of Angelo's voice slid under her skin.

The Dominguez case isn't what you think.

She ignored it. Or tried to.

Across the room, Hector Dominguez leaned back in his chair, a smirk tugging at the corner of his mouth. His expensive suit was a size too flashy, his tie too bright. But his eyes— sharp, black as wet stone— watched her with the patience of someone who already knew the ending.

"Ms. Vale," the judge's voice boomed as he entered, robes billowing. "Ready to proceed?"

"Always, Your Honor." Claudia's tone was crisp, controlled.

The hearing was a preliminary motion: Dominguez's counsel had filed to suppress key evidence, citing chain-of-custody concerns. A predictable move, but one that carried weight if the paperwork wasn't airtight.

Claudia flipped open her folder and felt her stomach tighten. The courier's signature stared back at her in sloppy black ink, circled faintly in pencil. A word whispered at the edge of memory: Careful.

"Your Honor," opposing counsel began, rising with theatrical gravitas, "the defense moves to strike Exhibit C from consideration. The evidence was mishandled, improperly logged, and cannot be trusted."

"That's not true," Claudia snapped, rising to her full height. Her voice cut clean through the room. "The evidence log is intact. The chain of custody is verified."

The judge gestured. "Proceed, Ms. Vale."

Claudia slid the document across the bench, forcing her hand steady. "The log shows transfer from officer to clerk to courier to filing, all within proper window. Every signature accounted for."

The judge peered at it. Opposing counsel smirked.

And Dominguez? He leaned forward, eyes narrowing, as if savoring a private joke.

The judge frowned. "Courier signature looks… irregular."

Claudia's pulse jumped. "Irregular does not equal invalid. The defense is grasping."

"Perhaps," the judge allowed, "but it does merit scrutiny. I'll allow Exhibit C provisionally.
But, Ms. Vale, be prepared to establish credibility at trial."

The gavel struck. A small victory. But it felt like losing ground.

Claudia gathered her papers, but her eyes betrayed her. They flicked toward Dominguez, and his smirk deepened, deliberate, like a man savoring the sight of someone slipping on ice.

As court adjourned, she slid her files into her briefcase and snapped it shut. The sound was too loud, too sharp.

"Rough day?"

The voice came from behind her. Gerald Marks, senior partner, hair silvered at the temples, reputation built on fifty years of courtroom swagger. He smiled too broadly, his tone honeyed with concern that felt like poison.

"You looked… distracted," he said softly, pulling her aside as the crowd dispersed. "That's not like you."

"I was not distracted," Claudia replied, cool.

"Mm." Marks tilted his head. "Funny. Because word around the firm is that you've been keeping unusual company. Names I don't need to say aloud."

Her skin prickled. "Excuse me?"

He leaned closer, lowering his voice. "If it's true, Claudia—if you've let yourself get tangled with men like Romano—you're not just risking this case. You're risking all of us."

She locked her jaw. "Careful what you imply."

"I'm not implying," he said smoothly. "I'm warning. Clean it up. Or step aside before someone cleans it up for you."

Then he patted her shoulder like a father giving advice and walked away, leaving the scent of old cologne and veiled threat in his wake.

Claudia stood frozen for a beat, her knuckles white around the handle of her briefcase.

When she finally turned back toward the defense table, Dominguez was gone. Only his absence remained—heavy, mocking, like he'd taken part of the floor with him.

She drew in a long breath, squared her shoulders, and walked out of the courtroom.

The city outside greeted her with the glare of noon sun and the weight of knowing Angelo had been right. The courthouse steps were a gauntlet of heat and noise. Reporters clustered like gulls, phones up, questions flung as offerings.

“Ms. Vale, is it true the chain of custody—”

“Are you seeking a plea from Dominguez—”

“Do you have a conflict of interest—”

Claudia didn’t slow. The trick was to give them your profile, not your face. She angled her body, so the sun burned their lenses and walked through the noise until it thinned to traffic and the staccato tap of her heels on stone.

Her car waited at the curb, black paint shimmering. She hit the unlock button and the sedan chirped back, obedient. The air inside was oven-hot; she cracked the windows and pulled the door shut with the careful gentleness of a person who had learned to measure force.

The engine turned over smoothly. A string quartet on low—last night’s playlist—stole a little of the courthouse off her skin. She checked the mirrors, shoulder-checked out of habit, merged.

Two blocks of ordinary. A bus belching heat. A food cart tipping steam into the sky. A woman laughing into her phone beneath a crooked awning.

Then the light turned yellow, and Claudia tapped the brake.

The pedal sank to the floor with the soft uselessness of a dream.

The light went red. The car didn’t slow.

The world compressed into a set of small, exact choices. Gear to neutral. Hazard lights. Pump the brake—nothing. Steering wheel into the empty lane—there, a gap, a van pulling out to leave her a sliver. She threaded the sliver. A horn bleated. Someone shouted a name that wasn’t hers.

The end of the block rose to meet her: a parked truck, a curb, a narrow mouth of alley hyphenating the buildings.

Claudia aimed for the alley. The tires kissed the curb and leapt. The car scraped a trash can and shouldered into shadow before it stopped with a violent shudder against a stack of pallets. The seatbelt bit her collarbone; her teeth clicked hard enough to sting through her skull. And then it was quiet, except for the furious beating of a heart that had learned too many metronomes.

She sat still for a count of five, hands locked to the wheel. The alley smelled of damp cardboard and the sour metal of old rain. A cat fled deeper into shadow like a retreating thought.

Her phone was on the passenger seat, facing down. She flipped it over with a thumb that didn't feel like it belonged to her.

Unknown Number: Don't move.

She looked up, breath catching without permission.

A shape detached itself from the shade at the alley's mouth, then another, men in jeans and work shirts, the city's uniform. One peeled off to redirect a curious passerby with a palm-out gesture that didn't invite argument. The second waved at a tow truck idling on the cross street as if this were any other Tuesday and not the moment after the floor gave way.

The first came to her window and knocked once with his knuckle. He didn't ask if she was okay. He looked at her face the way EMTs do—cataloguing color and focus—and then he nodded to someone behind him.

The passenger door opened, and Angelo slid in like he owned the air. He didn't crowd her. He didn't touch her. He took in the tilted angle of the hood, the red-light bleeding in from the street, the tremor she was burying in the tight hinge of her jaw.

"You drove it down," he said. "Good."

Claudia found her voice, ironed it flat. "Get out of my car."

He looked at her hands. "You're bleeding."

She followed his gaze; a half-moon of skin on her palm was scraped raw against the textured wheel. Blood beaded politely as pearls.

"Get. Out."

"You hit the curb to kill speed." He nodded to himself. "Smart. There's an empty loading bay behind the pallets—"

She turned the key, killed the engine that had nothing left to do. "Did you cut my brakes?"

Angelo's eyes lifted to hers, and whatever softness he'd brought with him evaporated. "No."

"Your people, then."

"No."

"Convince me."

He exhaled once, short. "If I wanted you dead, you wouldn't pick the alley. You'd take the intersection."

"My partner warned me someone would 'clean it up' if I didn't step aside," she said, ignoring the tremor that wanted to crawl into her voice. "Five minutes later, my brakes go out. You'll forgive me if Occam's razor cuts toward street kings with grudges."

Angelo leaned back, gaze moving to the rearview mirror. She realized he wasn't checking his reflection; he was watching the alley mouth behind them. "Look at the line," he said.

"What line?"

"On the passenger side. Under the glove compartment." He pointed to a teacher with infinite patience. "See the drip? Brake fluid. Fresh."

She looked. A dark tear traced the plastic edge of the dash and dropped to the floor mat. She hadn't noticed it because shock narrows the world to the size of a keyhole.

"You don't cut it up here," he said. "You cut it underneath. This is a puncture in the master cylinder feed. Delicate, fast. You hit the brakes a few times before it empties. Whoever did it knew you were driving out of the courthouse at lunch when you'd hit lights and stop signs. The timing matters."

"Meaning?"

"Meaning it wasn't random. And it wasn't meant to happen an hour from now. It was meant for this block." He pointed toward the intersection she'd escaped. "Public. Messy.
Memorable."

She stared at him, the realization slotting into place with a click she could feel in her bones. "You're telling me this was staged for publicity."

"For a message," he said. "Not for you. Through you."

"Dominguez," she said.

"Or someone who needs him free enough to owe them."

Her throat was dry. She hated how much sense he made. Hated that he made it while sitting in her passenger seat like a fact she couldn't unlearn.

The tow truck eased into the alley mouth, engine low. The driver climbed down and tipped two fingers at Angelo as if they were colleagues. Angelo nodded back without looking away from Claudia.

"Let them take it," he said. "My guy will trail. You'll get the report before the precinct files theirs."

"I'm not letting your 'guy' anywhere near a chain-of-custody story I have to explain to a judge."

Angelo's mouth ticked like he'd expected that answer and approved of it. "Then you'll get two reports."

"Independent."

"Independent." He glanced at the alley opening again; someone had stopped to stare, then thought better of it. "Can you stand?"

She unpeeled her fingers from the wheel. The tremor had stored itself somewhere no one could see. "Yes."

He reached for the door handle, then paused. "There's going to be a point," he said, voice low, edged with something like respect, "where pride gets you killed. Don't let it be today."

She snorted softly, humorlessly. "Says the man who refuses to admit he cares whether I live." A beat. "I admit it," he said. "I just don't advertise."

The passenger door swung open. The heat pounced. He was out, then at her door, then standing where anyone could see the distance between them. He didn't offer a hand. She didn't ask for one. She slid out, her heel finding uneven concrete, and stood while the tow driver and another man eased the car onto the winch.

The brake fluid made a thin ribbon as the sedan tilted, a dark throat cut that wouldn't stop bleeding.

A police cruiser nosed to the curb at the alley mouth. Two uniforms got out and stood with the careful casualness of men who know everything is being recorded, even when there's no camera in sight.

"Everything all right here?" one called.

Angelo's men became scenery—leaners, watchers, part of the brick, trash, and steam. Angelo himself turned his face to profile, harmless as a citizen. Claudia stepped toward the cops like her heels were ice picks.

“I lost brakes,” she said, neutral as case law. “I avoided a collision. I’d like to file a report and request a forensic inspection.”

The older cop nodded. “You pick a good lane.” His eyes flicked past her, took in the men, returned to her face. “You need EMT?”

“I’m fine.”

He studied her a second longer, then gave the tow driver a curt gesture. “Take it to City Lot first. Per procedure.”

He was already turning when Angelo said, conversationally, “Or you can take it to North Pier. Less bottleneck. Fewer cars today.”

The cop’s shoulders tightened. He didn’t turn back. “City Lot.”

“City Lot,” Angelo echoed, as if the words were a toast no one wanted to drink. He looked at Claudia. “Independent report. I’ll send you a copy.”

“You don’t have my email.”

He almost smiled. “You’re adorable.”

She wanted to tell him she wasn’t. That adorable was for people who hadn’t crawled under beds and learned to count storms. Instead, she said, “If you send anything to my office, send it to reception.”

“Noted.”

The cops took her statement against a hood that radiated heat. The tow rolled her car away, brake fluid tattooing the pavement behind it. When she looked back to the alley mouth, the men were gone—absorbed, erased. Only Angelo stayed, a silhouette pared out of light.

“You’re bleeding,” he said again, as if the fact were a dare.

She looked down at her palm; at the smear she had somehow managed not to wipe away. “I have Band-Aids.”

He shook his head once. “No. You have willpower. Band-Aids are for people who admit it hurts.”

She stepped past him, refusing to be pinned to the wall of her own body. “What do you want out of this, Angelo?”

He didn’t follow. “The same thing you want.”

“Justice?” The word tasted like something she’d once believed in without caveats.

“Leverage,” he said.

She stopped, a laugh escaping before she could fold it. “Of course.”

“Justice is a story we tell ourselves, “He added. “Leverage is the language power speaks when no one’s recording.”

She kept walking. “Then start speaking.”

“I already did,” he said to her back. “Step two: look at your own house.”

She didn’t turn. “My firm is clean.”

“Nothing is clean,” he said, not unkindly. “Some things are just less stained.”

The cruiser pulled away. The alley resumed its summer trance. Claudia reached the sunlit sidewalk and let the city noise wash over her like a lie she could breathe.

Her phone chimed.

Unknown Number: Neutral ground. One hour.

She stared at the screen. “No,” she said to no one, then typed it.

No.

A beat. Then:

Unknown Number: You're bleeding.

She deleted the message, then deleted the deletion, as if that would erase the correctness of it. She put the phone face down and walked toward the river. Sometimes the only way to make a decision was to move the feet until the head caught up.

The office smelled like lemon oil and the faint underside of printer ink. Claudia stepped into the lobby and the receptionist stood a little too quickly, smile a notch too bright.

"Ms. Vale, Mr. Marks asked if you could—"

"In a minute," Claudia said. "Where's Khan?"

"In the records room."

She took the stairs instead of the elevator, movement bled adrenaline. The records room was cool and dim, metal shelves marching like soldiers. Khan looked up from a cart stacked with red folders, his narrow face brightening and then clouding when he registered her expression.

"Everything okay?" he asked.

"How did the Dominguez packet leave this room yesterday?" she asked. No greetings. No cushion.

Khan blinked. "Courier pickup. Standard run."

"Who signed it out?"

He reached for the logbook, flipped pages with quick, careful fingers. "Me." He pointed to his signature. "Then Jo in Clerk. That's it."

"And the courier?"

"Same guy." He frowned. "Why?"

Claudia held out her hand. "Let me see yesterday's run sheet."

He hesitated a half-second too long, then handed it over. The paper was warm from his touch. She scanned names, times, and the shorthand that office life breeds. A small notation sat in the margin beside the Dominguez entry: a simple diagonal slash followed by a dot. Nothing, unless you know how to look.

She did. She'd seen the same mark in an organized crime file five years ago, a case that had taught her too much about how information travels when no one believes it's moving.

"What's this?" she asked, tapping the mark.

Khan's throat worked. "A check mark. It means I… checked it."

"You use check marks?" she said mildly. "Because all the others are boxes."

He didn't answer. The room seemed to narrow the way a throat does when a person is about to lie. She looked up into his eyes and saw fear there. Not of her. Of a story larger than either of them.

"Khan," she said softly. "Who told you to add that?"

"No one," he said too quickly. "It's nothing."

"Don't do that." Her voice stayed gentle, but it found an edge and rode it. "Don't call something nothing when it's the string that pulls a whole sweater apart."

Color rose in his face. He looked toward the door like a man checking the weather through a keyhole. "It's just a flag," he whispered. "For pickup. For… for the other route."

"What other route?"

He shook his head. His gaze slid past her shoulder, to a space she couldn't see. "Please don't ask me that."

"Too late."

"Ms. Vale," he said, almost pleading, "I have a sister. She needs it."

She closed the logbook and handed it back. "Understood."

He swallowed hard. "I didn't change anything. I never changed anything."

She nodded like she believed him because part of her did. "Where's the courier's intake today?"

"Reception," he said, voice small.

She left him in that refrigerated aisle of paper and went back downstairs. The receptionist flinched when she saw her return.

"Did the courier—"

"Left ten minutes ago," the receptionist said, now openly nervous. "He, um, dropped this." She slid a thick envelope across the counter. Claudia didn't touch it. The flap wasn't sealed. Inside, she could see the top edge of a photocopy: chain-of-custody, Dominguez, the familiar column of signatures.

A pencil line winked from the margin. Careful.

Claudia took the envelope, not because she wanted it but because not taking it would have been an admission of fear. She walked to her office with the slow gait of a person crossing a frozen lake on a day that shouldn't be cold.

Her phone vibrated again before she reached the glass.

Unknown Number: Neutral ground. Thirty minutes. Where God listens and no one else does.

She stopped in the hallway. The city moved through the glass like a tide.

Claudia typed, “No churches.

Reply: Then don’t call it one.

She stared at the wordless arrogance of it; at the way he made every instruction sound like a choice. She thought of the red light and the brake pedal sinking into uselessness. She thought of Marks’s hand on her shoulder, the way power learns to mimic care until you confuse the two.

She turned left instead of right and took the elevator to the street.

The building had lost its name a long time ago. Once it had been a parish where babies were baptized and vows stitched strangers into family. Now it was a hollowed-out brick echo chamber with stained-glass windows patched into squares of plastic like a child’s idea of first aid. The smell of candle wax lived under the smell of dust, a ghost insisting on its lease.

Angelo stood in the nave as if he’d been born there. He wasn’t alone, a woman in a
Dolphins’ sweatshirts swept the far aisle with a wide push broom, humming off-key. She didn’t glance up when Claudia entered; Angelo had chosen well. People who mind their own business are either the city’s saints or its accomplices.

“You’re late,” he said.

“I was busy not dying,” she said.

He nodded as if this were housekeeping. “You talked to Khan.”

She didn’t ask how he knew. “He’s scared.”

“Good. Fear keeps lies small.” He gestured toward a pew. She ignored the invitation and stood.

“Your brakes,” he said. “My report will come to you through the front desk. The city’s report will say what the city always says—mechanical failure, unfortunate incident, difficult to source. The truth is a pinhole cut in the line above the chassis. Clean. Not sloppy. Someone practiced.”

“Name,” she said.

“Soon.”

She let a breath out, controlled. “You dragged me here to tell me ‘Soon’?”

“I dragged you here,” he said quietly, “because if I said it anywhere else, the person we’re about to discuss would hear it before you did.”

The broom paused at the far end of the nave. The woman stretched her back, groaned softly, resumed.

“Your partner,” Angelo said. “Marks.”

She laughed once, and the sound made the rafters consciously not echo. “Gerald is a lot of things. Subtle isn’t one of them.”

“Gerald isn’t clever,” Angelo agreed. “He’s greedy. Greed learns clever friends.” He reached into his jacket, produced a folded sheet, laid it on the pew back the way a parishioner lays a hand. “Three years of quiet payments from a shell company tied to Dominguez’s larger world. They don’t go to Gerald. They go to a consulting outfit in his daughter’s name.”

Claudia took the paper. Read. Read again. Names that looked like fiction assembled into an arithmetic of shame. She felt the heat rise beneath her blouse, a tide she could not push back.

“This is fabricated,” she said, because if she didn’t say it out loud, she might never climb back out of the hole the words made.

“It’s verified,” he said. “You’ll get the numbers you need to verify them yourself. But you won’t do it through your firm’s servers.”

"Why?"

"Because someone at your firm likes to read your email."

She folded the paper small, smaller, a talisman having a seizure. "Why tell me?" she asked finally. "You get nothing out of this that I can see."

He tilted his head. "I get a prosecutor who won't be bought and a woman who owes me a favor."

"I don't owe you anything."

"You will," he said, and for the first time there was no heat in it. Just fact. "Not because I'll ask. Because you'll decide."

She hated the way the nave seemed to lean in, listening. Hated the way, the broom's rhythm had become the clock of her choices.

"What do you want me to do?" she asked.

"Nothing stupid," he said. "Which is difficult when you're brave."

"That's rich," she said. "From a man who thinks neutral ground is a church with a tenant sweeping secrets into piles."
He smiled without joy. "Neutral ground is any place pain taught you to whisper. For some of us, that's a church."

Her phone vibrated. She didn't look; she'd already decided that anyone who needed her could wait.

"Step one," he said. "Quarantine your case files. Print what matters. Walk it to someone who owes you nothing and owes the truth everything."

"Like whom?"

"An assistant district attorney with enemies," he said. "They're the only ones too angry to be bought."

She stared at him. "You know one."

"I know three."

"Of course you do."

"And Claudia?" he added.

"What."

"Tonight, when the office empties out, don't be there."

"Is this about the garage again?"

"It's about the fact that people who can't move you in court will try to move you with fire."

She laughed, but the sound wasn't brave. It was a reflex the body uses when teeth want to chatter. "You expect me to sprint out of my own building because a man I barely know likes to make metaphors?"

"I expect you to decide whether pride is a good tombstone," he said.

The broom squeaked over a rough patch of tiles. The woman cursed under her breath in a way that made Claudia like her.

"Fine," Claudia said. "I'll print what I need. I'll make copies offsite. I'll pretend to be cautious." She turned to go, then looked back. "And Angelo?"

"What."

"If you ever cut my brakes, I won't take the alley."

For the first time since she'd met him, he laughed. Not loudly. Not long. But it loosened something in the air had been too tight to breathe.

"Don't threaten me with being better at dying," he said. "Be better at living."

She left him in the nave with the broom and the ghosts and the taste of his laugh in her mouth like a coin.

Outside, the sky had decided to bruise. Clouds stacked like paperwork in an understaffed office. The afternoon had the specific tension of weather that wants to be blamed for more than it will do.

She walked fast because walking slow would feel like fear. At the corner, a bus exhaled; a man in a suit adjusted his tie like it might strangle him; a girl in a denim jacket hopped a puddle with the kind of grace the city forgets it can have. Claudia turned toward the tower that bore her name in glass and told herself she was going to pick up paper.

Nothing more.

Nothing less.

Chapter 4— The Client's Confession

The office should have been empty.
At half past ten, the Vale & Associates tower was a cathedral of silence, lights dimmed, the city beyond its windows a quilt of neon and shadow. Claudia sat at her desk with a single lamp burning, red folders stacked like soldiers awaiting orders.

She told herself she stayed because the Dominguez case needed her focus. But in truth, she stayed because leaving meant trusting the night. And the night had a way of proving Angelo right.

The floor groaned faintly as the HVAC kicked on. She rubbed her temple, turned another page—

Glass shattered.

Her head snapped up. Down the hall, the sharp percussion echoed, then the unmistakable low roar of flame blooming too fast. The fire alarm screamed awake, lights strobing red across the walls.

Claudia grabbed the Dominguez folder, clutching it like oxygen, and bolted. Smoke was already crawling along the ceiling, black and greasy. She ran for the stairwell, heels striking like gunfire.

Halfway down the first flight, another explosion shook the building. The stairwell was filled with a pulse of smoke and heat. Claudia covered her mouth with her sleeve, heart pounding, and kept moving.

The landing door burst open below her. A figure surged into the stairwell. Claudia froze, adrenaline clawing up her throat.

"Move!"

It was him. Angelo. His eyes locked on hers through the haze.

"What are you doing here?" she gasped, choking on smoke.

"Keeping you alive," he snapped, catching her elbow. His grip was iron, steering her down.

Another boom above them. Fire licked down the stairwell like a living thing. Claudia stumbled, coughing, and Angelo hauled her upright.

"Basement exit," he said, pulling her into motion.

"I don't need—"

"Save it for a courtroom. Not here."

They burst through the basement door into a corridor thick with smoke. Emergency lights flickered. The air carried the acrid bite of burning plastic.

Angelo shoved open a steel service door. Cool night air hit her like a slap. They staggered into an alley, the tower at their back glowing with fire's orange kiss. Sirens wailed closer.

Claudia braced against the wall, chest heaving. Her blouse was streaked with soot, hair half out of its bun. She still clutched the red folder like a lifeline.

Angelo's hand stayed on her arm a moment too long. "Told you not to be here tonight."

She shoved his hand away. "You expect me to believe you just happened to show up?"

He didn't flinch. "Believe what you want. You're not dead. That's the part that matters."

Flames climbed the tower, reflecting in his eyes. Claudia realized, with a jolt, that the building wasn't the only thing burning. They didn't go to her penthouse. Angelo steered her from the opposite direction, through a seam in the city only people like him knew.

"Walk," he said. "Holding that folder like it's your heart is announcing you have a heart."

Claudia tucked the Dominguez file beneath her jacket. "You don't get to bark orders at me."

"I get to keep you breathing," he said, not slowing. "Rank outranks manners."
They cut through an alley that smelled like fryer oil and rain and stepped into a cramped back lot with a roll-up door scarred by graffiti. Angelo banged twice in a rhythm that felt like a code and the door ratcheted up just enough to admit them. The room beyond was a garage, but not the kind that fixed cars. Metal cabinets. A battered couch. A wall of pegboard hung with tools that had names she didn't know.

A man with forearms like railroad ties nodded once and vanished through a side door. The roll-up clattered down. Quiet fell, heavy and padded.

Angelo turned to face her. Up close, soot smudged his cheek. A fleck of ash clung to his lash and refused gravity.

"You're bleeding," he said for the third time today. "Sit."

"I'm fine."

"You're stubborn," he corrected, and pointed at the couch.

Claudia sat because shock wanted her vertical spine to admit it was a lie. He returned with a dented first-aid kit and a cold bottle of water beaded with condensation.

"Drink."

"I don't—"

"Drink," he repeated, softer. It was amazing, she thought distantly, how easily obedience could feel like a gift when it was the right word at the right moment. She drank. The water hit her stomach like mercy.

He knelt, opened the kit, and took her hand. No gloves. No hesitation. His touch was careful in a way that felt studied practice hiding under nonchalance. He cleaned the tiny crescent of torn skin at her palm with saline and gauze that smelled like hospitals and the past.

"You ever been a medic?" she asked, hating how hoarse her voice had gone.

He shook his head, taping a butterfly neatly across the scrape. "I've been alive."
She breathed, slow and measured, as if oxygen had a price. "That wasn't a random fire."

"No." He met her eyes. The ash finally fell from his lash. "Two bottles through the east stairwell window. One into the paralegal bullpen. They wanted chaos, not a corpse count."

She pictured Khan's desk. The way he'd looked at the logbook like it might testify against him. "If they wanted me dead, they knew where my office was."

"They wanted to move you," Angelo said. "Flush the files. Break the habit of staying late.
Make you choose new routines so they can map them."

"How reassuring," she muttered.

He rose and tossed the bloody gauze into a trash can with a clatter that seemed too loud for the room. The big man returned with a small duffel and set it on a metal table, then melted away again, the door whispering shut.

"Shower's through there," Angelo said, nodding at a door with peeling paint. "Spare clothes in the bag. Nothing fancy."

"I'm not—"

"Claudia." He stepped closer, and the garage shrank until it had the dimensions of his breath. "You smell like smoke. If you walk back onto the street like that, you tell the city where you've been. Do you want to be invisible? Be ordinary. Wash. Change."

She stared at him for a heartbeat longer than she needed to. "Turn your back."

He turned without commentary.

The shower was a concrete stall and a contrarian miracle: hot water, steady pressure. She braced her hands on the wall and let heat beat the smoke out of her hair, the courthouse out of her bones. The room filled with steam and the sort of quiet that pretends to be safety.

She changed into the contents of the duffel: Black joggers with an anonymous drawstring, a soft gray T-shirt, socks that didn't match. She braided her wet hair into something that could pass for intention and gathered her soot-streaked blouse and ruined heels into the bag like evidence.

When she stepped back out, the garage looked different only because she did. Angelo had stripped off his jacket; the tattoos that crawled his forearms weren't a mess of ink but a language she couldn't read. He was rolling his sleeves down when he looked up and then didn't speak for a second.

"What," she said, suspicious of silence.

"Ordinary suits you," he said.

"It won't stick."

"We'll get you home," he said, "but not yet."

"We?" she asked, aware of the plural like a bruise she'd forgotten.

He ignored it. "Eat." He nodded at a metal tray that held two foil-wrapped sandwiches and a pair of apples polished to a shine. A glass bottle of Coke sweated beside them like a cliché that worked.

She unwrapped one sandwich and found grilled cheese—gooey, indecently comforting. She took a bite and had to close her eyes for a second because her body wanted to cry at the luxury of warmth. When she opened them, he wasn't watching her mouth; he was watching her knuckles, the way people do when they've learned tells.

"What?" she asked again.

"Counting," he said.

She looked down at her hand. She hadn't realized she was tapping her ring finger to her thumb. One-two-three-four. One-two-three-four.

She put the sandwich down. "You following me, Romano?"

"Sometimes," he said. "Sometimes I get there first."

"That's not an answer."
"It's the only one that doesn't get us both arrested."

She took another bite to avoid saying something imprudent. The Coke tasted like a childhood she didn't get. The apple she pocketed because it felt like planning.

"Who threw the bottles?" she asked.

"Two possibilities," he said. "Both ugly."

"Dominguez?"

"Dominguez doesn't touch glass," he said. "He hires men who like fire. But fire leaves witnesses. He likes lawyers too much to make enemies of insurance companies."

"Then who?"

"Friends of your friend," Angelo said, unwrapping his own sandwich with too much care for a man built by corner nights. "Marks."

Her jaw tightened. “You keep slandering my partners and I’ll file a motion for defamation in open court.”

“You’ll win the hearing,” he said, chewing, “and lose your office.”

“Prove it.”

“Working on it.”

“Work faster.”

He smiled without showing teeth. “I like you.”

“Distract someone else,” she said.

“For the record,” he said, “you’re not my type.”

“Gorgeous, stubborn, and alive?”
“Dangerous,” he said. “My type is people I can’t ruin by knowing them.”

She held his gaze because surrender is sometimes just blinking first. The air between them warmed up.

“You ruined my day,” she said.

“Better than the alternative,” he said.

The garage door made a small sound like metal remembering a storm. Angelo tilted his head and stilled. Outside, a car idled, then moved on. His body language returned to baseline—loose, predatory patience.

“Why help me?” she asked, softer now, because the shower had scoured the anger and left the question beneath. “You don’t get points from juries. You don’t get leverage if I live without owing you.”

“Leverage doesn’t need gratitude,” he said. “It needs memory. Tonight you remember who showed up when heat found you.”

"I also remember who knew to show up," she said. "If I find out you lit the match—"

"You'll prosecute me," he finished. "You're good at vows."

"Practice."

He nodded toward the duffel with her ruined blouse. "Let me have that. It'll smell like accelerant if they used what I think they did."

"Chain of custody," she said.

He lifted a palm. "We'll mirror. You keep one. I keep one. You can hand yours to whatever honest cop you still believe in."

She hesitated, then tossed him the shirt. He sealed it in a heavy plastic evidence sleeve like a man who had bought them by the pallet. He tagged it with a sticker that read only a date and time.
"You keep those on hand?" she asked.

"I live in a world where truth needs armor," he said. "Paper is the cheapest kind."

Her phone vibrated on the table. She glanced down.

Unknown Number: You alive?

She looked up, annoyed. "You text like a concerned parent."

"I text like a man who's seen women walk out of fires and run back into worse ones," he said.

She typed: Alive. Not grateful.

"Fair," he said.

She put the phone face down. "How long do you keep me in your little bunker before you return me to civilization?"

"A few hours," he said. "Then we take the slow roads."

“Home,” she said.

He didn’t agree. He also didn’t disagree.

“What if I say I’m done hiding?” she tested.

“Then you go to your penthouse,” he said, “and find out what they left for you there.”

“What would they leave?”

“Another kind of fire.”

“Meaning?”

“A camera you can’t see. A listening device that records the sound of you sleeping.” He held her eyes. “Your building has a vendor dependency list. Marks’s people have wanted access to it for a year.”

“Stop saying ‘Marks’s people’ like it’s a category.”

“It is,” he said calmly. “You’re just late to the taxonomy.”

She looked away because the alternative was showing him a flinch. The clock above the pegboard ticked a cheap, insistent rhythm. Somewhere in the walls, a pipe pinged like a trapped cricket.

“Tell me about the warehouse camera,” she said. “The one that didn’t malfunction.”

“I will,” he said. “But not everything now. You need sleep more than you need new nightmares.”

She laughed, genuinely this time. “You think sleep is optional. That’s adorable.”

He gathered the first-aid kit, as if cleaning up counted as empathy. “There’s a cot behind that door. The bathroom locks. I’ll be out here being ominous.”

“I don’t sleep where men tell me to,” she said, but the cot had already occupied a corner of her mind like a couch after an exhausting party. “We split the watch.”

He cocked his head. “You don’t trust me not to vanish?”

“I don’t trust you not to hover.”

He considered. “Fair.”

They didn’t sleep. Not really. He took the first “watch,” which consisted of him sitting in a folding chair, boots planted, eyes half-lidded, every muscle turned to a listening device. Claudia lay on the cot and pretended to drift while her mind replayed fire’s orange bloom behind glass.

She must have dozed, because at some hour that felt parentless she woke to quiet and found Angelo ten feet away, looking at her not with hunger but with the unmistakable relief of a man counting breaths he doesn’t own.

“What,” she said into the dark.

“You talk in your sleep,” he said.

“I don’t.”

“You said ‘under the bed,’” he said. “Then you counted to twelve.”

She swallowed. “Then let me sleep where I can see under it.”

He stood, slow so the chair wouldn’t squeal. “Take my spot,” he said, gesturing to the chair. “I’ll take the cot.”

“I’m not afraid of the dark,” she said.

“I am,” he said. “When it’s near you.”

The garage didn't shrink or expand. It just held the words between them like a candle cupped in two hands. He moved to the cot. She took the chair because power sometimes means letting someone else pretend you're safe.

The seconds added up. Dawn diluted the corners of the room from black to charcoal to the first draft of blue.

"Time," he said finally.

She stood, joints clicking a protest. "Where first?"

"Your office if the fire marshal's done. Then the place you print where nobody knows your last name."

"You have a suggestion," she said.

"I have a map," he said, and held the door for her.

They slipped back into the city dressed as nobody. The morning air tasted tin-clean after smoke. A delivery truck double-parked like a law of nature. Pigeons argued over something no living thing should eat.

At the curb, a newer sedan idled with the indifference of expensive engineering. Not hers. Angelo opened the passenger door.

"Get in."

"What happens if I say no?" she asked because she had to test it.

"You walk," he said, "and you'll still end up where I'm taking you. It'll just take longer, and you'll collect new risks like lint."

"Bossy," she said, and got in.

He pulled into slow traffic that had the weary optimism of ordinary people. For ten blocks, they were a pair of nobodies with a date with a printer. The banality soothed, then irritated.

"Last night," she said finally, "you said 'friends of your friend.' If you can tie Marks to
Dominguez by more than a daughter's consulting shell, do it."

"I can," he said.

"How?"

"Because I hired the accountant who scrubbed the books they think are clean."

She turned. "And this accountant is alive?"

"For now," he said.

"Name."

"Later."

She laughed once. "You think withholding names is a flirting technique."

"I think it's how we don't die."

They drove the last blocks in a silence that wasn't empty. When he parked, he didn't say 'we're here' because he knew she had already memorized the route.

The storefront looked like it sold nothing you'd want: vacuum parts, a faded sign for a brand that had died before phones learned to steal our eyes. Inside, a bell tinkled a sound that belonged in another decade.

The woman behind the counter wore readers on a chain and a T-shirt that said Everything Works, Until It Doesn't. Angelo nodded at her. She looked at Claudia like she was a puzzle that would solve itself if you stared hard enough.

"Back," the woman said. "Code's still the same."

Claudia raised an eyebrow. "You have a lot of 'neutrals' in your Rolodex."

He didn't answer. They passed into a back room with three printers, two copiers, and a smell like hot dust. The machines hummed with the self-importance of beasts of burden.

Claudia fed the Dominguez file into the feeder with a tenderness she refused to feel. Pages began to march into tidy stacks. She sorted them into piles: one to carry, one to hide, one to burn if the day required it.

While she worked, Angelo stood with his back to the door, hands in pockets, gaze loose. "After this," he said, "we go by your office. Then your apartment. You take thirty minutes to pack a bag like you're going to a conference. You carry nothing you can't explain."

"And if someone's waiting?"

"Then we see whether they came to watch or to speak."

"And if they came to do?" she asked.

"Then I ruin their day," he said simply.

The printer coughed the last sheet. She gathered stacks into manila envelopes and labeled them in block letters that belonged to her courtroom self. One she slid beneath a false bottom drawer the shop woman swung open with a flourish of indifference. One she tucked into her tote, the kind of bag women build lives in. One she handed to Angelo.

"Two mirrors," she said. "Chain of custody."

"Look at us," he said lightly. "Married."

"Annulled by lunch," she said.

They stepped back into the front room. The bell tinkled again; a man in a brown cap had just come in, holding a broken lamp like a child with a wounded pet. He blinked at them. Claudia tracked his hands automatically. The woman behind the counter didn't blink at all.

"Careful out there," the woman said, not looking up from her ledger.

"You too," Angelo said.

When the door shut behind them, the city recommenced its loud forgetting. Angelo opened the car door. Claudia paused with her hand on the roof.

"Angelo," she said.

He looked at her. The morning made the scar on his jaw less knife, more story.

"Last night," she said. "If I had stayed in my office two more minutes—"

"You'd have made it out," he said. "I'd have made sure."

She nodded once, a concession she didn't give lightly. "All right."

He studied her, then said, "You don't owe me."

"I know," she said, getting in. "I hate that you're right." The fire marshal's tape clung to the entrance of Vale & Associates like a wound dressing. Yellow, flapping in the wind, stamped with warnings no one in the city believed would keep danger out. Claudia and Angelo stood across the street, the tower rising above them in scorched dignity.

"Official word says electrical," Angelo murmured. "Shorted ballast in the stairwell. That'll be tomorrow's headline."

Claudia's mouth tightened. "And the bottles of accelerant?"

"They'll call it residue from cleaning supplies."

She adjusted the strap of her tote, knuckles pale. "That's not incompetence. That's a cover."

“Exactly,” Angelo said. “And covers need carpenters. Someone’s hammering inside your own firm.”

Claudia crossed the street. The guard posted at the door waved her through without argument—her name still had weight, even if ash stained the building’s bones. Inside, the lobby smelled of smoke layered under lemon disinfectant. Emergency crews had done their sweep, but the place felt hollowed.

Her office, thirty-two floors up, was worse. The door was intact, but the air inside was heavy with melted plastic. Her desk bore the faint outline where the Dominguez folder usually sat. A void.

Claudia dropped her tote in the chair and looked at Angelo. “You wanted me to see this. Why?”

He closed the door behind them. “Because it’s cleaner to confront betrayal when you’re already standing in the ashes.”

“Cryptic,” she said. “As usual.”

He moved to her window, hands in pockets, city glinting on his reflection. “Your senior partner, Marks—he’s not just compromised. He’s bought.”

Claudia felt her pulse tighten. “That’s a serious accusation.”

“I don’t accuse,” Angelo said. “I show.” He reached into his jacket and slid a slim envelope across her desk.

Inside: bank transfers. Amounts too neat to be random, too consistent to be oversight. The sender: a shell corporation out of Miami. The receiver: a consulting firm registered to Marks’s daughter.

Claudia read, reread, forced her lawyer’s brain to search for holes. “These could be fabricated.”

“Check the routing numbers yourself,” Angelo said. “They trace back to accounts used by Dominguez’s network. Offshore, laundered through shipping. I don’t bring you fairy tales, Claudia.”

Her jaw set. “So what? You want me to burn my own partner in open court?”

“I want you to know the truth,” Angelo said, stepping closer. “Because fighting blind gets you killed.”

She shoved the papers back at him. “Truth in your world is leverage. You keep it until it buys something.”

“And in your world?” he asked quietly. “Truth is whatever you can prove before the other side buries it.”

Their eyes locked. Neither gave ground.

Finally Claudia broke the silence. “Why give me this now? Why not wait until I’m too deep to crawl out?”

“Because you’re already too deep,” Angelo said. His voice was low, steady. “And I’d rather you hate me with both eyes open than trust anyone else with them shut.”

The words sank like stones. Claudia turned away, palms pressed to the cool glass of her window. Below, the city surged, oblivious. She could almost pretend she wasn’t standing on a fault line.

Her phone buzzed on the desk. A text from Khan. Need to see you. Urgent. Records room.

She showed Angelo. His expression didn’t change, but the stillness in him sharpened. “Go,” he said. “But not alone.”

Claudia hesitated. “If Khan’s compromised—”

“Then he’s about to tell you who owns him,” Angelo said. “And I want to hear it too.”

The records room was dim, half the lights out since the fire. Shelves loomed like shadows. Khan stood near the back, pale, hands jittering as though powered by too much caffeine.

“Ms. Vale,” he said, voice cracking. “I didn’t mean for it to go this far.”

Claudia stepped closer, Angelo behind her like a second spine. “What did you mean, Khan?”

“I thought it was just… flags. Small things. Marks said it was housekeeping. Just signals for routing.”

“Signals for who?” she pressed.

Khan’s throat bobbed. His eyes darted past her shoulder to Angelo. “I can’t say—”

“You’re already saying,” Angelo cut in, voice calm but razor-edged. “So finish it.”

Khan wrung his hands. “Dominguez. His people. They— they pay Marks. He pays me to keep the chain dirty, just dirty enough to kill a case if needed.”

Claudia’s stomach dropped. “And you did it?”

Tears clung to the corners of his eyes. “I have a sister. Hospital bills. I didn’t think—”

“You didn’t think you’d be burning down justice with your pencil marks,” she snapped.

Khan’s face crumpled. “I didn’t know about the fire. I swear—”

The overhead light flickered. A sound echoed from the hall—footsteps, then silence.

Angelo moved fast, pressing a finger to his lips. Claudia’s pulse hammered as the three of them stood frozen in the stale air.

The footsteps retreated. The silence returned.

Angelo leaned in to Claudia's ear, voice a whisper. "Now you know how deep the rot runs."

She turned to him, heat flaring in her chest—anger, fear, something sharper. "And you expect me to trust you?"

"I expect you to survive," he murmured.

For a heartbeat, the distance between them vanished. His breath was warm against her cheek. Claudia's lips parted—not in surrender, but in the dangerous space where fury and longing blur.

Then Khan made a sound, a choked sob, and the moment shattered.

Claudia stepped back, spine stiff. "We're not done."

"Not by a long shot," Angelo said. The records room seemed to breathe with the weight of secrets. Claudia stood between Khan and Angelo, the folder in her tote heavy as a weapon.

"Khan," she said, voice sharp as broken glass. "If you want to walk out of here alive, you'll tell me everything. Names. Dates. Every signal you've marked."

"I can't," Khan whispered, shaking his head. "If I do—"

"You already did," Angelo cut in. His eyes were flat, a tide too deep to read.

"I didn't know about the fire," Khan pleaded. "I swear it. Marks told me to flag files, nothing more. He said if I didn't—my sister—"

The overhead lights buzzed, flickered. Claudia felt it before she heard it: danger, rushing like blood in her ears.

"Shut up," Angelo said suddenly. He stepped forward, body taut, listening.

A soft thunk sounded in the hall. Then another. Claudia's chest clenched with recognition. Molotovs.

The door burst inward, smoke flooding the room. Shouts outside, boots pounding. Chaos.

"Down!" Angelo barked. He shoved Claudia to the floor, covered her with his body as glass shattered. Fire licked across a shelf, igniting old paper like tinder.

"Khan!" Claudia shouted, coughing. But the paralegal was gone — bolted into the smoke the moment panic cracked the room open.

"Damn it," Angelo cursed, hauling her to her feet. "Move!"

They ran through a side exit, flames snapping at their heels. Claudia clutched the folder to her chest, lungs screaming. The stairwell spat them out onto a lower level, smoke curling down the hall like a living thing.

They burst into the lobby. Outside, sirens wailed — fire crews arriving too late, again.

Claudia stumbled against the wall, coughing. "The files—my copies—"

Angelo caught her chin, forced her to meet his eyes. His touch was rough, urgent. "They're gone. Khan took them, or someone took him. Either way, you can't go back."

Her heart hammered. She shoved him away. "I don't need your protection—"

"You need the truth," he snapped. His voice was raw, stripped of its armor. "And you need to stop pretending the law will save you. It won't. Marks owns your house. Dominguez owns your court. And now they own your evidence."

Claudia froze. The words cut because they fit.

Angelo stepped closer, so close she could see the fine scar tissue at his jaw, the heat in his eyes. "You're out of options, Claudia. So I'll ask you once. Are you ready to choose sides?"

She stared at him, chest rising fast, caught between fury and the dark pull of something far more dangerous. Her lips parted—
The fire alarm shrieked again. Boots thundered down the hall.

Claudia swallowed the words. She didn't answer.

Angelo's jaw tightened, but he didn't press. He simply held her gaze, the question still burning there, until the world forced them apart.
The city glowed with fire behind them, sirens fracturing the night.
Claudia sat stiff in the passenger seat, hair damp with sweat and smoke, Dominguez's red folder clutched tight in her lap. Angelo drove with one hand, the other draped loosely across the wheel, as if chaos didn't exist outside the glass.

"Where's Khan?" Claudia demanded, her throat raw.

"Gone." His voice was flat, uncompromising.

"You let him slip—"

"I kept you alive."

She bristled. "He had the files—my mirrored set—"

"He was never going to keep them," Angelo said. His gaze flicked to her, sharp. "You think a paralegal runs with a folder like that and makes it out clean? Whoever owns him already owns what he carried."

Her hands tightened on the cardboard. "Then I have nothing."

"You have me."

The words landed between them heavy as a verdict. Claudia turned toward the window, jaw set against the heat rising in her chest. Outside, neon bled into rain-slick pavement, taxis hissed past, pedestrians scattered from the chaos they didn't want to see.

“You expect me to trust you,” she said, low.

“I expect you to survive,” he returned.

The silence after that wasn’t empty. It thrummed with unsaid things.

Angelo guided the car into a tunnel, shadows swallowing them whole. “They’ll tighten the circle now. No more warning shots. Next time, they don’t care if the fire eats you.”

“And you do?” she asked, unable to stop herself.

Chapter 5 — The Devil in Deposition

He didn't look at her. "Enough to pull you out twice."

Her pulse jumped. She hated that it did.

When they emerged into open air again, the skyline shifted—less towers, more brick. Angelo turned into a side street lined with shuttered shops and graffiti-scrawled steel. He parked beneath a broken streetlamp.

"This isn't my first choice," he said, killing the engine. "But it'll hold for the night."

Claudia looked at the building across from them: a narrow walk-up with barred windows and a metal door that bore no name.

"And then what?" she asked.

"Then you decide whether you want to keep bleeding alone or bleed with someone who knows how to stop it."

She stared at him, the words carving into her. The part of her that lived in boardrooms wanted to laugh, dismiss him. The part that had just run through smoke and flame wanted to believe.

Without waiting for an answer, Angelo stepped out. The street was empty, but he scanned it like a soldier. Then he came around to her side, opened the door, and held it—an invitation, not a command.

Claudia got out. The night smelled of rain and exhaust, of rust and danger. The folder weighed heavy in her hands.

The building swallowed them in shadow. They didn't stay in the warehouse. Angelo made a call whose ringtone she couldn't hear and fifteen minutes later they slipped into a car that had appeared with the confidence of a ghost. No plates she could memorize from one glance, no decals, nothing to hang a story on. He drove with that ruthless patience of people who know how to turn a city into a maze: no highways, no straight lines, a dozen right turns that left them somewhere no cabbie would find on purpose.

The safehouse was the opposite of his garage—cleaner, quieter, the kind of apartment you rent when you want to be a rumor. Third floor walk-up. Two rooms. A kitchen that pretended to be a shelf. Pale walls. One plant trying, with heroic optimism, to be green.

Angelo let her in first and did a slow, mechanical scan. It was the kind of check that said he hadn't been the one to open this door last, but he trusted whoever had.

"Whose place is this?" Claudia asked.

"Mine, for now," he said, which was not an answer so much as a refusal to give one. He locked the door with three different mechanisms. "Bathroom's there. Towels are clean. There's a sweater in the drawer if you get cold."

"I'm not cold," she said.

He looked at the way her fingers curled around the folder. "Your body disagrees."

She hated that he was right. Hated more that the room smelled like soap and the faintest ghost of lemon, and that it made a small traitorous part of her want to believe in the concept of safety. She set the folder on the table and stood with her palms flat on either side of it, as if steadying a map in wind.

"Tell me why Khan ran," she said.

"Because anyone who lives between two masters learns to sprint," Angelo said, unbuttoning his cuff and rolling his sleeve back like he was about to wash blood off his hands, even though there wasn't any. "If he vanished in the smoke, someone called him into it."

“Marks?” she said.

“Or one of Dominguez’s lieutenants, if they thought the room would unspool him.” He drew a chair out with his foot and sat, careful not to crowd her. “Either way, he’s not holding your papers. They are. By morning, any page that hurts them is already ash.”

Claudia closed her eyes, counted to four, breathed, counted again. The old ritual felt ridiculous in a room with no ghosts and one very real man, but it steadied the tremor in her hands. When she opened her eyes, he was watching the breath count happen, not with pity, but as if it were a language he already spoke.

“Don’t do that,” she said.

“Do what?”

“Make it look like knowing me is easy.”

“It isn’t,” he said, without humor. “But it’s familiar.”

She picked up the plant, turned the pot an inch, put it back, the meaningless movement of someone refusing stillness. “How familiar?”

“My father used to come home like a weather pattern,” Angelo said. “You could smell the storm three blocks away. If he made it to the kitchen, he’d sing. If he stopped in the hall, you learned where the knives were. People call what I am a talent. It’s not. It’s a childhood.”

Claudia looked up before she meant to. The tattoos on his forearms weren’t a costume. They were chapters.

“Your scar,” she said, and only realized after the words left that she’d asked a question he didn’t owe her. “Jaw.”

He shrugged a shoulder, the motion tugging the line pale. “Some men throw hands. Some throw bottles. Some throw boys. A fence taught me I can be cut and keep moving.”

The sentence landed with the kind of quiet a church recognizes. She had the absurd urge to apologize to the version of him who'd learned that lesson, like she could arrive late to the worst day of his childhood and pull him over the fence.

Instead: "In court," she said, "they call what we lived 'background.' As if it's paint."

"In my world, it's the whole wall," he said gently.

Silence sat with them, not awkward—alert. The city hummed beyond the thin windows, a thousand small lives refusing to be interesting. Claudia leaned her hips against the table's edge and felt the bruise blooming under her ribs complain. She'd wake tomorrow mapped in color.

He stood, opened a cabinet, and set a small pharmacy of honesty on the counter: ibuprofen, sterile wipes, water. "Sit," he said.

"You've said that three times tonight."

"And you've needed it all three."

"I don't—"

"Claudia," he said, and her name in his mouth made refusal feel juvenile. She sat. He tore a packet, the antiseptic smell a time machine. He cleaned a scrape she hadn't registered on her wrist, then another at the edge of her hairline where a shard had kissed her scalp. He worked without commentary, a man who had learned that narration spooks the body.

"Tell me about the Dominguez witness," he said, as if he were asking about the weather.
"The one who recanted. Why'd he fold?"

She kept her eyes on his hands. "His mother's pharmacy gets its shipments off the same truck every Tuesday. The truck stopped coming."

"Right," Angelo said, approving and grim in a single note. "Pressure. Always cleaner than a bullet."

"He cried in my office," she said, surprised at how quickly the memory rose. "Big man.
Calluses like shovels. He cried and apologized to the floor for wasting my time."

"You didn't fire him as a witness."

"Of course I didn't," she snapped. "You don't get to be brave for other people. That's not how consent works."

He made a small sound that might have been a laugh and might have been pain. "You and I agree on more than is healthy."

He finished with the wipes, palmed the ibuprofen, shook two into his own hand, shook two more into hers.

"I don't take—"

"You do now," he said lightly. "Or you won't be able to turn your head tomorrow without asking for help, and we both know how you feel about that."

She took them. The water tasted like nothing. It was a mercy.

"Marks will sell me to the board," she said, staring at the plant again because looking at something alive kept the room from tilting. "He'll call it crisis leadership. He'll talk about 'protecting the brand.' He'll do it with the cadence of a eulogy."

"He'll also file a quiet complaint with the bar," Angelo said. "Conflict of interest. Suggest you 'associated with known criminal elements.' He won't think he needs to prove it. He'll aim for stain."

"Then he'll aim true," she said, the iron returning to her voice. "Because I am sitting in a room with a known criminal element and taking pills from his hand."

He didn't flinch. "You're sitting in a room with a man who doesn't want you dead. That category is smaller than it should be."

"And in exchange?"

He took a breath like he was considering a lie and abandoning it. "In exchange, one day I'll ask you to look at a case the way I look at a street—sideways. I'll ask you not to hand a boy to a machine that will grind him into an example just because the paperwork says he fits."

She held his gaze. "If the boy put a bullet in someone's mother, I won't sell the universe your second chance."

"Good," he said. "Keep that. I need you to be harder than me in the right places."

It wasn't flirting. It was worse than flirting. It was faith.

The apartment's refrigerator whirred to life as if to remind them they were animals with bodies. He brought two bowls from a cabinet and poured cereal like it was an apology. She snorted and ate because the alternative was rehearsing tomorrow's starvation.

"Who pays the rent?" she asked, spoon balanced against her lip.

"No one who would enjoy meeting you," he said.

"Your accountant," she said, remembering the slip of paper in the church, the offshore routes he'd promised were real. "The one who scrubbed Marks's daughter's books."

"Ray," he said. "He's good with numbers and terrible with fear. I keep him alive by making his fear useful."

"Where is he?"

"Not here," Angelo said. "Which is why he's still breathing."

Her phone, dark on the table, lit with a single line of text from an unknown number that wasn't his.

I'm sorry.

Khan.

Claudia's spoon clinked against porcelain. Angelo saw the screen before she could turn it. He didn't reach for the phone; he didn't have to.

"Where is he?" Angelo asked.

"Unknown," she said, tapping the message open. The bubble hung there like a confession torn from a throat. She typed: Where?

Dots. Vanished. Nothing.

"He won't answer again," Angelo said. "He sent that from a borrowed phone at a gas station or a bathroom, and someone is already asking him why he stopped to breathe."

"He's not a criminal," Claudia said, anger flushing color up her throat.

"He's a citizen caught between billing cycles," Angelo said, merciless and right.
"Dominguez collects those like stamps. Marks uses them like paperweights."

She put the phone face down. "You talk like a man who despises the city and loves it more than anyone."

"I talk like a man who learned the city is an animal that eats, and I decided to feed it breadcrumbs I can track."

She looked at the clock. 2:17 a.m. Dawn felt like fiction. Court in seven hours was a different kind of fiction. Somewhere, a judge would sleep and wake believing in calendars. She envied that man in a complicated way—resentment braided with pity.

“Tell me about your people,” she said, because fatigue makes generosity a strategy. “The ones who orbit you in alleys. The ones who open doors without names.”

“They’re not mine,” he said. “They’re the city’s. I pay them. I keep cops away on nights when their sons need to walk home with a backpack full of tips. I show up at funerals even when there’s no priest. That buys loyalty that outlasts cash.”

“And when it doesn’t?”

“Then I bury them and don’t pretend it’s noble.”

She set the bowl down, appetite gone. “You’re asking me to choose you over the law.”

“I’m asking you to choose the truth over a theater that arrests the wrong people on time,” he said softly. “And I’m not asking tonight.”

The sweater in the drawer was, predictably, exactly her size. She wore it because cold had found her when she stopped running. Angelo took the couch because men who don’t sleep well often choose furniture that expects to be left. She took the bed because she had run out of clever ways to refuse help.

She didn’t turn off the lamp. He didn’t ask her to.

The ceiling had a crack that ran from corner to corner like a vein. She tracked it with her eyes while her body tried to measure whether the mattress was a trap. Somewhere between the first hundred heartbeats and the next, she slept.

In the threshold hour where the mind slides its mask half off, she dreamed the alley again—bottles, teeth of flame—and woke with the old instinct: under, small, quiet. Her hand reached down before she could arrest it and found nothing but floor.

“Claudia,” Angelo said from the couch, voice low and near, as if he’d been keeping a vigil without witnesses. “You’re here.”

"I know," she said, because admitting the opposite would make it truer.

"Three o'clock," he said, and she wanted to laugh at the absurdity of timekeeping presented like comfort, but the number anchored her. She breathed. He didn't get up. He didn't come closer. He just let the hour tick past like a bridge.

When morning arrived in that pale city way—gray before gold—she was already sitting on the edge of the bed, shoes beside her, folder on her lap. He was at the window, shadow against light, watching a world that had never once watched itself.

"Coffee?" he asked.

"Please," she said, and the word felt like a door she hadn't opened in years.

He handed her a mug and the barest smile. "You say 'please' like a challenge."

"I grew up earning my favors," she said. "Not being handed them."

"You still are," he said. "Earning them."

She sipped. The coffee was cheap and perfect. It put steel back in her spine.

"What's today?" she asked. "Step one."

"Step one," he said, "is you don't go to court."

She almost choked. "Excuse me?"

"You call in a fire. The courthouse will pretend to sympathize while they sharpen their teeth.
You stay off the record while we find the hole in your floor."

"'We,'" she said, but without enough bite to make it an objection.

"We," he repeated. "I'm going to peel Marks like paint. You're going to move everything that matters off anything he can touch. That includes your name."

"How do I move my name?"

"You lend it to someone who can spend it without getting you shot," he said. "An ADA who owes nobody. Or a reporter who's already been fired twice for telling the truth."

"Ray," she said. "Your accountant."

"Ray is step four," he said, amused. "Step two is the clerk's office. There's a woman named Jo who's honest even when it breaks her paycheck. We ask her for the login logs."

"She won't give them to you."

"She will if you ask."

"And step three?"

He opened the door, held it for her, and waited until she brushed past. "Step three," he said, with that almost-smile again, "is where you stop pretending you haven't already chosen."

They left the plant to keep trying. The city met them with a morning that had forgotten the night—or decided to lie about it—people in suits, people in uniforms, people in clothes that had learned to hide holes. Claudia tucked the folder close and let the street's noise drape over her like armor.

At the car, he paused, hand on the roof, eyes cutting toward the far corner of the block the way a wolf's ears tilt toward movement no human hears.

"What?" she asked.

"New tail," he said. "Clumsy."

“Marks?”

“Or Dominguez,” he said. “Either way, they’re about to learn the first rule.”

“Which is?”

He opened her door. “Don’t follow a woman who’s finally ready to stop running.” The courthouse clocktower loomed like a smug sentinel as Angelo guided the sedan through morning traffic. Claudia sat rigid in the passenger seat, folder anchored against her knees. To every onlooker, she looked like a professional on her way to argue motions. Inside, her pulse wrote a different story—fast, uneven, like it was late for its own hearing.

Angelo turned down a side street, easing the car between a bakery van and a delivery truck. “We don’t walk through the front,” he said. “Eyes are there. Cameras too. We go in quiet.”

“I’m a lawyer,” Claudia snapped. “Not a thief.”

“Today,” he said calmly, “you’re both.”

The back entrance of the courthouse smelled of bleach and resignation. Angelo’s contact—Jo, the clerk—met them in a stairwell with a stack of papers that looked too ordinary to be dangerous. She was older, hair pinned neat, glasses sliding toward the tip of her nose.

“You Vale?” Jo asked.

“Yes,” Claudia said.

“You didn’t get this from me,” Jo muttered, handing over the papers. Her hand shook once, then stilled. “Logs for the last three months. Who signed into your files, when, and from where.”

Claudia flipped through, eyes narrowing. “These show—”

“Slow down,” Angelo warned. “Don’t say it here.”

Jo's mouth pinched. "He's right. You'll want to read those somewhere that doesn't echo." She glanced at Angelo. "You owe me, Romano."

"I pay my debts," he said.

She vanished back into the stairwell, footsteps soft as erasure.

Claudia stared at the pages. Her own initials glared up at her from timestamps she knew were wrong. Weeks she'd been in trial. Days she'd been out of town. Her password. Her access card. Used like tools.

"They're framing me," she whispered.

"Marks," Angelo said. "He's already started."

Her throat tightened. "If the bar sees this—"

"They'll call it negligence," he finished. "Say you let your house get sloppy. They'll open an inquiry, suspend your license while they 'review.' You'll be a name on a boardroom agenda, not a person."

Claudia clutched the papers so tightly the edges bit into her palms. "Everything I built—"

"Is what he's dismantling," Angelo said.

She wanted to argue. She wanted to stand in a courtroom and shred Marks word by word until the truth was too sharp for him to hold. Instead, she heard herself whisper, "Why now? Why me?"

Angelo leaned back against the wall, watching her like a man who already knew the answer but wanted her to say it first.

"Because I don't bend," she said, bitter. "Because I don't take their money."

"And because you scare them," Angelo added softly. "You scare them because you remember what it's like to hide under the bed and you still stand taller than they do."

The words hit harder than she expected. She turned away, throat burning.

Her phone buzzed in her pocket. A number she didn't recognize. She answered on reflex.

"Claudia Vale," said a voice she knew too well. Marks. Smooth, practiced, the cadence of a man who'd been winning rooms for thirty years.

"Where are you?" he asked.

"Reviewing damages," she said evenly.

"Good. Keep your head down. The board's meeting tonight. There will be questions about last night's… mishap. I'll do what I can to protect you."

She froze. "Protect me?"

"Of course," he said, tone coated in false warmth. "But you'll need to show good faith. Step back from Dominguez. Reassign the case. It's too volatile. Let one of the partners with cleaner hands carry it forward."

Her vision blurred with fury. "Cleaner hands?"

"Don't be naive, Claudia," Marks said, voice tightening. "This firm survives because we know which fires to fight and which to let burn. You're too close to this one."

She wanted to scream. Instead she said, "I'll think about it."

"Do more than think," Marks replied. "Do what's best for the firm."

The line went dead.

Claudia lowered the phone with a hand that shook, just once. "He wants me out. He wants me quiet."

Angelo stepped closer, so close she could smell smoke still clinging to his shirt. “And what do you want?”

Her laugh cracked. “To burn the whole damn boardroom down.”

He smiled, faint and dangerous. “Now you’re speaking my language.”

She looked at him, really looked. Scar, ink, steady hands, the patience of a man who knew violence better than sleep. She hated that she needed him. She hated more that a small, traitorous part of her wanted him—not as leverage, not as protection, but as proof she wasn’t alone in the dark.

The papers trembled in her grip. She pressed them flat against her chest, as if that would keep her world from unraveling.

“I’m not yours,” she said, voice shaking with more than anger.

“No,” Angelo said softly. “But you’re not theirs either. And that’s why they’ll never forgive you.” They left the courthouse by the same back stairwell, papers buried deep in Claudia’s tote. Outside, the city hummed with the noon rush—trucks unloading, taxis snarling, hot dog carts perfuming the block with mustard and grease. To anyone watching, they were just another pair in suits. Inside, Claudia felt like she was walking a tightrope strung over fire.

Angelo guided her toward the car, his posture loose but his eyes alert. “Where to?” he asked.

She tightened her grip on the tote. “My office is ash. My home’s probably bugged. That leaves… nowhere.”

“Not nowhere,” he said. “With me.”

The words should have sounded like chains. Instead, they landed like a dare.

The safehouse they chose this time was above a closed bakery, the kind that smelled of yeast even in its sleep. A single narrow staircase led up to a flat with peeling wallpaper and windows that overlooked an alley full of trash cans and graffiti. It wasn't glamorous, but it was invisible.

Claudia dropped the tote on the table and pressed her palms against the wood until her knuckles blanched. "Marks is going to hang me with those logs. If I show them in court, they'll say I forged them. If I keep them hidden, he'll leak them himself."

"Then we don't play by his rules," Angelo said. He leaned against the counter, crossing his arms. "You want leverage? We create it."

Claudia looked up, eyes narrowing. "How?"

"Marks has been laundering Dominguez's money through his daughter's firm. You said it yourself—you don't bend. That means he's terrified of you finding proof. So we find it first. Then we choose where it lands."

Her pulse quickened. "That's blackmail."

"That's survival," he said.

"You're asking me to cross a line."

"No," Angelo said, voice low, steady. "I'm asking you to admit you've already crossed it.
You're in a burned office, running from men with bottles, hiding in rooms that don't exist. There's no line left, Claudia. Just which direction you walk."

She turned away, staring out the window at the alley. Graffiti bloomed on the brick like wildflowers—names, symbols, declarations. For a moment she envied their shameless permanence.

Her voice was quieter when she spoke again. "If I do this… if I work with you… what does that make me?"

He came up behind her, close enough that the heat of his body brushed her back. "It makes you alive."

She didn't move. The room held its breath.

"You think you know me," she said, her throat tight.

"I don't," he murmured. "Not yet. But I know what it costs to survive men like Marks and
Dominguez. And I know you've been paying it since you were small."

Her hand trembled against the window frame. She wanted to deny it, to put on the armor of the courtroom, the mask of the CEO. But she was tired, so tired, and the words slipped out before she could stop them.

"When I was eight, my father threw a bottle at me. It shattered over the bedpost. Glass in my hair. I didn't cry. I couldn't. Crying made it worse."

Angelo's reflection in the glass didn't flinch. He didn't pity. He just stood there, steady, a man who'd been cut and kept moving.

"That's why you don't run from fire," he said softly.

Claudia blinked hard, forcing the burn in her eyes back where it belonged. "That's why I can't stop."

Silence stretched. Then Angelo moved closer, his hand hovering near hers on the window frame, not touching, just near enough to feel like gravity. "So don't stop," he said. "But don't do it alone."

She turned then, sharply, facing him. They were too close, breaths tangling, the weight of everything they weren't saying pressing harder than the city outside.

Her voice dropped to a whisper. "If I work with you… it can't be about us."

"It isn't," Angelo said. His eyes flicked down to her mouth, then back up. "It's about surviving. Everything else is noise."
And yet neither of them moved. The noise between them was deafening.

Claudia stepped back first, dragging air into her lungs. "All right. We do it your way. We find the proof. We hit Marks where it hurts."

Angelo's smile was sharp, dangerous, but real. "Welcome to the other side, Vale."

"Don't get used to it," she said.

He poured them both coffee from a dented percolator. The taste was burnt, bitter, perfect.
They bent over the papers together, their shoulders nearly touching, plotting routes through offshore accounts, shell companies, and signatures Marks had never expected anyone to trace.

For the first time in days, Claudia felt something like momentum. She hated that it came from Angelo. She hated more that she liked the way his presence made her pulse steady, like maybe the tightrope wasn't strung over fire after all, but over something she might actually cross.
By evening, they had a plan. Angelo would track the accountant. Claudia would leverage her credentials to access restricted filings. Together, they'd build a case neither Marks nor Dominguez could bury.

But under the strategy, under the maps and coffee rings, something else had shifted.

When she stood to leave the table, Angelo caught her wrist lightly, the barest touch. Not possession. Not command. Just connection.

"You're not alone anymore," he said.

Claudia didn't answer. She couldn't. But she didn't pull away either.
The plan shouldn't have been risky. That was the lure.

Angelo had lines on Ray-the accountant with nervous hands and a genius for erasing footprints. Claudia had the credentials to request filings that no journalist could touch without a subpoena. They would meet in a neutral spot where Ray felt less visible: a public library branch on the river, third floor, reference section. Cameras but no guards, windows but no exits you couldn't predict. Noon the next day. Simple, contained, forgettable.

By the time Claudia and Angelo pushed through the library's revolving doors, the air conditioning had turned the place into a chilled cathedral. The soft thrum of vents, the hush of pages, the carefully modulated coughs of people trying not to be noticed. Sunlight sliced the stacks into measured geometry. It felt honest. It felt like a lie pretending to be honest.

"Third floor," Angelo said, eyes doing a lazy sweep that somehow recorded everything.
"North corner. Blue chairs."

They rode the elevator up with a mother and a toddler who was fixated on the numbers lighting, lighting, lighting. The doors sighed open to a room of study carrels, overwatered plants, and the faint antiseptic smell of new books. At the far end: blue chairs, river beyond glass, a man pretending to read a world atlas like it was a thriller.

Ray.

He saw Claudia first and didn't relax. His mouth made a shape that wanted to be a smile and thought better of it. His suit was too expensive for a man who claimed poverty and too wrinkled for a man who claimed ease. He clutched a portfolio like a priest guarding sacraments.

"Ms. Vale," he said, standing as if they were at a wedding.
"Ray," Angelo said, voice neutral.

Ray didn't nod. He angled his body so no one could see the portfolio's edge. "I shouldn't be here."

"Neither should we," Claudia said. "But here we are."

He swallowed. His Adam's apple bobbed like a buoy in a storm. "I brought what I could. It won't be enough."

"It'll be a start," she said. "Show me."

He opened the portfolio an inch and produced a single stapled packet as if the act cost him blood. Money moving from shell to shell—numbers that meant nothing until they meant everything. Names of subsidiaries tucked into the corners, signatures in the penmanship of men who'd learned not to press hard. On page three, a neat entry: Monarch Consulting (LLC) → $185,000, memo line: Compliance Retainer.

Monarch belonged to Marks's daughter.

Claudia's breath lengthened. "Dates?"

Ray tapped a column with a trembling finger. "Quarterly. Regular as tides."

"And sources?"

"Shipping. Warehouses that bill forty pallets and ship forty-two. Grocery chains that round up spoilage to hide a cut." His eyes flicked to Angelo. "You taught me to see it. You told me not to look too long."

"I told you to keep yourself alive," Angelo said.

Ray's laugh was brittle. "You send me into the dark with a pen and an abacus and call it mercy."

Angelo's jaw set. "You done?"

"No," Ray said, surprising both of them. He produced a second packet. This one was heavier. "Monarch paid out too. Not just to the daughter. To a political action committee that doesn't exist, except on paper. And to a charity whose only event is a dinner no one attends."

"Names," Claudia said.

Ray's finger found a line and rested there. Citizens for Urban Renewal. The Virtue Fund.

Claudia's brain catalogued, cross-referenced, plucked at threads. "Who signs for those?"

"The same man for both," Ray said. "He used to be a staffer. Now he calls himself a consultant. He sits in boardrooms and translates greed into strategy."

"Marks," Angelo said.

"Marks," Ray echoed, and the word seemed to fog the glass.

A librarian hustled past with a cart, shushing air that did not need to be shushed. The toddler from the elevator escaped his mother and thumped by like a small drum. The world insisted on its normalcy.

"Email?" Claudia asked. "Anything that shows intent."

Ray shook his head. "Nothing that says the quiet part out loud. He's not stupid. He learned from watching smarter men get indicted."

Claudia felt the old courtroom rhythm rise in her chest, the one that assembles fact into narrative, narrative into blade. "We don't need intent on paper. We need pattern. We need timeline. We need pressure points."

Ray closed the portfolio with a soft slap that sounded too loud. "You have them. Now I'm leaving." He stood too quickly, the chair legs rasping the carpet.

Angelo's hand landed on the portfolio. "Not yet."

Ray's expression curdled. "I brought your homework. I'm not staying after class."

"You're not walking into a net," Angelo said. "Someone followed you."

Ray's face drained. "How—"

"You checked your reflection too often," Angelo said. "You smelled like fear at the door and the man in the gray ball cap smelled it too. He's on the second floor now pretending to read microfilm. He'll come up when he thinks he has company."

Claudia's scalp prickled. "Can we move him?"

"Better," Angelo said, voice looser, smile that didn't reach his eyes. "We'll move us."

They threaded through stacks. Angelo didn't hurry. He never hurried. At the elevator, he thumbed the button and then didn't get in. "Stairs," he said. "Ray, you first. Claudia, behind him."

They went down a floor and bled out into reference again. Angelo looked like an off-duty cop who'd lost his badge and kept his authority. The man in the gray cap pretended to be enthralled by weather patterns from 1974.

"Don't look at him," Angelo said softly.

They reached the far stairwell, a concrete throat that smelled of mop water and age. Ray's breath turned audibly brittle. Claudia put a hand between his shoulders, not comforting, just present.

On the landing between floors, the door above them opened. Gray cap. His face was blank with professional boredom. He started down, one hand where a gun would be if this were a different building.

"Keep moving," Angelo said.

Gray cap matched their pace. Too casual. Angelo slowed a fraction, forcing the angle. The man lifted his chin, eyes flicking. Claudia's brain recorded details on habit: mid-forties, right-handed, knuckles scuffed, mouth a thin line used to clenching.

He moved on them at the next landing, speed blooming like a trap. A hand for Ray's arm. Another for the portfolio.

Angelo stepped into him, the violence quiet, efficient. Elbow to wrist. Knee to thigh. A twist that turned the man's momentum into the wall. The portfolio stayed with Ray. The gray cap's hand came out with a short black blade that looked like a letter opener and wanted to be more.

Claudia grabbed the rail with her left hand and Ray with her right. Angelo's forearm locked the man's knife arm high, the blade scraping concrete. The man headbutted without a tell. Angelo didn't take it—he rolled with it, bled it of power, answered with a palm under the chin that snapped teeth together hard enough to crack enamel.

"Run," Angelo said without looking at them.

Ray ran. Claudia didn't. She waited until gray cap feinted low and then kicked the knife the way soccer coaches warned you not to—hard and reckless. Metal clattered down the stairs, the sound ricocheting.

Gray cap snarled something in a language they all understood. He yanked free enough to shove Angelo into the rail. Angelo's shoulder hit steel and bounced. Gray cap reached for his belt.

Claudia didn't think. She grabbed a fire extinguisher from the bracket on the wall, yanked the pin with a ring finger that had remembered keys and locks its whole life, and fired cold white into his face.

The man gagged, blinded. Angelo took him down with a sweep that made pure geometry of gravity. He cuffed him with plastic ties as if zip-ties grew in stairwells.

"Now," Angelo said. "Run now."

They ran.

They poured out into the ground floor stacks like a story they weren't invited to tell, tripped another stairwell, found the loading bay. Sunlight slabbed concrete in sharp rectangles. A maintenance worker smoked like a character witness.

"Emergency," Angelo said, already sliding cash into a palm. "You didn't see us."

The worker nodded like everyone had homework. A door popped. They spilled into an alley that smelled of river and detergent. The car was a block away because Angelo never parked where the ending would be predictable. They hit the sidewalk at a controlled sprint that read like late-for-a-meeting if you weren't looking closely.

"Tell me you still have it," Angelo said, not winded.

Ray hugged the portfolio like a friend he didn't trust. "I have it."

They made it to the car. Doors open, bodies in, locks thumbed. Angelo pulled out into traffic without drama. Only then did Claudia let her lungful of air go.

Ray laughed once, a broken machine noise. "You two are insane," he said. "And I'm dead."

"No," Angelo said. "You're moving."

"Where?" Ray asked, terrified of the answer.

"Somewhere I can keep you until this lands," Angelo said. "Then as far out of range as you can stand."

Ray swallowed. "You'll keep me alive?"

"I'll try," Angelo said. "You'll meet me halfway."

"How?"

"Don't answer your phone," Angelo said. "Don't talk to anyone who says your middle name. Don't spend anything that can be traced. Don't be curious about the man who will follow you from the bodega to the bus stop."

Ray pressed the portfolio harder to his ribs. "I hate this."

"I know," Angelo said.

Claudia turned in her seat to look at Ray. "When this is over," she said, "you come with me to the DA. You tell them everything. You let me build you an immunity deal so strong it can hold even if a judge sneezes. That's your halfway."

Ray nodded, because hope is easier to accept when it sounds like paperwork.

They dropped him two neighborhoods away in a basement apartment with a door that stuck and a couch that had seen better sins. Angelo left a number on the table written in block letters like a scolding.

“Call only if you’re bleeding,” he said.

Ray looked like he might be already. “Okay.”

Back in the car, Claudia exhaled slowly. The city slid by wearing late afternoon like a clean shirt. “This isn’t sustainable,” she said. “Running. Hiding. Stairs.”

“It’s not a lifestyle,” Angelo said. “It’s a bridge.”

“To what?”

“To the moment when you stop fleeing and start hunting.”

“Then hurry,” she said.

They took the long way to the bakery safehouse. Angelo’s driving turned random into ritual—left, right, left, a pause at a light that didn’t need one. When they reached the back staircase, he killed the engine and didn’t move.

“What?” Claudia asked.

“Tail again,” he said. “Different flavor.”

“Marks?”

“Or Dominguez,” he said. “Or a freelancer who works for both.” He nodded toward the farmouth of the alley. A sedan idled there with the confidence of a car that belongs to the block. “Go upstairs. Pack what you touched. We’re burning it.”

She stared. “We just got here.”

“Exactly,” he said. “Someone knew where ‘here’ was. That means they knew where ‘before here’ was. No more breadcrumbs.”

She swallowed annoyance. “What about the plan?”

“We still run it,” he said. “But we run it on our feet.”

Upstairs, she stuffed what little she’d disturbed into the tote. The room already looked like they’d never been, which made it somehow sadder. She paused with her hand on the sweater drawer. Stupid, but the softness had meant something when the night was loud.

“Leave it,” Angelo said gently from the door. “Let the place keep some comfort.”

She left it.

Downstairs again, the alley had stretched thinner. Two men now, the shape of trouble trying to look like conversations. Angelo put the tote in her hands, and when she reached for the door handle, he closed his hand over hers.

“Stay on my left,” he said. “If something changes, you move without thinking. Don’t be brave. Be fast.”
“Is this the part where you tell me not to run into fire?” she asked.

“This is the part where I tell you not to run toward gunfire,” he said. “I’ll handle the romance of that.”

They walked into the alley like it belonged to them and always had. The sedan at the mouth idled, bored. The two men drifted a fraction closer, not enough to be charged with intent, enough to be charged with stupidity.

“Afternoon,” one said.

“Evening,” Angelo corrected pleasantly. “You’re early.”

“For what?” the other asked.

“The part where you pretend to have a reason,” Angelo said, and then the world bridged the distance between conversation and consequence.

The first man moved—center mass, arm swinging. Angelo stepped into him with a pivot that turned weight into absence. The second reached under his jacket and discovered, too late, that Angelo had closed the space where a clean draw lives. The gun cleared leather and met Angelo’s forearm; the shot went wild, popping glass out of a window two floors up. Claudia’s ears rang. She dropped low because bodies learn. The tote thumped her ribs.

“Go,” Angelo said, not looking at her.

She went sideways, not back, because law had taught her to never retreat into a narrative someone else wrote. The first man found a wall with his face. The second found empty air as Angelo removed the gun with the casual cruelty of someone removing a splinter. He popped the magazine, flung it. The gun, emptied, clattered into a drain.

“Tell Marks,” Angelo said into the second man’s ear, conversational like a weather report, “that if he sends staff, I send bodies. If he sends pros, I send flowers.” He released him. The man stumbled. The first had recovered enough to make a choice and he chose the oldest one—run.

The sedan at the alley mouth jolted awake, reversed too fast, clipped a garbage can, and fled the way cowards do—loud, messy, sure.

Angelo turned to Claudia. “You good?”

She nodded because words hadn’t found the room back yet.

“Then we’re done here,” he said. “Next place.”

They didn’t go to the garage safehouse. They didn’t go to the first apartment. Angelo chose a motel that rented by the hour in a district that didn’t judge. The room smelled like bleach and old decisions. He double-locked the door and slid a chair under the knob because ritual is how you tell fear you're still the one holding the pen.

Claudia set the tote on the bed and took inventory. Ray's packets. Jo's logs. The Dominguez file. A smaller envelope she had not packed.

"What's that?" she asked.

Angelo was at the window, slat of blinds tilted to see the parking lot. "What's what?"

She held up the envelope. No address. No seal. A single word in pencil on the front.

Careful.

Her stomach dropped. She turned it over with the dread of a surgeon discovering something missed. Inside: one photograph, glossy, new. A shot of her on the courthouse steps yesterday, phone to her ear, mouth a hard line. A red X marked the corner of her briefcase.

"Where did this come from?" she asked, voice low and even because panic is a poor listener.

Angelo crossed the room in three strides. He took the photo, scanned it, flipped it, scanned again. "They were inside the bakery," he said, fury under control because he fed it rules. "We were already burned before we got warm."

"And Khan?" she asked because the question had sat in her throat like a bone.
"Either he's a passenger," Angelo said, "or he's kindling."

The room seemed to tilt; she put a hand on the wall until gravity remembered her name. "I can't lose another person in this," she said, and hated the crack in it.

"You won't," he said. "Not to accident. Not to negligence. If you lose someone, it will be because we chose the cost and paid it."

"You talk like you can buy fate," she said.

"I talk like I can bargain with men," he said. "Fate doesn't return calls."

Silence swallowed the room and then handed it back. Claudia took the photo, slid it into a plastic sleeve from the tote, and labeled it the way she labeled all evidence—with date, time, and a thinly veiled prayer that truth still had a chance.

Angelo watched her, arms folded, the kind of patience you cultivate in cages. "This is the last night you'll pretend you have a choice," he said.

She looked up. "What does that mean?"

"It means tomorrow we stop reacting," he said. "We hit first. We go for the throat."

"Marks," she said.

"And the artery that feeds him," Angelo said. "We cut off the money. We break the wrists that hold the pen. We put someone in a room with a camera and make him say the quiet part where people can hear it."

"You want a confession," she said.

"I want leverage," he corrected. "Public. Viral. Unmistakable."

"And if we fail?" she asked.

"We won't," he said. "But if we do, we do it forward."

He stepped closer, and this time there was no smoke, no siren to break the moment. Just a cheap motel's hum and a woman who had run out of past tense.

"You asked me back at the lobby," he said, softer, "what I wanted out of this. This is it. I want you alive on the other side of a war you didn't start. I want you to keep your name. And I want to see what you do when the men who built this city out of fear have to watch it belong to someone who's not afraid."

Her breath stuttered. "I am afraid."

"Good," he said. "People who say they aren't are either lying or planning a funeral."

He lifted a hand and stopped it an inch from her cheek, like it belonged there and he had to ask permission from the air. She didn't move. He didn't either. The electricity between them was not a metaphor. It was a body remembering the physics of contact.

"Angelo," she said.

"Yes."

"If you kiss me now, I won't stop you."

He swallowed, the first unsteady thing she'd seen him do. "If I kiss you now, I don't stop either."

They stood in that dangerous mercy until the motel's refrigerator clicked on and the spell broke. He lowered his hand. She closed her eyes as if that could keep something from falling.

"Tomorrow," he said, voice rough. "We choose."

He turned to the window, back to patrol, because vigilance was the only acceptable substitute for touch. Claudia sat on the edge of the bed and opened the portfolio again, not because she needed to see the numbers, but because numbers were the story you could keep from changing if you stared hard enough.

In the parking lot, a car idled and moved on. Someone laughed three doors down. The world yawned.
Claudia looked at Angelo, and he looked like a man who had finally run out of places to put his hands.

"Ready?" he asked without turning.

"No," she said, honest as hunger. "But willing."

He nodded once, still facing the night. “That’s the only kind that works.”

Outside, thunder stacked somewhere far away, making promises the sky hadn’t decided whether to keep.

Chapter 6 — The Confession Room

The motel blinds let in a sliver of gray light. Claudia hadn't slept. The photograph marked Careful lay on the table between them like a third presence in the room. Angelo sat in the corner chair, boots planted, watching the window as though the glass owed him answers.

"You ever going to tell me what made you this way?" Claudia asked finally, breaking the silence that had been growing teeth for hours.

His jaw flexed, the scar along his chin catching the pale light. "Which way?"

"The man who moves like he expects the world to attack. The one who can't let his guard down, not even when the sun's barely up."

Angelo didn't answer at first. His eyes stayed on the parking lot. "You think men are born like this?"

"I think something forged you," she said. "And I want to know what."

He shifted, leaned forward, elbows on his knees. His voice was low, the cadence stripped of its usual confidence.

"My father was a soldier for Dominguez's predecessor. Not a boss. Not a leader. Just muscle. He bled for scraps and came home with rage instead of money. My mother tried to leave three times. Each time he found her, dragged her back. The last time, she didn't come back at all."

Claudia felt the air in the room sharpen. "What happened to her?"

Angelo's eyes flicked up, met hers for a heartbeat. "He happened. And when the cops came, they wrote it off as an accident. Stairs. Bruises. End of report."

Her chest tightened. "And you?"

“I was twelve,” he said. “Old enough to understand silence was survival. Young enough to believe silence was shame.” His hand flexed once, as if memory was something physical he could shake off. “I ran. Not far. Just to the next block, to the corner where the crew played cards. They took me in because I was angry enough to be useful.”

“And Dominguez?”

“Back then he was just a name whispered in alleys. By the time I was sixteen, he knew mine. By twenty, I was doing his work. Not because I wanted to be like him.” He leaned back, voice bitter. “Because I didn’t know how not to be my father.”

Claudia studied him. The tattoos on his arms weren’t decoration—they were ledger marks, each one a transaction of survival.

“You don’t answer to him now,” she said.

“No,” Angelo said. “But I still breathe in a city he owns. That means I’m never free of him. Neither are you.”

The silence after that was different. Heavy. Intimate. Dangerous.

Claudia folded her arms, but her voice softened. “You’ve been carrying that weight alone.”

“Better me than anyone else,” he said. “I can handle it.”

Her throat tightened. “That’s exactly what I used to tell myself.”

For the first time since she’d met him, Angelo’s mouth curved into something that wasn’t a smirk or a mask. It was small. Almost human. “Then maybe you understand why I don’t want to watch you carry it too.” Angelo leaned back in the chair, the wood creaking under his weight. His eyes weren’t on Claudia anymore. They were on a point beyond the wall, as if memory had painted a window only he could see.

“You asked what made me this way,” he said, his voice lower now, slower, every word pulled from somewhere old. “It wasn’t just my father. It was what came after.”

Claudia stayed quiet. In cross-examinations she'd learned when not to interrupt. This felt like one of those moments.

"I ran from home and found the crew," Angelo continued. "They gave me food, a mattress on the floor. But there's no charity in the streets. Everything's a transaction. My anger bought me a place. My fists paid the rent."

He rolled up his sleeve. A tattoo curled up his forearm: a snake coiled around a dagger. The ink was faded, older than the others.

"First mark I earned," he said. "Fourteen. They told me ink meant belonging. What it really meant was debt. You don't get tattoos like these unless you've spilled something to deserve them."

Claudia's chest tightened. "Blood?"

He nodded once. "The first time wasn't clean. It never is. Some kid from a rival block— seventeen, maybe. He pulled a knife. I reacted. That's all it takes. Reaction." His hand flexed, a ghost movement of the fight. "I walked away with a cut on my jaw and his blood on my shirt. They told me I'd proved myself. I went home that night and threw up until there was nothing left."

Claudia searched his face. The scar on his jaw wasn't just an old wound. It was the edge of a blade that had carved him into someone else.

"You kept going," she said softly.

"Because the alternative was being weak," Angelo said. "And in my world, weak meant dead. So I let them teach me. How to fight. How to collect. How to stand so no one tested you twice. By the time Dominguez called my name, I was already fluent in survival."

His gaze flicked back to her, sharp again. "That's what the tattoos are. Not art. Not pride. Just chapters. Every mark is a night I didn't die."

Claudia's throat felt tight. She wanted to reach across the table, trace the ink with her fingers, rewrite his story with touch. Instead she said, "Do you regret it?"

Angelo let out a sound that wasn't quite a laugh. "Regret doesn't put food on the table. Regret doesn't stop bullets. I learned early that you don't regret. You adapt."

"But you walked away," Claudia said. "You're not Dominguez's soldier anymore."

"No," he said. "But walking away doesn't erase what you've done. It just makes you the kind of ghost people remember when they need something ugly done right."

She leaned forward, elbows on the table, refusing to let him retreat into detachment. "And what do you want me to remember you as, Angelo? The boy who hid from his father? The kid with the first tattoo? The man with blood on his hands?"

His eyes held hers. For once, there was no mask, no smirk, no armor. Just raw truth.

"Remember me," he said, voice low, "as the man who's trying not to make the same mistakes twice."

The silence between them wasn't empty. It was thick, humming, charged with everything unspoken.

Claudia exhaled slowly, like she was letting out more than air. "That's the first honest thing you've said to me."

Angelo's mouth curved, small, almost sad. "Then maybe I'm learning from you." The motel room felt smaller the longer Angelo spoke. Claudia didn't interrupt; she let the silence pull the words out of him, like cross-examination without the gavel.

"My earliest memory," Angelo said after a long pause, "is of sound. Not sight. Sound."

Claudia tilted her head. "What kind?"

"Glass breaking," he said. "My father's voice after a bottle hit the wall. I was maybe five. Old enough to know my mother's hands shook when she touched my face after, but too young to understand why she couldn't stop him."

Claudia's chest tightened. Under the bed. Glass in her hair. She saw herself in him, mirrored in a different house, a different father.

"I used to hide in the closet," Angelo continued. "There was a hole in the back wall, just big enough for me to see the streetlight outside. I'd stare at it and count until I couldn't hear him anymore." His lips twisted, not quite a smile. "Funny thing is, I still sleep better if I can see light through a crack. Darkness isn't safe. It never was."
Claudia whispered, "Me too."

He looked at her, and for a second they weren't lawyer and gangster, weren't hunter and hunted. They were two kids, hiding from the same storm.

"My mother," Angelo said, voice lower, "tried to protect me. She'd sit me on the counter, give me a piece of bread, hum so loud I couldn't hear his footsteps. She called it a game— Sing with me, Angelo. But games end. He'd drag her out, and the humming would stop."

Claudia's eyes stung. "Where is she now?"

"She never made it past thirty," he said flatly. "By the time I was twelve, she was gone. Official story? Accident. Stairs. But I remember the bruise patterns. You don't get those from falling." His jaw clenched, scar tightening. "The cops didn't want to hear it. I stopped telling it."

Claudia wanted to reach across the table, wanted to touch his hand, but she stayed still. If she touched him now, it wouldn't be comfort. It would be confession.

"What about school?" she asked.

Angelo's laugh was short, humorless. "School was where you learned what kind of target you were. You wore the wrong shoes, you got jumped. You didn't fight back, you got jumped again. Teachers didn't care. Or they cared until my father came in, reeking of whiskey, and told them to mind their business. They minded."

"Did anyone… see you?" she asked carefully.

He blinked at her. "See me?"

"A teacher. A neighbor. Anyone who knew you weren't just trouble."

Angelo thought for a moment. His eyes softened at the memory. "Mrs. Delgado. Fifth grade. She caught me stealing lunch from another kid's tray. Instead of writing me up, she packed two sandwiches every day. Said her son didn't like ham, but I think he did. I ate them anyway." His voice grew quieter. "She called me Mi hijo.my boy I hadn't heard anyone say that without anger before."
Claudia smiled faintly, though her throat ached. "She gave you kindness."

"She gave me time," Angelo said. "But time runs out. She moved away by the end of the year. After that, no one packed sandwiches with me. So, I learned to pack my own. With my fists."

The words hung between them, sharp and soft all at once.

Claudia said, against her will, "You could've turned out different."

He shook his head. "No. Men like my father don't raise men who walk away. Unless something stronger than blood teaches them how."

"And what taught you?" she asked.

His eyes flicked to hers. The air tightened, heavy with something unspoken.

"You don't want the answer," he said.

"Try me."

He leaned forward, voice a whisper. “Violence. Violence taught me. First from him. Then from me. Then from anyone who thought I was small enough to break.”

Claudia swallowed. “And yet you don’t use it on me.”

His jaw flexed. “Because you’re the first person who looks at me like I don’t need it.”

Silence roared. The motel hummed. Her heart stuttered.

For the first time, Angelo looked vulnerable, not just scarred. And Claudia, God help her, wanted to step into that space. Angelo’s voice dipped lower, as if even the cracked motel walls didn’t deserve to hear what came next.

“You want to know the line?” he asked. “The one you don’t come back from?”

Claudia’s pulse quickened, but she nodded.
“I was fifteen,” he said. “Still small, still trying to act bigger than I was. I’d been running
errands for the crew—messages, money drops, packages I wasn’t supposed to open. Most days it felt like I was invisible. Until the night I wasn’t.”

His gaze went unfocused, locked on a memory so sharp it cut the room in half.

“There was this kid—maybe seventeen, maybe older, I never asked. Wrong block, wrong night. He had a knife, thought he could scare me into handing over what I was carrying. Just twenty bucks and a bag of cheap cigarettes. Nothing worth dying for.”

Claudia held her breath.

“He cornered me by the chain-link fence behind the bodega,” Angelo went on. “The streetlight was out. Just us, the smell of garbage, and the sound of my own blood in my ears. He shoved me, hard enough my teeth clicked. Told me to hand it over. I told him no."

"Why?" Claudia whispered.

Angelo gave a thin smile. "Because I'd rather bleed than be weak. My father taught me that much."

His hand flexed against his knee, muscle memory twitching.

"He swung the knife. Not smart, not trained—just wild. I grabbed his wrist. We fought like dogs, rolling in the dirt. I remember the grit in my mouth more than anything. Then I felt the blade slide. Not into me. Into him."

Claudia's stomach turned, but she didn't look away.

"He froze," Angelo said. "Like his brain couldn't process that metal could mean him. I held on. We both stared at the blood. Then he dropped, and I was still holding the knife. My hands wouldn't open."

The motel clock ticked too loud in the pause.

"I didn't plan it. I didn't mean it. But intent doesn't matter in alleys. The crew found me shaking, blade still in my hand. They pulled me up, clapped me on the back, told me I was one of them now. They said I'd proven myself. But I couldn't hear them. All I could hear was him choking."

His jaw tightened. His voice dropped to almost nothing.

"I went home that night and washed my hands until they bled. Didn't matter. I still saw it. Still hear it sometimes, in the quiet."

Claudia's throat burned. She forced her voice to stay steady. "Did you know his name?"

Angelo's eyes flicked to hers. There was no shield there now, no armor. Just something raw. "No. That's the part I hate most. If I'd known his name, maybe I could've carried him different. Instead he's just… the kid. My first ghost."

Claudia's chest ached. She wanted to argue that it wasn't his fault, that he was a child himself. But she knew words like that wouldn't land. He wasn't confessing for absolution. He was confessing because he wanted her to see all of him.

Slowly, deliberately, she said, "You were fifteen. He was older, armed. You fought for your life."

Angelo shook his head. "You can dress it up in courtroom language if you want, but I know what it was. The first time you cross that line, it doesn't matter why. You've still crossed it. And once you do, the world starts treating you different. People looked at me and saw what I'd done, not who I was. Eventually, I did too."

Silence stretched, thick and heavy. Claudia felt her hands tremble in her lap. She curled them into fists until they steadied.

"Why tell me this?" she asked finally.

Angelo's eyes burned into hers. "Because you need to know exactly to whom you're standing next. No illusions. No excuses. Just blood."

Her heart pounded. "And you think I'll run?"

His mouth curved into something like a dare. "I think you'll look at me different. That's enough."

Claudia leaned forward, voice low, dangerous. "You're wrong. I already knew you had blood on your hands. What I didn't know was whether you felt it. Now I do."

For the first time, Angelo's breath hitched. Just once. Then the mask slid back into place, but not fast enough to hide it.

And Claudia realized something that scared her more than any fire or threat.

She wasn't falling for Angelo despite the darkness.
She was falling because he let her see it. The motel's silence pressed on them after Angelo's words. Claudia sat still, hands curled on her knees, heart hammering like a verdict waiting to be read. She had wanted honesty — and he had given her more than she was prepared to carry.

Yet instead of breaking, something inside her felt steadier.

Angelo leaned back, shoulders tense, eyes unreadable again. "Now you know."

Claudia nodded slowly. "Now I know."

The words didn't frighten him the way he expected. They seemed to steady him too.

For a long moment neither spoke. Then Claudia rose, crossing the small distance to the table where the Dominguez folder still sat. She laid her hand on it.

"Marks isn't going to stop. Neither is Dominguez. They burned my office, they're watching my every move. If I don't fight back now, I'll never get the chance."

Angelo's gaze tracked her. "Fight back how?"

She looked up, meeting his eyes. "With you."

The air sharpened. His mouth curved, slow, dangerous. "Careful, lawyer. That sounds like an oath."

"It is," she said simply.
Something flickered in his expression — not triumph, not satisfaction. Something closer to recognition.

"Then we plan," Angelo said, his voice back to steel. He pushed away from the chair and joined her at the table. He opened the folder, scanned the pages with a practiced eye. "Marks's daughter. The shell companies. The charity. That's where we start."

Claudia frowned. “Evidence is one thing. But to bring them down, we need more than paper. We need a witness. Someone who can stand up in court, someone who doesn’t vanish the second Dominguez’s name is whispered.”

“Ray’s not enough,” Angelo said.

“No,” she agreed. “He’s already terrified. He’ll fold on the stand. We need someone higher. Someone closer to Marks.”

Angelo’s finger tapped the name on the page. Citizens for Urban Renewal. “I know a man who runs their security detail. He owes me. He’s not loyal to Marks — he’s loyal to his paycheck. If we press him right, he’ll talk.”

Claudia’s eyes narrowed. “And if he doesn’t?”

“Then we take away his reason not to.”

She held his gaze. “That’s the part that scares me. How easy you make it sound.”

Angelo shrugged. “Violence is easy. Living with it isn’t. That’s the part you keep forgetting.”

Her chest tightened, but she didn’t look away. “Maybe I don’t want to forget.”

The corner of his mouth twitched. “Then maybe you’re more dangerous than I thought.”

The folder lay open between them, the weight of two lives — hers of law, his of blood — finally aligning.

Claudia straightened. “Tomorrow. We go after Marks’s charity. I’ll handle the legal cover.
You handle the rest.”
Angelo nodded once, firm. “Tomorrow.”

The motel refrigerator clicked on. Somewhere outside, thunder rolled faintly over the city.

And for the first time, they weren't just two scarred souls orbiting each other. They were partners.

Not in law.
Not in crime.
In war.

Chapter 7 — The Motel and the Man

The sun hadn't cleared the skyline when they left the motel. The air was damp, carrying that gray, heavy quiet before the city woke. Angelo scanned the lot twice before unlocking the car.

Claudia's nerves buzzed. She had the Dominguez folder pressed to her chest like a shield. She was still replaying his words from the night before — remember me as the man trying not to make the same mistakes twice.

The sedan appeared before she could answer herself. Black, tinted, smooth. It swung across the alley, cutting them off.

The first bullet punched through their windshield.

"Down!" Angelo barked, shoving her flat against the seat as glass exploded. Claudia felt shards slice her cheek, hot blood trickling instantly down her jawline.

Gunfire shredded the car door, metal screaming. Angelo's pistol barked back. One shot, two. A window on the sedan burst red; the driver slumped, forehead painting the dash.

The SUV behind them slammed in — Claudia screamed as the impact jolted her spine. They were boxed.

Men spilled from both vehicles, masks down, guns up. The lot turned into a firing line.

Angelo moved like a storm given bone. He yanked Claudia low, crawled them out the passenger side as rounds stitched the car roof with sparks. His return fire was brutal — one man spun as a bullet tore through his throat, arterial spray misting the air before he collapsed, twitching in a wet gargle.

Another rushed them. Too close. Angelo slammed his face into the trunk corner, bone cracking, teeth scattering across the pavement like spilled dice. Blood poured down his chin as he sagged, half-conscious.

Claudia's hands shook, but she grabbed a loose brick from the lot and swung blindly when another shooter lunged. The corner connected with temple. The man went down, skull splitting against concrete. The sound was sickening, sticky. Claudia staggered back, bile rising.

But she didn't let go of the brick.

By the time the last shooter dropped — chest blooming scarlet as Angelo's round took him center mass — Claudia's breath was ragged, her blouse soaked with glass dust and someone else's blood.

The sedan roared off with the survivors, dragging a corpse half-in, half-out the door. The trail it left painted the lot in uneven red.

Angelo caught Claudia's arm. "You with me?"

She swallowed hard. "Yes."

His eyes searched hers, then flicked to the bodies cooling on the pavement. "Then don't look back."

She looked anyway. She saw blood seeping into cracks in the asphalt, smoke from the burning dumpster curling around dead men who'd been alive minutes ago. The smell was iron and gasoline, heavy and permanent.

And deep inside her chest, fear twisted into something else.
Not revulsion.
Not weakness.
Something sharper.

The sedan appeared before Claudia had even buckled her seatbelt. Black. Tinted. Silent. It swung across the alley like a guillotine blade, blocking their path.

The first bullet punched through their windshield. Glass turned to dust, slicing her cheek, hot blood rushing instantly down her jaw.

"Down!" Angelo barked, forcing her flat against the seat as gunfire shredded the car. Metal screamed. Tires popped. Her ears rang with the ricochet of death.

Angelo's pistol answered. One shot, two. A window on the sedan burst scarlet; the driver's skull snapped back against the headrest, blood painting the glass. The car shuddered but didn't stop.

Then came the SUV from behind. It slammed into their bumper, steel groaning. Claudia's spine jolted hard enough she bit her tongue. The copper taste flooded her mouth.

They were boxed.

Doors opened. Men poured out. Masks down. Guns up.

The lot turned into a firing line.

Angelo dragged her low, out the passenger side. Rounds stitched sparks across the roof where her head had been. His return fire was precise, merciless — a shooter staggered, throat torn open, arterial spray misting hot in the air before his knees buckled.

Another rushed. Angelo slammed his face into the trunk corner, bone cracking wet, teeth scattering across the pavement like dice. Blood gushed from the ruined mouth as the man sagged, half-conscious.

Claudia's body moved before her brain did. She grabbed a brick from the ground, swung blindly. It connected with temple — a hollow thud. The man dropped, skull splitting against the concrete. She saw the red halo spread, too wide, too fast. She gagged — but didn't drop the brick.

The last shooter fired wild. Angelo rolled, shot clean. Center mass. The man folded like paper, chest blooming scarlet, breath leaving in a wet cough.

Then silence.

Only the crackle of fire from the dumpster. The smell of gasoline. And blood — hot, metallic, unavoidable.

The sedan peeled away, dragging a corpse half-in, half-out the door. The body bounced against the asphalt, leaving a jagged smear of red like handwriting.

Angelo hauled Claudia up by the arm. Her blouse was soaked with glass dust, streaked with someone else's blood.

"You with me?" he demanded.

Her throat worked. "Yes."

"Then don't look back."

But she did. And what she saw would never leave her: men cooling on blacktop, their blood seeping into cracks like ink filling letters.

Fear twisted into something else inside her chest. Not revulsion. Not weakness. Something sharper.

—

The courthouse smelled sterile when she entered later that morning, but Claudia carried the stink of blood with her. Angelo had vanished into shadows after the ambush, promising they'd regroup. She went where she knew to go: law, her last weapon.

But law had already been turned against her.

"Ms. Vale," the bailiff said, tone clipped. "You've been subpoenaed."

Her stomach clenched. She took the envelope. Thick. Heavy. Too heavy.

She opened it at the defense table.

Not papers.

Flesh.

A finger. Swollen, purple, ring still tight around the bone. Her paralegal's wedding band.

Claudia's vision tunneled. Blood seeped into the manila. The smell was faint but undeniable.

A note slid free, scrawled in red ink — no, not ink. The edges were sticky.

"Keep talking, and you'll count the rest."

Her chest seized. She snapped the envelope shut, but the image was burned into her skull.

The judge banged his gavel. "Ms. Vale, is there an issue?"

She looked up. His eyes didn't ask. His eyes knew. He wasn't shocked. He wasn't outraged. He was complicit.

The gavel echoed. The note burned in her hand. And for the first time, Claudia realized courtrooms weren't sanctuaries anymore. They were just another battlefield.

Chapter 8— Red Silk, Red Blood

The Anselmo Hotel dressed its sins in crystal. Chandeliers the size of small suns flooded the ballroom in white fire; mirrors caught the light and multiplied it until the wealthy could mistake reflection for company. A string quartet sawed at a waltz like it owed them money. Claudia walked in on Angelo's arm and felt every eye decide a story about them. Her hair was a sleek weapon. Her dress was black, clean lines, slit high enough to run. Angelo wore a tux like a threat—ink just hidden, scar catching the chandelier light like a secret.

"Smile," he murmured without moving his lips.

"I don't do tricks," she said, and smiled anyway, the way sharks do.

Across the room, Gerald Marks held court beneath a banner that read Citizens for Urban Renewal. His daughter, all pearls and careful innocence, stood near the donation box, laughing at something a man twice her age said too close to her ear. Dominguez wasn't visible, which meant he was either upstairs or behind the glass of some private balcony, watching.

A waiter drifted by with champagne. Angelo took two flutes and sipped neither. "Ray's man is on the north wall," he said. "Security chief. Gray hair, cheap shoes, eyes like a dog that's been kicked too many times."

Claudia didn't look. "If he bolts?"

"I break his knees," Angelo said pleasantly. "Subtle."

They separated—parallel currents in a room that pretended not to be a river. Claudia wove through donors and city council members, caught a judge whose rulings always smelled like cigar smoke, and watched his face rearrange itself into polite surprise when he recognized her.

"Claudia! I heard about your… difficulties." His smile didn't reach his pupils. "How are you holding up?"

“Bad news travels fast,” she said, letting the words sit like a stain on his tie.

He patted his chest pocket—an old man’s tell when he’s carrying a favor—then mumbled something about catching up and evaporated toward the bar.

Angelo’s voice ghosted her ear through the comm bud. “Security chief is moving. East corridor. Two shadows behind him.”

“Dominguez’s?”

“Or Marks’s. Either way, they’re not here for canapés.”

Claudia drifted toward the east corridor as if she were bored of philanthropy. The hotel’s gilt gave way to narrower halls, patterned carpet, doors with brass numbers. She smelled fresh paint and the faint chemical bite of new carpet glue—renovations. A perfect place to hide something ugly under something expensive.

Voices ahead. One anxious, one flat. The flat one said, “You’re paid to keep quiet.” The anxious one said, “It’s getting loud.”

Claudia turned the corner and almost collided with the anxious one—Ray’s man—eyes too wide, breath sour with fear. He clocked her in a heartbeat, realized who she was, and tried to shoulder past. Angelo was already there, filling the hall with stillness.

“Talk,” Angelo said.

“I can’t,” the man whispered, glancing at the flat-voiced shadow behind him. “They’ll—”

A third voice cut through, amused and cold. “They’ll what, Tony? Kill you in your good suit?”

Gerald Marks stepped out of a service door with a smile he’d practiced since law school. He held a champagne flute like a prop. Two men in black stood behind him, hands loose, jackets too heavy for a ballroom.

“Claudia,” Marks said, delighted. “You look ravishing. I was just telling the mayor how proud we are of our young partners. Such resilience.”

“Is that what we’re calling arson now?” she said.

“Accidents happen,” he said, and sipped.

Angelo shifted a fraction. The goons noted it. The light in the corridor flickered as if the building itself wanted to wince.

“Walk away,” Marks told Claudia softly. “You don’t belong in these hallways.”

“Funny,” she said. “I’ve lived in hallways like this my whole life. I just stopped pretending the carpets were clean.”

He tilted his head, as if she’d told a charming joke. “We could still save you, you know. The board prefers a redemption arc. Resign quietly. We’ll call it burnout. In a year—two—you can open a boutique practice. Write a book. ‘How I Beat the Odds.’”

“And Dominguez?” she asked. “What do I write about him?”

Marks’s eyes cooled. “Who?”

Angelo smiled without warmth. “You brought your church voice to a whorehouse, counselor.”

Something clicked in the wall. A relay. A timer finding its mark.

Angelo’s head turned a degree, the way dogs hear thunder before the sky admits it.

“Down,” he said.

The blast rolled through the hotel like a giant exhaling fire. The chandeliers didn’t fall gracefully; they exploded, crystal turned shrapnel, light ripped into knives. Heat shoved the air into their lungs. The ballroom behind them became a mouth of smoke and screaming. A second blast answered from the west wing, painting the corridor in orange. Sirens in the ceiling woke, strobing red across expensive wallpaper.

Marks's champagne flew. He ducked and ran like a man who already knew the exits. His men drew and fired; the muzzle flashes were tiny suns. Angelo slammed Claudia into the service door, bullets chewing the corridor where her spine had been. Tony—Ray's man— made a sound that wasn't a word and dropped, a hole where his cheek had been, blood splashing the fire alarm box in a red handprint.

Claudia tasted copper in the smoke, realized she'd bitten her lip hard enough to bleed, and didn't care. She grabbed the brass doorstopper, jammed it under the service door before heat could fuse it shut.

"Kitchen," Angelo said, dragging her through steam and metal. Chefs shouted, ducked, scattered. A pastry chef stood frozen, sugar bubbling into a caramel that smelled absurdly like mercy.

Another blast. Closer. A panel of ceiling fell and smashed on the line. Gas hissed somewhere like a serpent.

A man in a mask lunged through the swinging door, blade low, eyes dead. Claudia didn't think. She snatched a broken stem from the floor, the glass jagged as guilt, and slashed across his forearm. Skin opened; blood ribboned down. He snarled, grabbed for her hair. Angelo's elbow answered. The man's head snapped. He fell into the rack with a clang and slid, leaving a smear.

They burst out into the loading bay. Night air knifed the smoke. Alarm lights washed the alley in pulse-red.

Two figures ran at them from the shadows. Angelo took the first center mass—three shots, tight. Claudia stepped into the second on instinct and jammed the broken stem into his throat. Hot arterial spray hit her wrist, hotter than the fire. He gurgled, hands clawing at the glass, then dropped, blood pumping in a rhythm that became obscene in how quickly it slowed.

Her stomach lurched. Her skin hummed. She had never been more alive or more afraid of herself.

Angelo's hand closed around her wrist, steadying, not prying. His eyes tracked her face, the tremor in her breath, the red on her fingers. He didn't flinch.

"Move," he said. Gentle, then harder. "Move."

Sirens converged—hotel security, fire, the kind of cops who answer for donors. Angelo yanked her into a service alley no one who'd ever given a speech would know. They ran until the hotel's heartbeat became a distant accusation.

They didn't talk on the drive. The city blurred, a smear of red and blue in the windshield. Claudia's hands wouldn't stop shaking. She held them out at one point and realized they weren't shaking because of fear. They were shaking because her body didn't know how to come down without shattering.

Angelo took them to an old rowhouse with a boarded first floor and a back door that remembered his knock. Inside: wide plank floors, dust polished by long absence, a couch too honest to be pretty. He locked three locks and set his gun on the table.

Claudia stood in the middle of the room like she was lost in a museum. Blood dotted her wrist. A line of it had dried on her collarbone, dark and already tacky. The smell of smoke lived in her hair.

"Sit," Angelo said quietly.

She didn't. "Tony's dead."

"Yes."

"I killed a man."

His eyes didn't leave hers. "Yes."

"I didn't hesitate," she said, voice thin. "I didn't even look for another way."

"You didn't have another way."

She laughed once, a sharp break in the air. "Maybe I wanted that." A beat. "Maybe I wanted the part where it was simple."

Angelo crossed the room without a sound and stopped a foot from her. He didn't touch her. He let the heat of him do the work.

"You're not simple," he said. "You're honest. Tonight, that looked like blood. I won't pretend it didn't." His gaze dropped to the line at her throat, back to her eyes. "Wash."

She shook her head. "I can't—" The word crumbled. "I can't get the smell off my skin."

He took her wrist, turned her palm up, and pressed her hand—blood, tremor, and all—flat against his chest. "Then use mine."

The thrum under his shirt wasn't calm. It was a controlled riot. She could feel it—his adrenaline, his restraint, the bridge between the worst of him and the man who had quietly put his body between her and a bomb twice in one night.

The room tilted.

"Claudia," he said, warning and invitation in the same breath.

"Don't tell me to be good," she whispered.

"I never have."

She reached for him first. Her fingers found the back of his neck, found the scar ridge at his jaw, found the place beneath his ribs where breath goes thin. His mouth hit hers like impact—hot, tasting of smoke and copper and the terrible relief of not being alone. He caught her waist and pulled, not tender, not cruel—hungry.

Buttons gave. Fabric complained. Skin found skin like a memory. She pressed him back against the wall, unsteady and sure at the same time, and he let her decide everything—the pace, the edge, the depth. When his hands slid beneath her dress and closed around her hips, she made a sound that wasn't pain and wasn't quite joy; it was what happens when a human body remembers it survived.

He lifted her. She wrapped around him. The wall held. The world narrowed to breath and heat and the way his mouth changed when she tugged his hair. She didn't want romance; she wanted proof. He gave it to her—rough, reverent, swearing once when she bit his shoulder. She answered with nails down his back and a whispered don't stop that wasn't a plea; it was a command.

They hit the couch, then the floor, then the kind of silence that doesn't mean "over." When he rolled, when she pulled him back, when they burned through the last of their adrenaline on each other, there was no performance left. Just two people with smoke in their lungs and blood on their hands choosing a different way to shake.

When the quiet finally found them, it wasn't gentle. It was earned. Claudia lay on the floorboards, hair a dark stroke against the wood, chest rising in a rhythm that hurt. Angelo sprawled beside her, one arm flung over his eyes, throat working.

She turned her head. "We're not good people."

He didn't move his arm. "We're alive people."

"Is there a difference?"

"Sometimes."

She looked at the ceiling. A crack ran from corner to corner like a vein. "I liked it," she said to the crack, to the room, to him. "Killing him. I liked the part where it was simple."

Angelo's arm lowered. He looked at her like a man who's been given a confession he won't waste. "Then we tell the truth about that. To each other. To no one else."

A knock, sudden and hard, rattled the back door.

They froze. The pistol was in Angelo's hand before the echo died.

"Stay," he whispered, and stood. He moved like the floor belonged to him. The door creaked. He opened it a sliver.

"Delivery," a voice said, muffled and wrong.

Angelo shoved the door wide and his training stopped him half a second before his stomach could. A man lay on the stoop like a package badly wrapped. His throat was cut so deep it was almost neat. His abdomen was open, a red, obscene mouth; entrails slicked the wood in ropes. Someone had arranged them with the care of a florist.

Pinned to the corpse's shirt with a steak knife: a Polaroid of Claudia and Angelo leaving the gala kitchen. Her broken stem-weapon in frame, a red arc midair.

A word scrawled across the photo in a looping hand.

Yours.

Claudia's body reacted—gasp, cold, a flood of adrenaline her muscles didn't want.

Angelo stepped into the threshold like a wall and scanned the alley—no footsteps, no engine retreating. Whoever delivered the message knew how to walk in silence and leave in none.

He closed the door. He locked every lock. He turned back to Claudia and didn't hide his fury.

"This ends," he said. "Tomorrow. No more reaction. We go first."

She pushed herself upright, dragged the sheet around her because bodies need something to do when minds stagger. The Polaroid burned in her hand.

"How?" she asked. Not doubt. Logistics.

“We gut the charity,” he said. “Live. On camera. We pull the feeds. We pull the donors. We pull the cops who took checks and the judges who blessed it. We force Marks to choose between drowning and naming who held his head under.”

“And Dominguez?” she asked.

Angelo’s eyes were coal. “I take him off the board.”

She stood. Her legs held. Barefoot, blood still drying along the line of her collarbone, she crossed to him. He was still heat and iron and the one person in the city whose lies she could catalog.

“Then we do it,” she said. “We stop pretending the law will save us. We build our own.”

He lifted his palm. She lifted hers. He drew a knife—a small one, clean—and nicked his skin. She didn’t flinch when he nicked hers. They pressed the cuts together. Warmth. Salt. Promise.

“Partners?” he asked.

“In war,” she said.

He kissed her once more—short, brutal, sealing—and then stepped away before wanting more made them stupid.

“Sleep two hours,” he said. “Then we hunt.”

She looked at the door, at the dark beneath it, at the memory of a body arranged like punctuation. “I won’t sleep.”

“Good,” he said. “Neither will they.”

Outside, sirens stitched the night into something jagged. Somewhere, a city rich with light pretended nothing burned. Inside the rowhouse, blood dried on skin and floorboards both. Two people who weren’t good and weren’t finished stared into the dark and decided to make it blink first.

Chapter 9 — The Devil's Ledger

The world believed Rafael Dominguez was a ghost. He liked it that way. A man with no face could wear them all.

Tonight, he sat in his penthouse above the city, curtains drawn, lights dim, only the skyline burning in glass. A cigar smoldered between his fingers, sweet smoke coiling around his tailored suit. He was not young, but power made age irrelevant.

Below him, the Anselmo Hotel was still a wound in the city's skin, smoke crawling into the dawn. The news called it an "electrical fault." Dominguez smiled at the insult. He hadn't ordered the blast, but he understood why Marks had. Fear was a currency. Marks had spent too much of it.

A knock at the door. Soft, precise. One of his lieutenants entered—Carlos, loyal, quiet, face scarred from the old days. He carried a leather case.

"From Marks," Carlos said, setting it down.

Dominguez flipped the clasps. Inside: bundles of cash, still warm from the counting machine. On top of the money lay something smaller. A necklace, broken, with flecks of blood still clinging to the pearls.

He plucked it free, turned it in the light. "Sloppy," he murmured.

Carlos said nothing.

Dominguez rose, walked to the window, and looked down at the city that whispered his name like a curse. His empire ran under the streets: ports, police, politicians, every artery that mattered. Angelo Alvarez thought leaving had severed that grip. Claudia Vale thought law could cut it clean. Both were wrong.

"Have them watched," Dominguez said softly. "Not killed. Yet. I want to know who they trust. Who they call. Where they bleed."

Carlos inclined his head. “And Marks?”

Dominguez exhaled smoke. “Marks believes he is my equal. He believes money makes him untouchable. Remind him what money cannot buy.”

He closed the cigar cutter with a click, severing ash like a throat.

“His daughter will do.”

Carlos’s jaw tightened. He nodded, left.

Dominguez turned back to the window. The city was a chessboard, its pieces oblivious. Angelo and Claudia thought they had chosen war. They hadn’t. War was Dominguez’s native tongue.

He smiled into the glass until his reflection blurred with the skyline, and whispered, “Let them come.” Carlos returned less than an hour later with two men dragging something between them. Dominguez didn’t rise. He sat in his leather chair, cigar smoke curling, glass of brandy untouched.

The something hit the marble floor with a wet sound.

It was a man. Or what was left of one. One of Dominguez’s collectors who had thought he could skim off the docks.

Blood matted his hair. His hands were bound, knuckles split, shirt torn down the front. He wheezed, a wet rattle in his chest. His left eye was swollen shut; his right found Dominguez and flinched like a child caught stealing.

Dominguez took his time. He trimmed the cigar, flicked the end into a crystal ashtray, leaned forward. “Do you know the difference between debt and betrayal?”

The man coughed red onto the marble. “Please… I—”

"Debt can be paid." Dominguez's voice was silk. "Betrayal demands interest."

He motioned. Carlos handed him a tool: not a gun, not a knife. A set of bolt cutters, black steel, jaws already slick.

Dominguez knelt beside the man, brandy close enough to smell but not to drink. "Hands," he said.

The two guards forced the man's wrists flat. He screamed, tried to curl, but Dominguez's calm cut through it like scripture. The bolt cutters closed on the first finger. The crunch was obscene: bone and tendon snapping, blood spraying his cuff. The scream rose and cracked; the body convulsed.

Dominguez dropped the severed finger into the brandy glass. It plinked like ice. He swirled it once, watching the liquid blush. "Skimming, my friend, is small theft. But stealing faith?" He set the glass down in front of the man, who stared, sobbing, at his own digit floating in amber. "That is something I cannot forgive."

He clipped another. The finger landed on marble this time, rolling toward the rug. The man shrieked, voice breaking, snot and blood mingling.

Dominguez straightened, wiped the cutters with a handkerchief as if polishing silver. "Send him to the docks," he said. "Tie him to the nets. Let the tide decide if he still belongs to me."

Carlos nodded. The guards dragged the man out, his screams echoing off the marble, then thinning into the night air.

When the door shut, Dominguez sat again, brandy glass before him. He plucked the finger out, dropped it into the ashtray, and drank the liquor down slow.

He didn't wince at the taste.

The skyline winked back at him from the window. In his reflection, he saw himself steady, composed. Not a man committing cruelty. A man correcting accounts.

That was the truth of Rafael Dominguez. He wasn't a monster in his own mind. He was an accountant of pain. And every debt would be balanced. The penthouse doors opened again, softer this time. Carlos returned with a girl in a white dress that was meant to be elegant, though the dirt and sweat streaks made it look like surrender. Gerald Marks's daughter.

Dominguez didn't stand. He let her walk into the room between two guards, wrists bound, hair loose and tangled like a puppet dragged by its strings. She tried to lift her chin, but fear betrayed her. It always did.

Dominguez poured another brandy, gestured at the empty chair across from him. "Sit, Niña."

She hesitated. A guard pressed down on her shoulder until she obeyed.

Her lips trembled. "My father—"

"Your father is a clerk," Dominguez said, voice flat. "He signs papers. He cashes checks. But power?" He tapped the desk with one thick finger. "Power doesn't sign. Power doesn't ask. Power takes."

He studied her face, delicate, trembling. Not ugly. Not remarkable. Simply his leverage.

"Do you know why you are here?" he asked.

She shook her head, eyes darting toward the guards.

"You are here because your father owes me. And he has grown arrogant. He forgets who puts the roof over his head. Who pays for his mistakes." Dominguez leaned back. "You will remind him."

He motioned. Carlos placed a phone on the desk, speaker already live. Gerald Marks's voice filled the room, sharp with panic: "If you've touched her, Dominguez, I swear—"

“Swear quieter,” Dominguez interrupted. “Your daughter can hear you.”

A sob cracked through the line. The girl squeezed her eyes shut.

Dominguez reached into his pocket and pulled free the bolt cutters again. He laid them on the table with care, their jaws gleaming red from earlier. The girl’s breath hitched, fast and shallow.

“Choose, Marks,” Dominguez said calmly. “Do I take her hand, or do you take mine?”

Confusion, static. “Your—what? Please, don’t—”

“Your loyalty,” Dominguez said, smiling without warmth. “Her hand for your silence. One keeps her pretty. The other keeps her alive.”

On the line, Marks choked on words. The girl whimpered, wrists straining at rope.

Dominguez stood, walked behind her chair, and rested one heavy hand on her shoulder. She froze. He leaned close enough that his lips nearly touched her ear. “You will be delivered back to him when he remembers how to kneel.”

He straightened, signaled Carlos. The call cut.

The girl sagged, tears streaking down her face.

Dominguez looked at her the way a butcher looks at inventory. “Do not cry. Crying does not change math.”

He nodded. The guards dragged her out.

When the door closed, Dominguez returned to his chair, lit another cigar, and stared out over the city. Claudia and Angelo thought they had declared war. Gerald Marks thought his money mattered. None of them understood.

War was not noise. War was subtraction. And Dominguez was always willing to balance the equation. The smoke from Dominguez's cigar hung thick, a shroud between him and the skyline. He didn't wave it away. He liked the veil—it softened the city; made it look more obedient.

"Angelo Alvarez," he murmured aloud, as if the name itself were a nuisance in his teeth.

Carlos glanced up, silent, waiting.

"Once he was my right hand," Dominguez said, voice carrying that soft amusement that always preceded violence. "I taught him how to make men disappear without a ripple. How to pull out a tongue so cleanly the lungs collapse before the scream. How to make a debt collector out of a boy with nothing but fire in his eyes."

He tapped ash into the crystal tray. "And now? He plays hero with a woman who thinks laws are shields."

A pause. Dominguez's mouth twitched—not quite a smile, not quite a snarl.

"She looks like her," he added softly.

Carlos tilted his head. "Who, patron?"

Dominguez's eyes narrowed on memory. "The lawyer who tried to indict me in '92. Pretty. Fierce. Thought her voice in the courtroom meant something. Do you know what became of her, Carlos?"

Carlos waited, though he already knew the story.

"I had her brother brought in from Veracruz," Dominguez said. His voice was matter of fact, as if reading from ledgers. "Kept him in a basement six weeks. Sent her a letter every third day with a piece of him inside. A tooth. A fingernail. The last envelope was heavier." He exhaled smoke, slow and steady. "When she opened it, she stopped coming to court."

He tapped ash again. "She killed herself two months later. Saved me the effort."

Carlos's jaw flexed, but his face didn't shift.

Dominguez leaned back, savoring the memory of the way others savored wine. "Claudia Vale carries the same arrogance in her bones. But arrogance is fragile. All it takes is one fracture."

He raised his glass. The brandy caught the skyline like a burning horizon. "And Angelo—" He chuckled once, low, and dry. "Angelo will learn again what it means to be fatherless."

Carlos's gaze sharpened, the scar on his cheek pale in the lamplight. "Do you want him brought in alive?"

Dominguez smiled, slow, predatory. "Alive, Carlos. Always alive. Dead men can't watch me break what they love."

He stood, heavy with calm, and walked to the window. The city spread beneath him, thousands of lights blinking like weak stars.

"Tell Marks to prepare the gala accounts for audit," he said. "Then remind him what happens when he hesitates. His daughter is fragile. Fragile things break."

Carlos bowed his head once and left.
Dominguez pressed a hand to the glass, palm leaving an oily smear over the city. "They believe they've declared war," he whispered. "They've only signed their names in the ledger."

His reflection in the window grinned back, smoke curling around it like a crown.
Dominguez's hand slid down the glass until his fingertips rested on the cold sill. The skyline pulsed, a map of arteries he already owned. Somewhere in that glitter, Angelo thought of himself as a wolf again. Somewhere, Claudia Vale believed she could sharpen the law into a blade.

Dominguez smiled.

“They bleed before they break,” he whispered to the glass. “And I always collect.”

Behind him, the brandy glass still carried the print of his lips. The ashtray still cradled the severed finger like a relic. The ledger—his true scripture—lay open on the desk, pages waiting for two more names.

He turned away from the window at last, leaving his reflection grinning in the dark city.

Chapter 10 — The First Strike

The rowhouse was a lung that had forgotten how to breathe. Dust hung in the air, and the iron tang that lived in the floorboards rose whenever the heat kicked on. Claudia sat forward on the couch, elbows on her knees, watching the morning news without sound as a helicopter camera loved Anselmo's wound a little too much. The chyron said ELECTRICAL FAULT in honest white letters; the plume of smoke in the frame made it a punchline.

Behind her eyes, Dominguez's voice lingered like cigar smoke: They bleed before they break. And I always collect.

Glass cracked in her hand. Whiskey ran warm across her palm and dripped to the floor in slow amber beads. She didn't flinch. She set the ruined tumbler down and wiped her hand on a dish towel gone gray from a life it hadn't chosen.

At the window, Angelo lifted his shirt to hold a rag over the cut that the stairwell blade had left. The wound had the shape of a grin that didn't belong to him. He watched the street with the patience of a man who had outlived impatience.

"Dominguez won't stop," Claudia said at last, voice ground down to bone. "He'll escalate until we're not just bait. Until we're examples."

Angelo turned, the scar along his jaw a chalk stroke in the dim. "Then we escalate first."

They cleared the table. Files bloomed and overlapped until the wood disappeared—donor ledgers, bank transfers, shell-company maps. Claudia's handwriting tangled with Angelo's hard slashes: names, dates, vessels, alleyways. Ray's photo lay in the center: Marks's daughter, wrists bound, head bent as two men hustled her toward a van. The image felt cold even in the warm pool of the lamp.
"A daughter isn't collateral," Claudia said. "It's a leash."

“Dominguez doesn’t have daughters,” Angelo answered. “He has entries.”

“Then we burn the ledger.”

She pulled the laptop close. The screen light caught the faint scar at her collarbone where a chandelier star had chosen her and been plucked free. Her fingers moved like memory. “Finance mirrors on twenty-nine. Legal backups on twenty-seven. I still know how to sing to their doors. We breach tonight. We flood the city with their rot.”

Angelo slid a magazine home; the click made the lamp tremble. “And if he expects you to think like that?”

“Good,” she said. “I’m tired of disappointing him.”

They left at 11:53 p.m. in a car that had forgotten all its previous names. Fog made halos of the streetlights; rain freckled the windshield and the silence between them.

Angelo took a long way of rights and lefts that meant something to him. Claudia sat with a messenger bag between her feet, laptop cocooned, cables coiled like veins. She stared at her hands until they became hands again and not the red tools she’d met in the loading bay.

The tower knifed up into glass-black sky. In the lobby, a cleaning crew’s citrus couldn’t quite drown the smell of fresh wax. Behind the desk, Artie slouched over a sports feed in the glow of his phone. A Monster can sweat neon rings on the counter.
“East service door,” Claudia murmured. “Camera drifts for four seconds when the west elevator pings.”

Angelo opened the door with a sliver of plastic and gentle impatience. Inside, air conditioning hummed like a verdict. The elevator doors parted on brushed steel. In their reflection, Claudia recognized a woman whose edges had stopped apologizing.

“If we walk into a gun,” Angelo said, not taking his eyes off their doubles, “you go low and left.”

“And you?”

“High and through.”

The car climbed. Numbers blinked. Her heart kept time until she told it to stop.

Twenty-nine breathed cold air. Carpet softened their steps; framed awards lined the wall—cases Claudia had once broken the city with and had framed like hunting trophies. Tonight, they were an exhibit of a life that no longer fit.

She keyed an override on the server room door. New access hung over old like wallpaper; she peeled it back with a rhythm her fingers remembered. The light blinked green. Inside, rows of steel racks purred and blinked, blue LEDs like winter stars.

Claudia knelt and fed her device to the right port. Directories unfolded in clean, cruel lines: Donors.csv. UR_Shells.xlsx. Qtrly_Transfers.pdf. Her pulse made a metronome in her wrists as she compressed, encrypted, and seeded copies across twelve inboxes at once—two local TV desks, three city reporters who still paid in shoe leather, a state AG intake, a blogger with a fox avatar and an axe, a public defender who refused to be tired, and three blind drops that would scream if anyone tried to smother them.
“Two minutes,” she said.

Angelo didn’t move. “One.”

Footsteps ghosted down from thirty-one—lazy at first, then curious. She watched the bar climb. 76%. 91%. 100%. She yanked the drive, tucked it inside her hoodie, and killed the screen.

The server room door breathed open an inch. A man in a balaclava slid through with knife reversed—a pro. He slashed for Angelo’s gut—blocked. Cut again and printed a red smile along Angelo’s side. Angelo didn’t give him a sound. He turned the man, hip-shift, weight steel—

Claudia had the extinguisher off its hook before the knife found skin a third time. The first swing caught the temple. The thud was wet and private. The second swing broke something that sounded like a promise. The man crumpled in a trickle of red that shone under blue LEDs.

She raised the extinguisher again, distance gone from her eyes.

Angelo caught her wrist. "Enough," he said, voice low enough to thread adrenaline.

Enough. Not mercy. Not yet.

They took the stairs because elevators remembered who rode them. Stairwells are honest. They echo what you put in. On twenty-seven, radio chatter buzzed above them: "Server room… check twenty-nine… hallway's clean… you see anything?"
Another man waited on the landing, knife held blade-down, body turned narrow, the stance of someone who had learned to end arguments. Angelo moved firsthand to wrist, twist, shoulder to wall. The knife clanged to concrete. Claudia drove a heel into the instep and felt bones shift under rubber. The man howled. Angelo put him quiet with a short punch that took the lights out without breaking the bulb.

On twenty-six a camera winked alive. Angelo shot it without looking, and sparks fell like fat snow.

They pushed through a dark floor mid-renovation where drywall dust tried to make footprints tell a story. Angelo kicked a bucket and dragged a boot through a smear, turning their line into nonsense. Claudia didn't smile, but her brain did. Freight elevator, then the loading bay, then air that didn't feel recirculated.

At the bay, a janitor smoked with half a soul. He looked at them—at the red drying on Angelo's shirt, at the truth in their hands—and chose a version of the night that wouldn't cost him sleep. Angelo pressed bills into his palm and a finger to his lips. The man nodded like a prayer with teeth and turned away.

They slid into the car. Claudia counted turns as she had been taught: right, left, left, pause. Her hands shook only when she let them.

The city woke up on a diet it didn't want and couldn't refuse.

At 6:43 a.m., a local anchor called it "breaking" with the voice she used for weather. Graphics made rot look respectable. Donor names crawled across the screen under a headline that tried to be calm: URBAN RENEWAL DONORS UNDER SCRUTINY. By 6:50, the national morning show had their patriot blue on it. By 7:02, the fox-avatar blogger had mirrored the spreadsheets and red-circled a judge's fishing buddy. At 7:17, a hacktivist collective with a habit of winning posted three torrents and an insurance file with the key split twelve ways.

At 8:30, protesters gathered outside the tower with signs that still smelled like Sharpie: NOT WITH OUR TAXES. WHO OWNS WHO? MARKS = MASKS. A man with a bullhorn mispronounced Dominguez and didn't care.

Marks hit a podium at 10:03 in front of two flags and a lawyer who had the face of a hunger strike. He said the words men like him learn early: shocked, saddened, cooperating, rogue staff, integrity, trust. He didn't say Dominguez. His sweat said everything else.

"Bleeding yet?" Claudia asked the TV.

"Everywhere he cares about," Angelo said. He'd let her sew him at the kitchen table with a boiled needle and the tip of her patience. He sat paler than the wall, pistol on the table because rituals matter.

Her burner buzzed. Unknown. Do you think cameras save you? They only make the blood look brighter. —R.D.

Claudia stared at the letters until they drifted out of focus. She set the phone down face first. Angelo smiled without warmth.

"He's watching," he said. "He wants us to see the teeth before the bite."

"Then let's break them," she said.

The second burner buzzed harder, frantic. RAY: You started a war. They're moving money. And they're moving HER.

A photo followed: grainy, timestamped. Underground garage. Two suits, one van, a girl in a white dress with her wrists bound. Her head down the way prey learns. Marks's daughter.

Claudia felt the floor tilt and then right itself. Angelo read over her shoulder, breath sharp through his nose.

"Leverage," she said.

"Ledger," he answered.

They didn't need to say Dominguez.

They went live at 1:37 p.m. from a municipal hearing room that smelled like disinfectant and fear. The seal hung on the wall. A flag drooped in the air like a tired witness. Claudia had chosen the room because the camera angles were already tested and the microphones told the truth if you fed them.

The stream title was bureaucratic enough to slip past spam filters: PUBLIC INTEREST HEARING: UR ACCOUNTS. The chat filled with exclamation points and name-calling; then it stilled like a congregation when she stepped into frame.

"My name is Claudia Vale," she said. The lens didn't scare her anymore; it just listened. "You know where I worked."

She held up papers that made the soft sound of knives. "This is the donor ledger for
Citizens for Urban Renewal. These are the shell entities that laundered the money— Monarch, Virtue, Easton Ferry. These are the quarterly transfers from city contracts. They are cross-signed by the board, including Gerald Marks."

A murmur ran through the chat even though it had no throat.

"I have sent copies to the Attorney General, the State Bar, three newspapers, a television station, the public defender's office, and three public repositories with split keys and Deadman triggers. If anything happens to me or to my witnesses, the next release is worse."

Off-camera, Angelo stood with one hand on the tripod and one under his jacket. Jo—the clerk—sat on the floor out of frame, knuckles white around a glass of water. Her phone vibrated on the tile like a small animal trying to warn them about weather.

Claudia read amounts. She read dates. She read names she had once written thank-you letters to. She didn't let the lens blink without blinking first.

When she finished, she killed the stream with a thumb that wanted to tremble and didn't.

Angelo lowered his hand from the tripod. "You just set the city on fire without lighting a match."

"Matches are for people who like control," she said.

The knock came like punctuation. Three hard raps on the rowhouse door. Angelo went to the peephole with the muzzle first. "Jo," he said, surprised into an extra syllable of caution.

He set the chain and opened the door a hand's width. Jo's face was wrong—glass-eyed, sick with apology. "They took my brother," she whispered. "They made me call you. I'm sorry. I'm so—"

"Inside," Angelo said, and tugged the chain free.

She stumbled past him and the air behind her changed shape. A van engine throbbed at the curb. Four men poured out wearing city jackets that fit men who carried other men's guns. One pointed and laughed. The others raised weapons like they were saying hello.

The first round turned the door into lace. Angelo yanked Jo flat; the second round powdered a family photo that had never hung there. Claudia rolled behind the kitchen wall and tore a shotgun free from the cabinet where Angelo had taped it. The tape took paint and a curse with it.

“Left,” Angelo snapped, and fired twice through the door hole. A scream. A porch board thundered. Claudia pumped once and leaned out. The shotgun’s roar flung a man off the steps and through the railing; he hit the yard the way trash cans do on bad nights and didn’t get up.

The van tried to back on a blown tire. Angelo put the tire out of its misery and then put the driver’s nerve out with a round that took the mirror into the street. Sirens braided at the far end of the block—late as always, honest as ever.

Jo sobbed once like a machine with a cracked gear. Claudia crawled to her and put a hand on her shoulder. “You did right.” It was a good lie. “You’re safe.”

“They said your name,” Jo whispered. “They said you weren’t a lawyer anymore.”

“Then they’re about to meet whatever that makes me.”

Angelo didn’t smile, but his eyes did. “We can’t hold,” he said.

“We won’t.” Claudia stood, rolled stiffness out of her neck, and grabbed the duffel with law books that had lost their priesthood. The shotgun went in on top. “We have a press to feed.” He nodded, bleeding through his shirt but vertical because gravity had learned to bargain with him. “My favorite meal.”

By midafternoon, the city had two stories to chew and one stomach to hold them. Outside the tower, a council member tried to outrun a microphone and discovered that cameras don’t tire. The mayor called for “full transparency” and blinked wrong on the word full. A judge posted a photo of a grandchild and turned off comments when the first forty-seven mentioned the Virtue Fund.

Claudia’s burner lit up again with Ray: Police scanner: vans moving to Dock 19. Two black, one white. River side. And… six-figure contract on A. A second later: Don’t be heroes. A third: He wants you to come.

Angelo read it. “Invitation,” he said, and there was that small, feral curve to his mouth again. “How polite.”

Claudia felt the cold find her spine and sit there like a friend. “Then we RSVP.”

On their way out, she paused at the sink. The two halves of the kitchen Polaroid were still curled in the dish where she’d left them. She struck a match and held the flame under the gloss until it blackened and folded in on itself. Smoke rose in a thin line and vanished like it owed her.

“Ready?” Angelo asked from the door.

She looked at the stitches she’d tied into his side, at the jaw scar that had learned to hold light and threat at the same time. “Ready.”

They stepped into a city wearing afternoon like a scab. News vans clogged intersections. Protest signs bobbed like buoys in wake. The river smell thickened into diesel and old rope the closer they got to Dock 19.

A text bubbled on the dash-mounted burner as Angelo didn’t slow for a yellow light.

Unknown: You are very brave. Bring him. I will teach you what brave costs. —R.D.

“Teaching moment,” Angelo said, almost cheerful.

“Office hours,” Claudia said, rolling the window down to let the cold grab her face. “Let’s not be late.”

The tower shrank in the rearview. Ahead, cranes cut the sky into teeth and the water waited with its old patience. Dock 19 was where money learned to hold its breath and men pretended they could swim. The car slid into the shadow of stacked containers painted in colors that had names once. A gull screamed like a bad omen or a good witness.

“Low and left,” Angelo said, checking the pistol one more time.

"High and through," she answered, and found she was smiling, not because this was sane—because it was honest.

They rolled toward the river and the next page of the ledger. The war had found daylight. The rest would not be polite. The river air grew heavier with every block. Diesel clung to the night like grease on skin, layered with the salt-rot of nets that hadn't seen fish in years. Containers stacked three high leaned into the fog, their faded paint peeled into hieroglyphs of a commerce no one tracked.

Claudia cracked the window. The cold stung her cheek, sharpened her thoughts. She counted every container they passed, every shadow that shifted where shadows shouldn't. Her hand never left the duffel at her feet. The shotgun waited inside, wrapped in a sweatshirt that smelled faintly of detergent, home, a life that had been forfeited weeks ago.

Beside her, Angelo drove with one hand on the wheel, the other resting loose on his pistol. His stitches seeped under his jacket, darkening fabric, but his face betrayed nothing. The scar along his jaw looked carved deeper under the glow of the dock lights.

The burner on the dash buzzed again. Claudia flipped it.

Unknown: Dock 19 has always been a ledger. Tonight, I write your names. —R.D.

The message sat there, glowing like an omen.

"He knows we're coming," Claudia said, voice calm, almost too calm.

"He wanted us to." Angelo's smile was a scar's echo—sharp, humorless. "That's the mistake."

The road narrowed to a lane of cracked concrete where the streetlights ended. Darkness pooled thick, broken only by the sulfur glow of lamps humming high above the stacks. The river lapped at the pilings below, patient as a metronome keeping time with their steps.

Angelo cut the engine. The sudden silence made Claudia's pulse sound loud in her ears. She pulled the duffel onto her lap, unzipped it, and laid her palm on the shotgun's cold steel. Not comfort—certainty.

She looked across at Angelo. His eyes burned steady, black glass with no give. He nodded once. "Low and left."

"High and through," she answered.

The car doors opened, sound ricocheting too loud into the emptiness. They stepped out, boots on damp concrete, fog curling at their ankles like smoke.

Shadows shifted between the containers. The faint glint of gunmetal winked under lamp posts. Men were here already, breathing the same cold air, waiting like wolves circling in silence.

Claudia inhaled through her nose. The taste of salt and oil hit her tongue. She tightened her grip on the duffel. The fear she expected didn't come. What rose instead was clarity.

Beside her, Angelo rolled his shoulders once, stretching against the pull of stitches. His grin surfaced again, brief, and feral. He looked like a man who had spent his life walking into traps and surviving just to spite them.

A gull screamed overhead, jagged, and wild. The sound carried, echoed, died against steel walls.

Somewhere ahead, Dominguez's men shifted their weight. Somewhere higher, a sniper exhaled slow. And in the water beneath, the river made room for new names.

Claudia and Angelo walked forward together, into the dark geometry of containers. The war had left whispers and shadows.

Now it was written in open air.

Chapter 11 — Dock 19

Dock 19 rose out of the river mist like something half-remembered from a nightmare. Cranes stood frozen with their necks craned toward the water, steel skeletons rusting at the joints. Containers towered three high, painted once in blue and red, now chipped to gray scars and graffiti tags that looked like hieroglyphs to another century. The smell was part diesel, part brine, part rot.

Claudia climbed out of the car first. Her boots hit the cracked concrete, and the fog curled low around her ankles. She pulled the duffel strap higher on her shoulder. Inside, the shotgun was a familiar weight, reassuring and merciless at once.

Angelo eased out the driver's side with his pistol in hand, his other arm pressed casually over the stitches tugging at his side. He didn't mention the pain. He never did. He let the night wrap around him like an old suit he'd once tailored in blood.

The silence wasn't natural. Not here. Not with men hiding somewhere among the stacks. Claudia knew it. Angelo knew it. The whole dock felt like a mouth held closed too long.

"Cigarette ash," Angelo murmured, his eyes cutting toward a container gap. Claudia followed his gaze. A faint ember hit the ground and was crushed too quickly. Someone was already watching.

A gull screamed overhead and vanished into the dark. Then—nothing. Even the water's rhythm seemed to hush.

Angelo's scar pulled tight as he muttered, "Trap's sprung."

Claudia's throat tightened, but her hands stayed steady. "Then we write our own ending."

They moved forward together, the fog swallowing them into steel corridors. Headlights detonated behind them—twin white flares that carved their shadows long across the concrete. In the same heartbeat, the dark erupted with muzzle flash from three angles. Bullets chewed steel; sparks flew like angry fireflies off the container walls.

"Low-left!" Claudia dropped, pivoted on her knee, and slid behind a stack as rounds stitched the space where her spine had been. The duffel thumped down beside her. She yanked the zipper and felt the cold, clean certainty of the shotgun's receiver in her palm.

Angelo went high-through—two long strides and a leap onto a knee-high pallet, using the elevation to angle fire down. His first two shots cracked and placed. One mask disappeared backward, a spray of red misting the fog; another spun with a shoulder blooming dark and fell hard against corrugated steel.

"Three more, right flank!" Claudia called.

She stepped out and fired. The boom flattened the night. A man jerked as if hooked by the chest and vanished behind a stack with a sound like meat dropped on tile. Return fire hammered the corner she'd been hugging. Concrete spat chips into her cheek. She tasted dust and iron.

A shape lunged close—too close—for the barrel. Claudia reversed her grip. The stock smashed into a mask; plastic split; bone underneath did, too. The man folded, hands grasping at air that wouldn't hold him.

Angelo vanished into the slots between containers like water finding its level. Gunfire followed, then stopped—replaced by a wet grunt and the sick clack of a jaw breaking. He reappeared at Claudia's shoulder, breath steady, blood soaking his side darker.

"You're hit," she said.

"Later," he said, and glanced past her. "Listen."

They heard it then under the echo of shots: engine idle, heavy doors creaking open, metal chain rattle. A van reversed toward the river with a slow, confident beep. Floodlights on its roof flared to life and burned through fog, making the dock a white stage.

Inside the van: a cage bolted to the floor. A girl in a white dress, wrists raw from rope, hair plastered to her face. Marks's daughter. Her eyes found the light and flinched, then found Claudia and didn't.

"Move," Angelo said. They ran low. Rounds sparked on the dock at their heels. Claudia ducked into a gap and nearly tripped over a body that tried to breathe and failed. Warm splash across her boot. She didn't stop.

Two men came around opposite sides of the same container—coordinated, rifles high. Angelo cut left, Claudia right. The shotgun boomed; the left man's chest cave-in bucked him backward. Angelo caught the right man's barrel mid-raise, torqued, smashed the stock into teeth, and buried a knife point under the ribs with the practiced contempt of someone who had done this too many times. The man sighed, knees went wrong, and he slid down the container wall leaving a vertical smear.

The van's cargo doors yawned wider. A third man inside raised a pistol toward the cage. The girl threw herself against the bars. Angelo fired twice through the open doors. The pistol clattered to the floor. The man folded on himself and didn't move again.
Claudia reached the bumper, breath hot in her throat. Another shooter popped from behind the wheel well. She caught a glimpse—bald scalp, tattoo like a hook—and then his muzzle flash was all she could see. The shockwave shivered her arm; her shoulder screamed. She swung the shotgun one-handed like a bat and felt the ugly give of cartilage. He went down. She racked, leaned, and finished it. The blast blew the fog apart in a ring.

"Behind!" Angelo barked.

She turned in time to see a figure at full sprint, knife low, eyes starved. He hit Angelo in a tackle that drove them both into a stack. Angelo rolled, a grunt forced out of him, and took a wild slash across his already-bleeding side. He answered with a headbutt that turned the knife-man's face to slack meat, then locked a forearm around the throat and squeezed until the fight went out like a bad light.

Silence didn't return. It crouched, waiting to be allowed.

A single shot cracked from high—different note, clean as glass. A puff of splinters jumped from the van door a hand's width from Claudia's face. Sniper.

"Down!" Angelo shoved her, grabbed the van's door, and dragged it closed enough to break the line of sight. Wood chunked again—another shot, an inch lower. The round caught the lip of the door and ricocheted whining into the dark.

"Angle's north crane," Angelo said, eyes cutting the geometry. "Halfway up. Light wind left to-right."

"How do you—"

"Because I taught them," he said, a flat admission, and holstered his pistol. He took the shotgun from Claudia gently, checked the load, handed it back, and nodded toward the cage. "Get her."

He melted left—into shadow—vanishing as if the steel itself swallowed him. Three breaths later, a shout jerked from the crane's direction. Then a muffled scuffle. Then a scream that ended too fast. A small shape fell from the rigging with a sound that didn't belong to anything that was going to stand up again.

Claudia found the cage latch and swore. Padlock, heavy, old-school. She holstered, dug in the duffel for the bolt cutter they'd brought out of ordinary paranoia and set the jaws.

"Hey," she said, soft, eyes not leaving the lock. "Look at me."

The girl did—slow, a flinch hiding inside the movement.
"My name is Claudia," she said. The cutters bit. The lock's bow groaned. "We're taking you out of here."

The lock gave with a cough of metal. Claudia wrenched the door and caught the girl as her legs forgot how to choose.

"Can you run?" Claudia asked.

The girl nodded, a lie children tell to be brave.

“Then we walk fast.”

Angelo reappeared with a sneer of blood drying at his temple and something grim under his nail beds. He scanned, listening the way men listen when they know the dock is a throat and someone is still holding it closed.

“More coming,” he said. “Different boots. Police?” A beat. “Or men who rent the uniforms.”

As if summoned, red and blue flickered at the far end of the lane. Sirens didn’t wail; they panted. Cars with light bars but no conscience.

“We don’t have time,” Claudia said.

“Into the stacks,” Angelo said, and took point. They cut a zigzag through the container maze. Angelo kept them to shade and non-lines. The girl moved on new legs and old fear, fingers white on Claudia’s sleeve. They passed three bodies that wouldn’t be testimony again. One tried to be and failed—blood bubbling at lips, eyes wide in the wrong kind of pleading. Claudia didn’t let the girl look.

Headlights swung wide at the far end—two cruisers fanning, trying to box lanes. A bullhorn lied about hands in the air. Boots hit concrete in rhythm that said training.

“Trap-within-trap,” Angelo said. “They want us in the open with a witness and a story that can’t survive a press conference.”

“They want us to shoot at badges,” Claudia said, and set the shotgun down for half a second to tie the girl’s wrists free. The skin there was flayed to angry pink. “Stay behind me. Eyes on my back. Move when I move.”

The bullhorn commanded again. Words about “safe surrender” and “no one has to get hurt.” A rifle bolt racked behind the voice.

Angelo's mouth twisted—humorless. "I could shoot the speaker from here."
"Save it," Claudia said. "We need cars, not martyrs."

He blinked once: agreement. "Left," he said, pointing with his chin. "Service stair on the seawall. Drops to the lower dock."

They ran. Voices rose behind them. A round snapped past, taking a chip out of steel that whined as it fell. Angelo turned and fired twice—not at men, at a floodlight. It burst. Darkness tilted the field in their favor.

The stair was slick and narrow, concrete sweating river. They slid down to the lower dock where the water licked pilings like a patient animal. Above, boots thundered in disagreement about which way they'd gone.

"Boat?" Claudia asked.

Angelo's eyes scanned the black water and found shapes that didn't want to be names.
"Skiff," he said, pointing at a shadow tied loose to a cleat. "Lucky us."

"Luck is for people who like odds," Claudia said, and helped the girl in, then shoved off while Angelo jumped and caught the bow line with a grunt that sealed his stitches with pain.

He found the starter rope by feel. Two pulls. The engine coughed awake too loud. Shouts above. Muzzles peered over the lip of the dock like curious snakes. Angelo threw them into the swell and the skiff nosed out.

Rifles cracked. Bullets snapped the water in angry dimples around the hull. Claudia lay over the girl and counted shots the way she counted steps at night when sleep pretended it would come.

The skiff drifted into darker water between the pilings of an old pier. Angelo killed the motor. Silence returned—fake, temporary.

Above, the bullhorn lied to itself. "We have you surrounded."

"Not tonight," Angelo said into the engine's casing, and met Claudia's eyes. "You good?"

She nodded. "She's breathing."

The girl made a noise that was almost a laugh and almost a sob. "He said you would come," she whispered into Claudia's shoulder. "He said you would come so he could count you."

Claudia's jaw tensed. "Who said?"
"Dominguez," the girl breathed, as if the name itself could tilt the boat. "He said you were already on his paper."

Angelo's eyes lifted past them, past the skiff, past the water, to the black against black where the pier met the night. A silhouette stood there that hadn't been there a breath ago. Broad shoulders. Hands in pockets. A red ember brightened on a cigar end, then went dark beneath a palm.

"Go," Angelo whispered, and nudged the throttle. The skiff, obedient, slid like a thought.

The silhouette didn't follow. It just watched. The ember brightened again. A hand lifted—not a wave. A mark, like a clerk checking a box. They cut a zigzag through the container maze. Angelo kept them to shade and non-lines. The girl moved on new legs and old fear, fingers white on Claudia's sleeve. They passed three bodies that wouldn't be testimony again. One tried to be and failed—blood bubbling at lips, eyes wide in the wrong kind of pleading. Claudia didn't let the girl look.

Headlights swung wide at the far end—two cruisers fanning, trying to box lanes. A bullhorn lied about hands in the air. Boots hit concrete in rhythm that said training.

"Trap-within-trap," Angelo said. "They want us in the open with a witness and a story that can't survive a press conference."

"They want us to shoot at badges," Claudia said, and set the shotgun down for half a second to tie the girl's wrists free. The skin there was flayed to angry pink. "Stay behind me. Eyes on my back. Move when I move."

The bullhorn commanded again. Words about "safe surrender" and "no one has to get hurt." A rifle bolt racked behind the voice.

Angelo's mouth twisted—humorless. "I could shoot the speaker from here."

"Save it," Claudia said. "We need cars, not martyrs."

He blinked once: agreement. "Left," he said, pointing with his chin. "Service stair on the seawall. Drops to the lower dock."

They ran. Voices rose behind them. A round snapped past, taking a chip out of steel that whined as it fell. Angelo turned and fired twice—not at men, at a floodlight. It burst. Darkness tilted the field in their favor.

The stair was slick and narrow, concrete sweating river. They slid down to the lower dock where the water licked pilings like a patient animal. Above, boots thundered in disagreement about which way they'd gone.

"Boat?" Claudia asked.

Angelo's eyes scanned the black water and found shapes that didn't want to be names.
"Skiff," he said, pointing at a shadow tied loose to a cleat. "Lucky us."

"Luck is for people who like odds," Claudia said, and helped the girl in, then shoved off while Angelo jumped and caught the bow line with a grunt that sealed his stitches with pain.

He found the starter rope by feel. Two pulls. The engine coughed awake too loud. Shouts above. Muzzles peered over the lip of the dock like curious snakes. Angelo threw them into the swell and the skiff nosed out.

Rifles cracked. Bullets snapped the water in angry dimples around the hull. Claudia lay over the girl and counted shots the way she counted steps at night when sleep pretended it would come.

The skiff drifted into darker water between the pilings of an old pier. Angelo killed the motor. Silence returned—fake, temporary.

Above, the bullhorn lied to itself. “We have you surrounded.”

“Not tonight,” Angelo said into the engine’s casing, and met Claudia’s eyes. “You good?”

She nodded. “She’s breathing.”

The girl made a noise that was almost a laugh and almost a sob. “He said you would come,” she whispered into Claudia’s shoulder. “He said you would come so he could count you.”
Claudia’s jaw tensed. “Who said?”

“Dominguez,” the girl breathed, as if the name itself could tilt the boat. “He said you were already on his paper.”

Angelo’s eyes lifted past them, past the skiff, past the water, to the black against black where the pier met the night. A silhouette stood there that hadn’t been there a breath ago. Broad shoulders. Hands in pockets. A red ember brightened on a cigar end, then went dark beneath a palm.

“Go,” Angelo whispered, and nudged the throttle. The skiff, obedient, slid like a thought.
The silhouette didn't follow. It just watched. The ember brightened again. A hand lifted—not a wave. A mark, like a clerk checking a box.
They cut along the shadow of the seawall, keeping the pier’s rotten teeth between the skiff and the mouths with badges above. A warehouse door ahead hung crooked over a private slip. Angelo eased them into the black throat of it and killed the motor.

Inside, the dark smelled of rope, oil, and rats old enough to pay rent. Angelo tied off and listened hard enough his scar tightened. Claudia helped the girl onto the dock and felt her knees try to forget. She made them remember.

“We can’t take her to the house,” Angelo said. “It’s a landmark now.”

Claudia nodded. “I know a church that keeps its doors open. The priest does math in confessions.”

Angelo raised an eyebrow. “And he likes you?”

“He likes lost causes.” She touched the girl’s cheek, made her meet eyes that had decided about mornings. “You’re going to see someone kind. He’ll ask you nothing you don’t offer.”

The girl gave a small, tight nod. “My father—”

“Is on a stage,” Claudia said. “He’ll keep kneeling until we’re finished.”

Angelo’s phone buzzed once—Ray. Dock 19 losing cops to the tower. Your feed is killing them. Move while they argue. A second message: And the bounty just doubled.

Angelo exhaled almost a laugh. “I’m popular.”

“Get in line,” Claudia said. “Let’s go.”

They slipped out the far door into an alley that smelled like dead brine and old promises. Angelo stole a pickup with a screwdriver and the practiced ease of a man who had once made keys to cities. The engine coughed alive. Claudia buckled the girl in and climbed into the passenger seat with the shotgun laid across her thighs like a sleeping animal.

As they pulled out, she looked back. The docks receded into fog and flicker. For a heartbeat—just one—she saw the same silhouette on the pier, ember bright, a hand raised like a blessing or a tally mark. Then it was gone, or the night chose not to show it. They didn’t go to the church. Not yet. Halfway there, the girl’s head lolled and a sound came

out of her that wasn't decision. Claudia checked her pulse. Too fast. Skin cold and sweat-slick. Shock trying to edit her.
"Hospital?" Angelo asked.

"They'll call it in," Claudia said. "We get a nurse without admissions."

Angelo turned two streets early and slid behind a clinic where the paint flaked off the sign and the light over the back door stuttered. The door opened for Angelo's knock after a pattern of silence. A woman let them in wearing scrubs printed with cartoon bears that wouldn't sleep after this shift. She didn't ask questions until the office door closed.

Angelo peeled cash from a roll and set it on the desk like it was trying to apologize. The nurse—Elena, Claudia remembered—took it, counted with her thumb and not her eyes, and pointed to a cot. She cleaned the girl's wrists with saline and salt words, checked pupils, checked breath, checked for breaks. "She'll live," Elena said softly, then let steel into her voice. "But if the men who did this come to my door—"

"They won't," Angelo said, and meant it in the way men mean weather.

Claudia took Elena's hand. "Thank you."

Elena held it a second longer than a handshake and then let go. "Leave the back way," she said. "Don't make me remember your faces if I don't have to."

They left the girl sleeping and closed the door soft.

In the alley, the pickup clicked as it cooled. Angelo leaned on the fender and lifted his shirt enough to look at the cut. The stitches had torn. Blood patterned his side in a spidering bloom.

"Sit," Claudia said.

He did, which told her more about the hurt than anything. She cleaned him with bottled water and gauze, then re-stitched him there in the alley while a cat watched with the bored disdain of a god who had seen better sacrifices.

"You're getting good at this," he said, voice rough.

"Don't make me prove it on you again," she said, knotting the thread. "Hold still."

He did. Streetlight burned copper on his cheekbone. When she finished, he let out a breath he hadn't wanted to admit he was holding.

"What now?" he asked.

"Now," Claudia said, wiping her hands, "we go home and make the next move hurt."
He nodded. "He saw us," he said, and didn't have to say who.

"I know," she said. "He wanted to."

Angelo straightened and looked down the alley like it could choose to be longer. "We didn't die in his ledger tonight."

"No," she said, and thought of the hand lifting in the fog, checking off boxes. "But he wrote us in."

They climbed back into the truck. The engine turned. The city ahead was lit and loud and very interested in other people's lives. Behind, the river kept its patient math.

They drove into the noise.

Chapter 12 — The Blood Beneath the Briefcase

The sky over the city hadn't decided on a color yet.
A thin gray seam divided river from smoke, morning from whatever came after nights like Dock 19. The truck's engine coughed tiredly, the sound of metal reconsidering loyalty. Angelo drove one-handed, his other pressed against the stitched side that kept trying to open again.

They hadn't spoken since the clinic. Silence rode with them like a fourth passenger who didn't believe in seatbelts.

Claudia watched the lights roll past her window—orange, white, then nothing. She thought of the girl sleeping on that cot, of the nurse's steady hands, of how every rescue cost the same: a piece of whatever you were pretending not to miss.

"Turn here," she said.

Angelo eased the truck down a side street lined with shuttered warehouses. The dawn light made their rust look holy.

"You sure about this?" he asked.

"No." She pointed ahead. "Park there."

They stopped outside a motel that had given up pretending to be one. Half the sign's letters were dead, leaving only the word MOT. Claudia got out and stretched, feeling the stiffness set in her shoulders, the kind of ache that wasn't asking to be healed. She grabbed the duffel and the case from behind the seat. The case hummed faintly, like it remembered something before she did.

"Inside," she said.

The room smelled of lemon cleaner and resignation. One light worked. She locked the door, checked the blinds twice, and set the briefcase on the table. It looked ordinary—gray metal, brass corners, unbothered by murder and paperwork.

Angelo dropped onto the chair by the window. He pulled his shirt up to inspect the stitches. Blood had seeped through the gauze, a black flower spreading slow. Claudia dug a first-aid kit out of the duffel and knelt beside him.

He watched her hands. “You always sew this quiet?”

“Only when I’m scared,” she said.

He smiled a little. “So all the time.”

She didn’t look up. “Hold still.”

When the needle broke skin, he flinched and pretended he hadn’t. She tied off the thread and taped a fresh bandage. “That’ll hold until you decide it shouldn’t.”

“Thanks,” he said, and meant it in the way he rarely did—with weight.

Claudia sat back on her heels. The case on the table gave a small metallic sigh, like a thing that knew it was being ignored.

She stood, walked over, and popped the locks.

The hum deepened. Inside, the Dominguez file lay on top—edges curled, paper damp as if it had sweated through the night. The top page showed a blank space where a signature should be, but under the light, faint red lines appeared—capillaries in ink.

“Angelo,” she said quietly. “Look.”

He rose, leaned close. The lines pulsed, spreading into letters written in a language that didn’t care if she understood.

Latin, or something pretending.
Sanguis servabit legem.
Blood preserves the law.

She traced the words with one fingertip. The ink felt warmer than paper should.
"You ever see anything like this?" she asked.

"I've seen files that burned from the inside out," he said. "But not ones that wanted to."

The page shifted, curling at the edges. Beneath it, more papers rearranged themselves, like a deck cutting under invisible hands. Claudia flipped through: police transcripts, court seals, witness statements—each overlaid with faint impressions of other documents, older, written in fountain pens that hadn't existed in decades.

In the center, a photograph—sepia, cracked, the kind you'd find in a courthouse archive. A woman in black stood on courthouse steps, eyes sharp as verdicts. She could have been Claudia's twin, save for the century between them.

On the back, a name written in a heavy hand: Maria Vale.

Claudia felt the breath leave her chest. "My family didn't keep records this old."

"Guess they didn't need to," Angelo said. "You're the record."

The clock on the nightstand ticked once, hard, then stopped. The air thickened—the moment before storm or sentence. The light over the sink flickered and stayed dim, throwing their shadows long.

Claudia closed the case slowly. "We're not done with Dominguez."

Angelo gave a small laugh that wasn't humor. "We were never going to be." They cleaned up, packed light, and left the motel before the city remembered their names. In the truck, Claudia's phone buzzed—no caller ID, just a voice that carried the echo of a courtroom microphone.

"Counselor Vale."

Claudia's grip tightened on the phone. "Who is this?"

"You filed a motion last night," the voice said. Calm. Almost kind. "You don't remember, but we received it."

"What motion?"

"Continuance," the voice said. "Against oblivion."

The line clicked dead.

Angelo glanced over. "Bad news?"

"Worse," she said. "Administrative." By noon they were under fluorescent lights again, back in the city's belly where records went to molder in peace. Claudia still had clearance—old habits die politely. They slipped past the security desk, down a hall where the tiles had learned not to echo.

The archives were cold and endless. Boxes stacked to the ceiling, rows labeled in handwriting that had outlived the clerks. Claudia found Dominguez easily. She opened the first folder and froze. Inside weren't affidavits or exhibits—just a single sheet of vellum so old it smelled of candle smoke.

Across the top: The Docket.

Below, in Latin and English interwoven, were four headings: Sentence. Motion. Affidavit. Appeal.

"This isn't a file," Angelo said behind her. "It's a spell written by lawyers."

Claudia laughed once, brittle. "We specialize in curses."

The vellum flared faintly under her hand. For an instant, ink burned gold, showing words behind words:
All signatures shall return to their source.

The air changed pressure, like the room had remembered it had lungs. Every fluorescent light flickered in unison. The hum of electricity pitched lower, the sound of language thinking.

Angelo stepped closer. “We should go.”

She closed the folder, slid it into her briefcase, and shut it with a snap that sounded like contempt. “We can’t.”

“Why not?”

“Because the law’s written in blood,” she said, and glanced at her wrist. The birthmark there—circle, hook, three slashes—glowed faintly beneath her skin. “And I think mine’s on the docket.” They reached Helena’s cabin at dusk. The woods hummed low, the way forests do before they decide whether they’re going to let you in. Inside, the air smelled of cedar and ink. Claudia placed the briefcase on the table. The latch clicked on its own.

Helena poured whiskey instead of coffee. “You want to tell me why your suitcase is breathing?”

Claudia opened it. The pages fluttered once, a sound like paper inhaling.

“This case was never about Dominguez,” she said. “It’s about jurisdiction.”

Helena frowned. “Between what and what?”

“Between us and whatever wrote us.”

Angelo watched from the window. “You’re losing altitude, counselor.”

“No,” Claudia said. “I’m remembering gravity.”

The file glowed again—soft red through the paper. One phrase pulsed at the bottom: Custodia sanguinis.
Custody of blood.

Helena took a slow sip, eyes narrowed. "If that thing starts talking Latin, I'm burning it."

"Don't," Claudia said. "It talks back." That night, the forest filled with headlights.

Three SUVs parked in the clearing, engines idling low. Shadows moved between them—men in suits without insignia. Angelo cocked his head. "Uniform boots, private rhythm."

"They found us," Helena said.

Claudia closed the case. The glow dimmed, but the air in the cabin tightened, every nail remembering tension.

Glass shattered in the next second. Shouts followed—muffled orders, flashlights slicing the dark. Helena grabbed her revolver from the mantle and muttered, "Every damn time."

Angelo pushed Claudia toward the back. "Run."

"I'm done running," she said, but he was already moving, already turning the table on its side as cover. The first round splintered the door. Wood exploded across the floor.

Claudia ducked behind the case. The metal vibrated once, then flared with light. The men hesitated—confused, maybe blinded—and she felt the same strange pull as the night before at Dock 19: the world inhaling, waiting.

She spoke without thinking, the words pulled from somewhere deeper than language. "Affidavit admittitur."

The bullets stopped midair. Just stopped—hanging, quivering like insects caught in amber. The light from the briefcase intensified; the room burned white.

Then silence.

When the light faded, the men were gone. Only the forest outside, perfectly still. Not a leaf moved.

Angelo turned to her, face pale. “What did you just do?”

“I think,” she said slowly, “I cited precedent.” They didn’t stay. Helena gave them the truck and two new names. “If the papers start asking questions,” she said, “lie beautifully.”

Claudia looked back once as they left. The cabin stood intact but hollow, as if every echo had moved out. The case on the seat beside her hummed again, low and satisfied.

Angelo drove until the road turned to mist. Neither of them mentioned Dock 19, the girl, or the man with the cigar. Some truths needed to ferment.

“What happens now?” he asked finally.

Claudia looked down at the case, at the faint red line still pulsing under the latch. “Now,” she said, “we find out who signed it first.

Chapter 13 — The Inheritance of Ash

The highway wound along the river like an unspooled vein. Dawn hadn't found the courage to show up yet; the world existed in the gray pause between crimes and confessions. Angelo drove without music. The briefcase on Claudia's lap vibrated faintly with every mile marker, as though counting.

She tried to convince herself it was the road. The road didn't answer.

When she finally spoke, her voice startled the silence.
"Maria Vale," she said. "Do you believe in ghosts?"

Angelo's scar caught the first hint of morning. "I believe in consequences."

"Same thing," she said.

He smiled at that—one of his rare, human ones. Then he nodded toward the glove box. "Open it."

Inside lay a folded photograph, edges scorched. The image showed a courtroom from a century ago—twelve jurors in black coats, their faces blurred by motion. At the bench, a woman stood with her hand raised in oath. Claudia recognized the jawline before her brain caught up.

"You had this?" she asked.

"I found it in the crane's control box at Dock 19," he said. "Looked like a warning."

The briefcase hummed louder, an insect trapped in metal. Claudia set it on the floor and pressed her heel against the lid until it quieted. They reached the edge of the old district—brick buildings stitched together with telephone wire, alleys full of last night's news. Angelo parked beside a boarded-up café with City Records Annex still faintly visible above the door.

Inside, the air smelled of paper turned to dust and promises. The lights didn't work, but the windows were generous enough. Claudia followed the path of daylight across stacks of files until she found the section marked Historic Court Documents — Pre-Federal Charter.

She tugged one drawer. It rolled open smooth as memory.
Within: boxes stamped with the same sigil branded into her wrist.

She lifted the top one. Dust fell like verdicts.

The first folder contained hand-written minutes from The People v. Salazar, 1847.
The ink shimmered faintly gold, identical to the Dominguez file.

Halfway down the page, in smaller handwriting—her ancestor's.

If guilt is hereditary, then so is grace. Let this clause stand until someone braver argues otherwise.
— M. Vale

Claudia traced the words. They burned cold.
"She was a defense attorney," she whispered. "Arguing against original sin."

Angelo leaned on the cabinet. "Looks like she lost."

"Maybe not," Claudia said, lifting another file. Beneath it lay an envelope sealed with dark wax stamped Docket No. 1.

She cracked the seal. Inside were four parchment leaves, thin as breath. The Latin was newer than she expected, written as if the hand that wrote it still existed somewhere:

Sentence of Forever — hereby binding all witnesses of flesh and word to the preservation of equilibrium. Breach shall call the Redaction.

Claudia read the last word twice.

“The Redaction,” she said. “It’s not metaphor, it’s a clause.”

Angelo frowned. “Meaning?”

“Meaning if someone tries to erase what’s written, the erasure fights back.” They spent the rest of the day there, chasing fragments. When Claudia finally dozed in the chair, exhaustion pulled her into a dream that didn’t feel borrowed.

She stood in a courtroom with no ceiling. The benches were carved from salt. A judge sat faceless behind a curtain of smoke.
“State your name,” the voice commanded.

“Claudia Vale,” she said.

“Occupation?”

“Counsel.”

“Client?”

“The City.”

The judge leaned forward. Behind the smoke, she glimpsed a thousand faint silhouettes—every person she’d defended, every witness she’d silenced. Their mouths opened, releasing moths instead of words.

“You inherit the Docket,” the voice said. “Do you plead comprehension?”

She tried to answer, but the air filled with ash, swirling, forming words she didn’t want to read:

Every verdict leaves an echo. You are the echo.

She woke with a gasp, a taste of dust and ink on her tongue.
The briefcase on the desk had opened itself.

Inside, the Dominguez file now lay blank—every word gone except three carved into the paper’s surface:

Remember me. Night again. They left the annex and drove to the river's edge, following instinct more than plan. The water moved slower here, thick with reflected light from the refineries upstream. Claudia set the case on the pier and sat beside it.

Angelo lit a cigarette and offered one; she shook her head.

"You ever think," she said, "that maybe the case isn't about Dominguez at all? Maybe he's just a name the curse uses when it needs an alias."

He exhaled smoke that turned red in the taillight glow. "If that's true, what's it want from you?"

"Continuity," she said softly. "Someone to finish the sentence."

Wind rose from the river, cold and articulate. The surface rippled, forming brief lines of reflected moonlight that looked like handwriting. For an instant, she saw words skimming the current.

Custodia sanguinis.

The same phrase that had appeared in Helena's cabin.
She whispered it back. The river answered with a single sound—like paper tearing underwater.

When it subsided, the briefcase latch clicked open again.
Angelo drew his pistol automatically.

Inside the case, a single page glowed. Its header read:

Affidavit of Sin — draft one.

The rest was empty, waiting.

Claudia stared at it, throat tight. "It's already naming the next case."

Angelo holstered the gun. "Then you better win this one first." They left the pier before dawn. By the time the sun broke over the skyline, the briefcase had stopped humming, though the smell of smoke clung to the air around it.

On the dashboard, Claudia spread the old photograph of Maria Vale beside the new one from Dock 19—the cigar ember marking the man on the pier. Under the changing light, faint gold lines connected them, invisible at night but alive now, sketching a pattern like genealogy rewritten in flame.

Angelo nodded toward it. “Family tree?”

“Family sentence,” she said.

They drove until the city thinned into fields and silence. Ahead, the road split—one branch leading back toward law, the other into whatever counted as legend.

Claudia folded the photograph and slipped it into her jacket. “Pick a direction.”

Angelo smiled without humor. “You’ll pick anyway.”

She did. Toward the horizon that looked most like a question.

Behind them, Dock 19 was already rubble. But under the water, buried in silt and salt, words carved themselves into the pilings in letters of fire:

All signatures shall return to their source.

Chapter 14 The Box

The safehouse walls pressed in like a coffin. Claudia's blouse clung damp against her back, streaked with dust and someone else's blood. The church's echo still lived in her ears— glass shattering, boots pounding, the sharp crack of gunfire.

Marks sat on the rug, shoulders curled inward, a cigarette trembling between his fingers. Smoke curled, then broke apart in the draft from the rattling fan. His tie dangled loose around his neck, stained with sweat.

"You're not smoking it," Claudia said.

Marks blinked, then stared at the ember like it was foreign. He raised it to his mouth, coughed on the inhale, dropped it into a paper cup of stale coffee.

Angelo leaned against the wall, his torn sleeve rolled past his elbow. The tattoos were black vines, thorns tangled with knives. He didn't speak. He didn't need to. The scar along his jaw told enough stories.

Claudia tossed her briefcase onto the table. The wood shuddered. "He knew," she said. "Every move we made tonight was predicted. That wasn't coincidence. That was choreography."

Marks buried his face in his hands. "You think I don't know? You think I don't feel it every time he breathes before I do?"

Claudia's jaw tightened. "Explain."

Marks's laugh cracked, bitter and raw. He dug in his pocket and pulled out a folded scrap of lined paper. His hand shook as he passed it across.

Claudia unfolded it. The letters were neat, blocky, deliberate:

PAGE 51: THE BOX CLOSES.

Her stomach sank.

"What is this?"

Marks's eyes glistened red. "He calls it La Caja. The Box. You don't see the walls until they're already shut around you. Every contact, every move, every choice—he lays them out. You think you're chasing him, but he's already written your story."

Angelo finally spoke, voice flat. "And we're in it."

Marks nodded, jerking like a marionette with snapped strings. "You don't get it. None of you do. He doesn't just trap bodies. He traps minds. Judges, cops, lawyers, me. You. Once he says you're in the box, you don't climb out. You scratch at the walls until your nails break, and still—it closes." Marks stared at the scrap like it might start speaking for him. When it didn't, words spilled anyway.

"He keeps two books," he said. "The one the accountants show auditors, and the one he calls the Box. The Box isn't numbers. It's people. Levers. Weaknesses. Favors that felt harmless when you said yes."

Claudia folded her arms. "Names."

"Rector," Marks said first, as if anything else would be a lie. "Dominguez found him in a credit union that never recovered from 2008. Fired for 'process irregularities,' which means he was too good at catching other people's theft. Dominguez hired him to catch ours. Rector hates messy money. He thinks order is sacred."

"Then he and I have something in common," Claudia said.

Marks shook his head. "You have rules. He has rituals. He hums hymns under his breath while he balances the Box. He'll walk into a room and name every variable: who's scared, who cheats, who wants, who can be bought cheaper next time." A sad laugh. "He hums 'Jesus, Remember Me' when he writes a name in. He says it keeps him humble."

Angelo's gaze flicked to Claudia. Hymn. She filed it next to other small knives.

"What did you give him?" she asked.

"Introductions. Then signatures. Then silence." Marks rubbed his eyes. "You think you're keeping control because you only move one inch at a time. But the Box doesn't measure distance. It measures direction."

"Where does he keep it?" Angelo asked.

Marks swallowed. "Not digital. He doesn't trust screens. Ledgers bound in leather. Corrections writ by hand. He keeps them near the water. Underground. The air smells like old paper and iron."

"The customs house," Claudia said. It wasn't a question, just a slotting of weight into structure.

Marks flinched. "He calls it a museum so people will stop looking." Claudia spread a legal pad and drew three squares in a row. "He corrals, he constricts, he collects," she said, writing the verbs over the boxes. "Corrals: leak, rumor, 'street' pressure—push us where he wants us. Constricts: smears and police attention, ambushes in sanctuaries, messages that pretend to be destiny." She tapped the third box. "Collects: the Box. Evidence, signatures, names. The thing that makes all his threats true."

Angelo pointed to the first square. "Corralling started when he used Marks to pull us to Bart's."

"Constricting when he sent the ledger," Claudia said. "When he put 'TOGETHER' on a page and made us watch each other for weaknesses we don't have time to indulge."

Marks looked between them like a man watching a surgeon remove something he'd thought was part of his body. "You can't get to the Box," he said. "Even if you find a way in, Rector will have already moved the most important pages."

Claudia met his eyes. “Then we don’t go for the pages first. We go for Rector. He’s the hinge.”

Angelo nodded once. “He’ll be at the customs house tonight. Reconciliation nights are calendar holy days for men like him.”

Marks flinched. “He’ll expect me.”

“Good,” Angelo said. “Expectation is a handle.”

Claudia flipped the page. “We need locations, hours, routes, and—” The light above them buzzed, dipped, came back. Angelo’s head tilted. “Car outside,” he murmured. “Same engine as the SUV at the garment district.”

Claudia palmed the shotgun. Marks went pale. Angelo went to the window without being seen by it.

“Two men,” he said. “Not in a hurry.”

Claudia breathed once through her nose and made the call in her head she’d already made. “We move safehouses again.”

“Tonight?” Marks squeaked.

“Right now,” Angelo said. “Fear is a compass if you use it right. Get your coat. Padre Emil opened the side door of the rectory with a look that said he would prefer less drama and fewer bullets. “Your timing is uncharitable,” he said, stepping aside. “But the guest room is empty.”

They threaded into a narrow back room with a small bed and a big crucifix. Claudia set her bag down, then set the shotgun under the bed as if the floor needed to know what it was sleeping over.

Emil folded his arms. “You’re bleeding again,” he told Angelo.

“It’s fashionable,” Angelo said.

Emil handed him a roll of gauze and a look that could have been a prayer or sarcasm. “There are two cops on my front steps pretending they're lost. If you plan to introduce them to theology, do it somewhere else."

"We plan to introduce someone to arithmetic," Claudia said. "Do you know the customs house?"

Emil's mouth quirked. "I know where they kept the stories we wrote when ships were louder than planes." His face sobered. "Be careful with fire down there. Stone remembers."

"Stone will have to make room," she said.

Emil nodded at Marks. "And him?"

"Witness, for now," Angelo said. "Bait, if necessary."

Marks gagged. "I'm in the room."

"Then listen," Claudia said. "You call Rector. Ask for 'reconciliation' the way you always do.
If he tells you the hour and the place, you show up—exactly as asked. We'll be there first."

Emil rubbed his temples. "You people break into my house, bleed on my floor, and recruit God's building for arson. You know what that makes me?"

"A good man," Claudia said.

"A tired one," Emil said. "Get out before I remember I believe in rules
Back in the car, Claudia buckled in and didn't start the engine. Angelo watched her in the mirror.

"What," he said.

"You keep throwing yourself toward the bullet first," she said. "In the nave. In the alley. At
Dock 19. That's not bravery. That's habit."

His mouth twitched—almost a smile, almost a snarl. "Habit kept me alive long enough to meet you."

"It'll get you killed before we finish this."

He turned to face her fully. "I'm not planning on finishing this alone."

The truth of that hit harder than the argument. Claudia looked away first, at the river, at the city pretending to be asleep. "Good," she said quietly. "Because if you die before I do, I'll drag you back long enough to yell at you."

A beat. He huffed once—something like a laugh. "Duly noted."

She started the car. They parked three blocks from the customs house and walked the rest under awnings that dripped yesterday's rain. Claudia narrated the way prosecutors do when they're building a case for a jury that doesn't know it believes her yet.

"Corridor access points," she said, counting on her fingers. "Public museum stairs with a shut gate; staff elevator off the loading bay; river intake—old records chute; and a maintenance stair we found last time."

Angelo added, "Traps: trip wire on the first gate, a breaker that kills the smoke detectors but not the cameras that matter, and a plainclothes guard who wants to be seen enough you'll think that's all there is."

"And Rector himself," she said. "He's a walking alarm. Notices the wire moved a millimeter.
Notices a breath that doesn't belong."

Angelo's head dipped. "He'll smell cheap tobacco and fear. We give him neither."

"Speak for yourself," she said.

He grinned. The scar bent with it. "We're going to do something ugly, Vale."

“We’ve already done ugly,” she said. “Tonight we do necessary.” Marks made the call from a payphone that a developer had left standing because it looked good in brochures. Claudia watched him through the window of a laundromat across the street, pretending to be interested in a row of washing machines that had forgotten their manners. Angelo stood with his back to the detergent shelf, scanning reflections in the glass.

The line clicked. Rector’s voice folded through in that quiet, patient tone. “Page.”

Marks swallowed. “Fifty-two.”

“Same hour,” Rector said. “Same place.”

“Alone?” Marks asked, because he had to.

Rector hummed a bar of the hymn. The line went dead.

Claudia exhaled. “He believes his own rules,” she said. “That’ll kill him.”

Angelo shook his head. “Rules don’t kill men. Exceptions do.” They used the same access badge Claudia had conned from the city and the same service corridor that still smelled like lemon wax lying about being clean. Down the stairs. Past the capped lens. To the trip wire.

Claudia didn’t lift it this time. She added a second loop of wire, taped invisibly to the wall, that would give when the first one did—returning to rest with the same angle, the same tension. If Rector touched it, it would sing the right note.

Angelo killed the auxiliary lights for twenty seconds and brought them back, enough to make the cameras stutter. He chalked a tiny line on the floor at the point where the guard’s boots had scuffed last time. If the chalk smeared, they’d know who stepped where.

“You look like a man setting a stage,” Claudia murmured.

“I am,” he said. “Actors think they own the show. The stage knows better.”

“Marks?” she asked into the mic.

His voice crackled back like a man trying to become a signal. “In position.”

Claudia checked her watch. 9:57. He didn’t make a sound at first—just that not-silence of a presence that belongs in a place and therefore doesn’t broadcast itself. Then the faint squeak of nitrile. The hymn under his breath. …remember me…

Two men flanked him: heavy and light, as predicted. Rector paused at the trip wire and— tell it true—smiled behind the cotton mask when the loop swayed perfectly and settled exactly as he’d left it the night before. He touched the chalk with a toe, found it unchanged, and hummed louder, pleased to be confirmed by the world.

“Page,” he called down the corridor.

“Fifty-two,” Marks answered from the corner, voice steady once and then less so.

“Alone,” Rector said.

Claudia slid her thumb over the mic switch and cut it. “Now,” she whispered.

Angelo moved first, low, and fast, taking the heavy man’s throat in the same motion as the muzzle found the light one’s center mass. Claudia came opposite, shotgun leveled at Rector’s sternum from a slant that put her outside both men’s peripheral vision. Rector froze with polite surprise.

“Hello again,” he said, calm as key clicks. “You’re punctual.”

“Keys,” Claudia said.

“I brought my hands,” he said, and offered them.

Angelo stripped the ring from his glove, found a second ring inside the coat, and a single plain key taped to the inner seam. "Door and core," he said.

Rector's eyes warmed. "You learn quickly."

"We'll test whether you do," Claudia said. At Vault 3B the air changed from museum to engine room. Angelo slid the plain key into the hidden lintel lock, then the ring into the visible one; the wheel answered like a beast woken with flattery. Claudia held Rector at gunpoint while Marks hovered at the corridor mouth like someone waiting for a verdict.

Inside, the room yawned cool and dry. Leather, paper, time. Not a shrine—an operating theater. Claudia's eyes landed on the spine with a red thread and felt something mean and satisfied tighten in her chest. Corrections.

"Step in," she told Rector. "Tell me which book kills you if I burn it."

He nodded at a ledger bound in dark calf, unmarked. "That one kills you," he said pleasantly. "The one with the judges. Burn it and the city spends ten years tearing up its floorboards to see what squeaks. Meanwhile, men like me simply change the names on the tabs."

She didn't blink. "And this one?"

She tapped Corrections. He hummed the hymn again, softer. "That one kills me."

Angelo didn't take his eyes off the corridor. "Then we'll keep it for last."

Rector tilted his head. "You think there's a last page."

"There's always a last page," Claudia said. "You either write it yourself or you let a man like Dominguez write it for you."

He lowered his eyes, as if to the book. "Ms. Vale," he said softly, "you of all people should know—books don't end. They balance."

Her anger rose like a tide. She kept it caged behind her ribs and did the math. Time. Motion sensor. Smoke. Marks's nerve. Police response. Dominguez listening for the precise moment to move his next piece.

"Bag it," she told Angelo, chin to the Corrections ledger.

He slid it into a fireproof sack and sealed the lip with tape. Rector's humming faded another degree, as if distance from the book weakened him.

"Now what?" Marks whispered.

"Now we leave—quiet," Angelo said.

They did not get quiet.

Two floors above, alarms began as a rumor and became a choir. Someone had noticed the breaker's flirtation. The guard in the lobby had decided to stop yawning. Outside, the first siren wound itself into a scream.

Rector's eyes brightened. "See?" he said gently. "The Box closes."

Angelo shoved him forward. "Not tonight."

They moved as the corridor filled with a mechanical cough that meant fans waking to move smoke that wasn't there yet. At the trip wire, Claudia nudged the secondary loop so it sang the same little nothing as before. At the service stair, she paused and listened to the building breathe.

"Elevator," Angelo said.

"No," she said, at the same time. They looked at each other. He shrugged: Your call. They took the stairs.

At the landing, two men in city jackets appeared with hands out like traffic cops. Angelo's shot was clean and mean; Claudia's was ugly and effective. Rector flinched—not at the violence, at the noise.

“Down,” she said.

They burst out into the loading bay as two cruisers rolled to the curb. Angelo threw the fireproof bag into a laundry cart and pushed. Claudia shoved Rector face-first into the same cart and threw a sheet over the lot. Marks stumbled like a man told to pretend not to be himself.

“Badge,” Claudia said.

She flashed the city laminate and shouted over the alarms, “Sprinkler fault—archives—get me a tech who can count to ten!”

The guard blinked at chaos and did what people do when a woman with authority and fury points: he got out of their way.

They rolled the cart into the alley, pushed it twenty yards, and only then did Angelo let the grin show up. The scar bent with it, wicked and alive.

“Page fifty-two,” he said, breath fogging in the night. “Addendum.” They didn’t go to the safehouse. They didn’t go to Emil. They went to a storage unit two neighborhoods away that Angelo kept for days when the city needed a lie told gently.

Inside: a metal table, a wheeled chair, a coil of rope, a first-aid kit, and a coffeepot that had no business being as clean as it was.

Rector sat in the chair with his wrists tied, mask off. His mouth was small, neat, the mouth of a man who liked precise bites. He watched Claudia as if she were a ledger with an interesting error.

“You have a choice,” she said. “You can help us burn the Box. Or you can watch me rip out pages until the city starts screaming.”

He hummed, very faint. …remember me…

Angelo set the fireproof bag on the table. “You know what’s in here,” he said.

Rector's eyes warmed. "I know what you think is in there," he said. "But a man like Dominguez never keeps only one hinge."

Claudia leaned down, close enough to see the pale ring a mask leaves on a face. "We don't need every hinge," she said. "We need the one that breaks him in public."

Rector considered that long enough to test her patience. Finally, he nodded—once. "Then you'll want the judges. The donors. And the line that changes the air in a room: the union man with the keys to the port."

"Names," Angelo said.

"Later," Rector said. "After you make a promise."

Claudia smiled without heat. "We don't make promises to accountants."

"You do if you want the Box to open," he said pleasantly. "Page fifty-four, Ms. Vale. It's titled Pledge for a reason."

The burner on the table buzzed. Unknown number. Angelo flipped it, put it on speaker.

Dominguez's voice came through smooth as oiled rope. "Page fifty-three was Ash," he said. "I smell smoke and it doesn't belong to me. Naughty."

Claudia pulled a chair beside the table and sat, elbows on her knees, eyes on the phone like a gun sight. "You built a box," she said. "We found the hinge."

He laughed softly. "You always were good at reading frames. Shame there won't be a book club where you're going."

The line clicked. No threat. No time. Just the promise of motion.

Claudia looked at Rector. "Your hymn," she said. "Sing it all the way through."

He smiled with small teeth. “Only if you intend to listen.”

Angelo rolled his shoulders and cracked his knuckles. “Talk,” he told Rector. “Or hum. We’ll make it music either way.”

Rector studied them, then the bag, then the rope at his wrists. “Very well,” he said. “Let’s balance.”

Claudia opened her notebook and wrote a single line at the top of the page, above all the others: Chapter 14 — The Box.

Then she turned the page and held the pen ready.

Chapter 15 — The Motion Filed

The storage unit swallowed their footfalls when they stepped out, the metal door dropping behind them with a groan that sounded too much like relief. The night had a wet throat. Fog lay low, slick on the asphalt, curling around ankles like a habit you were trying to break.

Angelo kept his hand on Claudia's back until they reached the truck. Not possessive—practical, like he was making sure the city didn't take a bite on the way. He checked the mirrors, checked the quiet, checked the air itself as if air could hold a weapon.

"Go," she said, and the word came out level. That counted as victory.

They slid into the seats. The cab smelled like cordite and burned paper. Angelo turned the key. The engine turned back.

They pulled onto the avenue. The streetlights blew halos through the mist, sick yellow moons. Rain came in a grudging spit—just enough to make the wipers squeal and the road oily. Claudia cracked the window for the cold; it sharpened her thoughts the way a whetstone makes a knife honest. She set the fireproof bag at her feet, one palm flat over it like you steady a book during an earthquake.

The radio woke, uninvited. Angelo hadn't touched it. Static first, then the middle of a hymn from a station nobody sane listened to after midnight.

He hit the power and killed it. Static bled through anyway for a breath, like a whisper pressed against a wall. Words almost but not quite.

She counted under her breath. Four in, hold, four out. The way the therapist had taught her to stack ghosts into neat little boxes. It didn't banish anything. It made it organized.

A group of men on a corner laughed too loud, then stopped as the truck rolled by. The city was always full of audiences trying to choose between silence and courage. A tag glared from the brick behind them—paint so new it glistened wet: a rough circle, a hooked tail, three short slashes. She'd seen the mark a hundred times without seeing it. Tonight it looked back.

"You know that one?" she asked.

Angelo glanced, kept driving. "Kids call it the Watcher. Means someone's got eyes on the street. Or wants you to think they do."

"Which is safer?"

"Neither."

They hit a light that refused to turn. Claudia's reflection hovered faintly in the windshield, layered with the ghost of the street. The red stayed red. Somewhere a gull screamed like metal tearing. She rubbed her thumb along the crease of the bag. The ledger inside shifted—she felt it, absurd as the idea was—paper breathing.

She let memory unclench in small, controlled releases. A courtroom, air-conditioned and smug. A judge with eyes that looked like closed doors. Men who deserved to be afraid of her and weren't because men like that outsource fear. And under all of it, the old house: a kitchen chair on its side, a bottle shattering like ice, her father's voice thick with liquor and grievance. Debt, he'd said once, not to her but at her, as if he could bruise the air in front of her face. There's always a debt, little mouse. The world is a ledger. You'll pay yours.

The light turned. Angelo didn't floor it. He slid forward the way men move when they've learned the city's patience is a trap. The fog grew teeth in the alleys. Street after street, more tags—circles with hooks, slashed three times—sprouted like mushrooms after rain. Not new paint. Old scars. She wondered if she'd never actually looked at the walls of the place she'd made a life in.

"What did Padre Emil tell you about symbols?" she asked, half to puncture the quiet, half because she wanted the room inside the question.

"That all languages were drawn before they were spoken," Angelo said. "That people make marks to teach the dark to remember them."

“And this one?”

His scar tugged when he almost smiled. “He said the men I knew used it wrong.”

“Is there a right way?”

“There’s a right person to ask,” he said. “And she doesn’t work for heaven.”

Claudia looked at him. He didn’t look back. The scar tracked along his jaw like a reminder. Ink climbed his forearm, the edges of it vanishing under the sleeve. She knew the map well enough to draw it in the dark: thorns, a blade without ornament, a clock with no hands. Crew marks layered over something older. He’d told her once that time didn’t help if you were counting the wrong thing. The wrong thing had a name again tonight: debt.

A police cruiser cut across two lanes ahead and vanished into the fog. No siren. City magic—now you see it, now you don’t. Angelo took a longer route than made sense on paper, then another one. He liked to arrive at places sideways, like he could convince fate to miss them if they didn’t announce themselves head-on.

The safe apartment crouched over a bodega that sold lemons, cigarettes, and hope printed on lottery slips. The sign out front blinked the way tired eyes blink. Angelo killed the engine and let the silence equalize.

They got out. Somewhere above, a fan hummed like a faraway hive. The bodega bell chimed twice and an old man in a track jacket stepped into the fog with a paper bag. He didn’t look at them. Good manners in this city aren’t about greetings; they’re about willful blindness.

Up the stairs. Second landing smelled like boiled coffee. Third smelled like bleach and a memory of something fried. The hallway light flickered once, then steadied. Claudia could feel the ledger through the bag—like a heartbeat under her hand, or maybe that was just her own pulse relocated.

At the door, Angelo reached for the knob and then didn't. He stood still a second, listening to a frequency she couldn't hear. Claudia watched the length of that stillness and thought about how a man builds a life out of not trusting the parts of the world that want to be trusted most. He turned the key. The deadbolt thunked back. They slipped inside.

The apartment was square and plain—a couch that had never been told a story, a table too honest to wobble, a bed you could make in under a minute. A window looked over a brick wall, generous in how little it offered. She liked it for that. Rooms with too much view ask for too much confession.

She set the bag on the table. The zipper rasped like a match starting. Inside lay the ledger pages they'd taken from the dock and the small black book with red thread in its spine—the one that breathed like it had lungs. Angelo washed his hands at the sink; the water came brown, then cleared. The hiss of it sounded like a crowd hushing itself before a verdict.

"Let me see," he said.

"I'm fine," she said, and tasted the lie. Fine is a word you put on a wound to make it stop asking for a name.

"You're bleeding."

She looked and found the thin brown seam down her sleeve where the day had written its notes. She turned her arm. He took her wrist and peeled back the cuff. His hands were careful in the way careful men can be when they've had to teach themselves gentleness so it didn't go extinct.

Saline. Gauze. The soft reprimand of alcohol, a sting that meant clean. He taped the cut and then sat back on his heels, eyes scanning her face like an exit map. He was always inventorying: doors, windows, weapons, expressions.

"You," she said, "are leaking too."

His half-smile was a scar's echo. "Fashionable."

She lifted the hem of his shirt; stitches tugged across his ribs, purple halos blooming in tidal pools around the thread. She cleaned him. He watched her the way a man watches a fuse he knows won't reach powder but respects anyway.

Silence in the room rearranged itself into something companionable. The city noise outside kept its distance, as if it had been paid to.

"Sit," she said finally, and he did, which told her more about pain than any question would have. She finished the last gauze, pressed her palm over tape as if sealing a pact.

The apartment felt colder than it should. She turned to the small heater and twisted the dial. The burner caught. Blue flame. For one second, a shape licked along the metal—curve, hook, three small slashes—and then it was only heat again. The human brain is a good editor; it removes things that want to ruin the story.

"Did you—" she began.

"What," he said.

"Nothing." A lawyer's answer. A survivor's.

The mirror above the sink coughed a fog bloom, then cleared. Claudia's reflection looked back, eyes too bright, wet hair marking her temple like a question. The glass had the oddest lag, a fraction of a second where the world seemed to think about whether it wanted to keep up. Then everything snapped precise.

"Shower," she said.

He nodded. "I'll take the chair."

"You'll take the water after me," she said, and meant both the literal and the thing beneath it.

She walked to the bathroom and undressed like she was filing a brief—deliberate, clause by clause. Bruises written in purple cursive on her ribs, a scrape at the shoulder that would turn a deep good blue by morning. She turned the hot until it hissed; steam rolled up the glass and wrote on the mirror in a hand she didn't recognize. Three strokes. A crooked circle. A hooked tail. She wiped it away. The steam wrote it again slower, as if trying to teach a child to form the letters.

She stepped into the water. Heat took the edge off the world. The noise in her spine unwound a notch. She put her forehead against cool tile. The tile hummed and went quiet, the way tile does when you are too tired to argue with physics.

The door opened, careful. Angelo set his pistol on the sink, the knife beside it, the way a man empties his hands to tell the room he means no harm. He didn't cross the line; he waited at the threshold.

"Company?" he asked.

Claudia closed her eyes. There was no word for the ache that wasn't pain. "Yes," she said. "But don't fix me. Not here."

He undressed with the economy of someone shedding a uniform that the skin itself had been. Ink moved when he moved—vines waking, not wiggling; that would be superstition and she did not afford superstition. He stepped in under the spray without flinching. Heat crawled over old scars and wrote new steam on the glass.

They stood with the distance of honest people. Then they didn't.

He reached first for her wrist, the lightest touch, an offer, not a claim. She turned and the distance closed without negotiation. Kiss, yes. Mouths, yes. But the part that mattered most was the press of forehead to forehead, bone to bone—the reminder that their skulls had done their job a long time: kept what needed keeping.

Under the water, the apartment made a sound like a pipe learning a tune. It was almost a hum. It stopped when Claudia stilled, then resumed when she moved again, curious as a child.

"Static," he said, because giving something a name makes it smaller.

"It feels like the opposite," she said, and that was too large to keep in the room. She let it pass between them and go.

When they were done being careful with each other and careful in that room, they shut off the water. Towels. Steam thinned. Claudia wiped a strip on the glass and looked at herself. Not a stranger. For a fraction, the reflection lagged again—her mouth a heartbeat ahead of her face, then perfect. The brain is merciful.

From the other room, the phone vibrated once—her private line, the one no one was supposed to reach. She let it buzz. It stopped. It started again, patient, and certain.

"Rector," she said, reaching for a shirt.

"Or someone who signs his checks," Angelo said, dragging on a black tee that hung like it had been manufactured to argue with his bones.

The phone buzzed a third time. That was insistence, not luck. Claudia crossed to the table and picked up. The line breathed. No voice. Just the sound a match makes when it wants to be rubbed against stone.

"Speak," she said, a lawyer's command put into a room that pretended it was a phone call.

A man's whisper emerged, delicate as ash. "Page fifty," he said. "Inheritance."
"Who is this."

"You were born owing," the whisper said, tender as a threat. "And he was born to collect."

The line went dead. Claudia lowered the phone. Angelo watched her face like it was a street he planned to cross without dying.

"Marks?" he asked.

"Accountant with poetry," she said. "Dangerous species."

She pulled the ledger toward her. The top page had not been the top page when she set the stack down. That was a problem for people who liked their worlds crisp and orderly. She lifted it. Legal parchment, old glue in the scent, a salt taste in the back of the throat like the river room had found a way to breathe up through the bodega floor.

An entry in neat church-hand:

VALE, CLAUDIA — off-hours investigations; therapist, 2:07 p.m. Wednesdays. Witness intimidation (indirect). Margin: COMPULSION.

She angled the lamp and light slid across the paper. Letters rose, thinner than veins, as if someone had written with pressure only and trusted the page to remember the bruise:

Linea peccati — sanguis debitum.

Her Latin didn't deserve a parade, but it showed up to work: line of sin — blood debt.

She didn't say it aloud. The room might hear. The room already heard too much.

Angelo leaned in. For the smallest instant, real recognition crossed his face, raw as a nerve. He put it away. "Seen that tag on brick," he said. "Means a post is watched."

"This isn't a post," she said. "It's paper from a dead library under a river."

"Dominguez likes redundancy," he said.

"This isn't his redundancy," she said. "It's older."

The heater clicked and the small blue flame licked again into a curved hook before it steadied to ordinary blue. Angelo didn't look. He didn't have to; he had already decided which parts of the world he would not let in, because letting them in meant they could never be put back out.

Outside, the bodega's bell rang. Voices. Laughter that didn't belong to people who had seen blood tonight. And still, a pressure in the room like a church's—between prayer and answer.

"Question," Claudia said, eyes on the ledger. "If sin leaves signatures, who taught the city to read?"

"Witches," Angelo said, too flat for it to be a joke.

"You don't believe in that."
"I believe in what people will do to get what they want," he said. "The name you put on the wanting is your business."

She turned the page. A smear in the margin—dried wine colored, or something that liked to pretend. A shape in it. The circle, the hook, the three slashes. She set her thumb on it. Heat breathed against her skin, not hot enough to burn, just enough to be acknowledged.

"Don't," Angelo said, quicker than he meant to.

"Tell me why."

"Let's not have our first fight about religion," he said.

"Whose religion?"

"The city's," he said, and the word was large enough to cast a shadow across the table.

She let her hand hover a fraction above the mark without touching. Even air has rules. Even air can write.

The room rearranged itself into purpose. Guns checked. Bag zipped. Street re-entered. Rector would still be tied to his little chair, dreaming up numbers to weigh against the future. The ledger would still be a throat asking for the right knife. The city would still be a choir that liked to sing off-key until somebody tuned it with a little blood.

At the door, Angelo paused long enough to touch two fingers to the ink at his shoulder—the thorn-curve that mirrored the hook on the page. He didn't make it a ritual. He didn't have to for it to be one.

"Pride kills," he said. "Tonight we let it live."

She met his eyes. "Thought you didn't advertise that you cared whether I do."

"I'm advertising that I enjoy when you prove me wrong," he said, deadpan soft.

The hallway had new quiet in it. On the second landing, an open door framed an old woman in a housecoat. She traced a small shape in the air absently with two fingers—curve, hook, three slashes—like scratching an itch that lived behind her knuckles. When she noticed them watching she folded her hands and smiled like she'd forgotten the gesture as soon as she'd made it.

"Arthritis," she said, by way of apology.

"Isn't it always," Claudia answered, and kept moving.

On the street, steam rose from the grates like the city was an animal letting off tired breath. A tag on the opposite wall winked in the wet light. The truck started the way it always did: loyal, without questions.

As they pulled from the curb, Claudia set her palm on the ledger bag and felt, for a single unkind heartbeat, a second pulse underneath her own. She counted four. Count four, hold, count four, hold—the prayer she didn't call a prayer. The Latin lined up behind her teeth like a verdict waiting for its reading.

She did not speak it.

The light turned green. They went to fetch a man who hummed and a box that wanted to be a mouth. The bathroom was a square of wet breath and tile. Steam should have risen in sheets, obedient to heat. Instead, it moved like it had found a reason. Tiny rivers crawled across the mirror and then reversed course, drops running up the glass as if gravity had grown bored and stepped out for cigarettes.

Claudia planted her palms on the sink, breath fogging the surface until her reflection blurred to a ghost with sharp shoulders. The bolt was half-thrown—neither locked nor open, the posture of someone who trusted only tension. The heater in the corner ticked a counting rhythm. The pipes inside the wall hummed like a throat warming to sing.

Angelo set his pistol on the porcelain, then the knife, metal kissing ceramic with small, honest sounds. He didn't enter yet. He leaned on the frame, humidity flattening the rumple in his shirt, tattoos dark as fresh ink where the sleeve had ridden up. The thorned band at his shoulder seemed brighter with the wet.

"Company?" he asked.

"Yes." Her voice had no courtroom polish on it now, just the sanded-down truth. "But don't fix me."

He didn't. He shed the rest of the day: shirt, holster, the uniform of a man who expected rooms to argue. The ink across his ribs moved when he did—not writhing, nothing childish—just the natural flex of skin over muscle, lines curving to fit new angles. It would be easy to say superstition, to call the shifting a trick of light and want, and she was still the kind of woman who preferred the easy answer until it cut her hand.

He stepped into the spray. Heat crawled over both of them. She had left space, a sliver between bodies, a courtesy. He stood in that space like it had weight and then set it down, closing an inch, then another, until they could feel each other's breath without borrowing it. The shower drummed a beat they could have pretended was rain outside. She didn't pretend.

"Tell me when it hurts," she said, glancing at the stitches.

"It hurts."

"Then tell me when it matters."

“I will,” he said, and she believed him in the exact way a person believes a cliff edge—useful, dangerous, true whether you respect it or not.

Her fingers tracked the seam of gauze, then the unstitched skin, then the edges of old scars that had made their peace with being permanent. The intimacy was plain, not showy; it felt less like desire and more like two people laying down a load for the length of a breath. His forehead found hers. It clicked into place, skull to skull, as if bone recognized bone.

The pipes behind the wall picked up a second note. Not louder—lower. It nested under the water’s hiss. A vibration. Claudia stilled and it stilled with her, then resumed when she moved again, like a patient mimic learning a step. She angled her head. The sound tuned itself to her pause and went perfectly quiet, obedient.

“Static,” Angelo said, because that was his name for anything he refused to argue with.

“It isn’t,” she said softly. “Static is random.”

“What is it, then?”

“Pattern.” The word tasted like iron.
On the mirror, a clean oval formed in the fog without a hand to make it. At first it was just absence. Then it wrote—the glass showing through in thin strokes where no towel had wiped. Linea peccati. The letters were neat, a schoolteacher’s hand taught by a priest. Beneath it, slower, as if the steam needed reminding: Sanguis debitum.

Her scalp prickled. She didn’t look away from the mirror to ask if he saw it. She already knew the answer from the habit of every courtroom she’d ever dominated—how to read a face without moving her own. Angelo hadn’t turned. He was watching the door, always the door, steam skimming the slope of his cheekbone like a veil.

“Your hand,” he said, and it took a heartbeat to realize he meant hers, not the words.

She followed his gaze down. A red ghost of a symbol burned faintly beneath the skin at the hinge of her thumb and palm: a crooked circle, a hooked tail, three small slashes. Not a cut. Not paint. A heat-mark, like the way a ring leaves a line after years. She pressed it and the sting answered, not pain, but acknowledgment. As if the mark had a nerve.

She lifted her hand. Water beaded. The mark did not wash.

“Looks like irritation,” she lied.

“Irritation usually doesn’t stare back,” he said.

“Everything stares back if you hold still too long.”

“Then don’t,” he said.

She reached up and wiped a line in the fog with her wrist. The Latin blurred and then vanished, steam reclaiming its surface as if embarrassed at having been literate in public. The water made a short brown thread down the drain—rust, she told herself. Old pipes. The color cleared, and the hum behind the wall swallowed itself until the room was left with only heat and their breathing.

She stepped closer because stepping away would have been a sermon and she wasn’t in the mood to preach. Their mouths met without theater. It wasn’t tenderness exactly and it wasn’t hunger either. It was something that understood both and refused to vote. His hands found the backs of her arms just above the elbow—anchor points. She set her palms at his jaw, fingers slipping to the corded muscle behind his ear, and they stayed there, balancing, like people who knew what happened when you let go too fast.

When they broke, it was a clean break. No flinch. They stayed close, foreheads resting, the water tracing routes it had traced already across their shoulders and chest, as if even the shower knew repetition makes meaning.

From somewhere—inside the wall, inside memory, it was impossible to say—a voice made a shape. Three syllables, breathed and gone, a cadence she had not heard since the floorboards of a childhood bedroom taught her to stay very still. Ledger's due. The words didn't sound like her father, and yet her bones knew his weight inside them.

She opened her eyes. The mirror was blank again. She looked at Angelo and he was already looking at her, eyes narrowed a fraction, not suspicious of her but of what the room had the nerve to do in front of her.

"What did you hear?" he asked.

"The shower," she said.

"Try again."
She didn't. Names make things heavier, and she needed light hands right now. "Finish," she said, meaning the water, the cleaning, this small remaking of skin and nerve.

They shut off the tap. Silence thudded into the room, too big at first, then shrinking to fit. Towels. Cloth on wet. She dragged one over her hair, then flattened another against her ribs and shoulder, inventorying what needed covering when the world came back in. He worked the towel with one hand and the other came up without thought to touch her wrist where the faint mark lived. He didn't press. Just mapped it gently with a thumb, as if learning a route he planned to avoid.

"Burn?" he asked.

"Not from heat."

"From what?"

"From attention," she said, and found she was suddenly done talking.

They dressed. The bolt on the door stayed neither—just shy of locked, just shy of trust. As they stepped back into the main room, the city outside seemed to notice them again. A car passed. Someone laughed in the hallway. The little heater made an honest click. Nothing spooky, nothing dramatic. Just life refilling itself with noise like a lung that had been held too long.

On the table, the ledger waited with prim patience. Angelo reached for his pistol the way a man reaches for an old friend: without looking, certain of where it lives. Claudia rubbed the last damp out of her hair with the towel and ignored the mirror's clean face behind her in case it had decided to learn new tricks.

"Ready?" he asked.

"No," she said, and felt the relief of being accurate. "But we go." The phone buzzed a third time. Insistence, not luck. Claudia thumbed it open and let the line breathe first. Silence is a shape; she'd learned to hear what people put inside it.

A whisper slid in like ash. "Page fifty," the voice said. "Inheritance."

"Who is this."

"You were born owing," the voice murmured, tender as a threat. "And he was born to collect."

The line died. The dial tone returned with the bored civility of bureaucracy. Claudia lowered the phone and the room seemed to lean back, disappointed it wouldn't get to eavesdrop more.

"Marks?" Angelo asked.

"Accountant with poetry," she said. "Which should be illegal."

She drew the ledger toward her. The stack had resequenced itself—she could feel it in her bones the way a woman knows someone has moved her things. The top page wasn't the top when she'd set it down. She flipped. Legal stock, old glue in the scent, a salt note like the river basement had found their lungs and set up home.

Neat church-hand met her. VALE, CLAUDIA — off-hours investigations; therapist 2:07 p.m. Wednesdays. Witness intimidation (indirect). Margin: COMPULSION.

She angled the lamp. Letters rose thin as veins where no ink lived—pressure writing, the page remembering the bruise of a pen. Linea peccati — sanguis debitum.

"Read?" Angelo asked softly.

"Enough," she said.

He nodded, as if the word had weight he could measure. His fingers hovered over the margin but didn't touch. "Seen that mark on brick," he said, eyes on the faint hook-and-circle ghost. "Means eyes are on you."

"This isn't spray paint," she said. "It's older than brick. It's older than Dominguez."

The heater clicked. A blue tongue of flame licked into a familiar curve and retreated, pretending it hadn't meant anything at all. Outside, the bodega's bell chimed, and a woman laughed in a key that used to mean safety.

Claudia set her thumb above the hook and did not press. Heat breathed up—not burn, not sting, just acknowledgement. She withdrew her hand and the warmth followed an inch, then settled back into the page like a cat agreeing to stay on its own side of the couch.

"Don't feed it," Angelo said. It wasn't a joke.

"Religious objection?"

"Practical. Things you feed follow you."

"Things?"

He didn't answer. A muscle in his jaw wrote its own confession.

She turned another sheet. A smear in the margin the color of dried wine formed the crooked circle again, the hook, the three slashes. Beneath, a date. Not printed. Written with a hand that had practiced steadiness.

The date matched neither court calendar nor news cycle. It matched her mother's birthday.

The room got small. "Coincidence," she said aloud, to bully the air back into shape.

"Maybe," Angelo said, and meant no.

Claudia flipped further. Names unspooled. Judges who'd recused without reason. Donors with funds that changed color in daylight. A nurse with a habit of writing the time of death before the last breath left the room. Each entry carried a thin cousin beneath it, pressure-writing that only revealed itself when light angled just so: debts, bloodlines, Latin that pretended to be dead while doing pushups in the basement.

She set both hands flat on the table as if bracing it to keep from tilting. "If this is a ledger," she said, "who audits it."

"Witches," Angelo said again, and this time the word didn't land like folklore. It landed like logistics.

"You don't believe in—"

"I believe in who gets paid," he said. "Dominguez pays men with envelopes. Somebody pays him with promises. Somebody older."
The mirror over the sink shivered as if the building had exhaled. Claudia caught her reflection at the edge of her eye. For a breath, the other her tilted her head first. Then the glass snapped obedient and she was alone again.

"All right," she said, speaking to the room, to the page, to the part of her own mind she trusted to run toward fire with a plan. "We use it."

"Use what."

"The page. The mark. If it watches, it learns. If it learns, it can be taught."

Angelo's mouth did the almost-smile that never quite qualified. "Teach away."

She lowered her head to the ledger until her mouth was inches above the margin. She didn't intend to say it; she intended to think it hard enough that the room would get the hint. The thought slipped anyway, a whisper that barely qualified as sound: "Linea peccati. Sanguis debitum."

Nothing dramatic. No lights stuttered. No door slammed. Just a change in pressure, like weather turning in a room. The blue flame in the heater shivered to the hook for a heartbeat and went honest again. The mark beneath her hand warmed enough to register.

"Noted," she said to nobody.

"Don't do it again," Angelo said, quiet.

"Why."

He looked at her in a way that made the apartment feel smaller. "Because if it answers, we won't like the terms."

The phone on the table—a cheap burner, not the private line—buzzed once, then twice. Unknown number. Angelo flipped it open and set it between them without speaking. The voice that came through was too pleased with itself to be human or too human to be safe.

"Page fifty-three was Ash," it said. "I smell smoke that doesn't belong to me. Naughty."

Claudia leaned in, elbows on her knees. "You built a box," she said to the air. "We found the hinge."

A soft laugh. "You read frames well. Shame there won't be a book club where you're going."

The line clicked dead. No threat. Just the promise of motion.

Angelo rolled his shoulders like a man checking the seatbelt before a crash. "Two hours," he said. "Rector will still be breathing."

“Let’s go teach the box,” she said.

They moved—reload, repack, rearm—the quiet choreography of people who had practiced not dying and found it useful. At the door, Angelo touched two fingers to the thorn-curve ink near his shoulder. He didn’t cross himself. He didn’t have to for it to count.

In the hallway, the old woman across the landing lifted a hand and traced a small shape in the air—curve, hook, three slashes—absently, like scratching an itch she couldn’t name. When she saw them she smiled and folded her hands. “Arthritis,” she said.

“Isn’t it always,” Claudia answered.

They took the stairs two at a time. The city met them at the curb with breath steaming from under grates, tags glinting wet on brick, and a wind that smelled faintly of river and something copper that had never been filed properly.

“Low and left,” Angelo said when the truck door shut.

“High and through,” Claudia answered.

The light stuttered green. The ledger settled in the bag with the careful dignity of a legal document that knew its soul was older than law. They pulled into the street. The drive back toward the storage district ran like a pulse through the damp veins of the city. Steam clung to the truck’s hood. Every sign they passed had learned a new word—the hook, the circle, the three slashes—and painted it over its own name. Claudia didn’t point them out anymore. Noticing was permission.

Angelo kept one hand on the wheel and one near the pistol wedged between seat and thigh. His eyes moved more than his mouth did. He didn’t speak until they’d crossed into the block where the river smell turned metallic.

“You know what this is,” he said finally.

“Patterns,” she answered.

“Patterns are what we call the rules we can’t write down.”

She thought about the mark on her hand, now gone pale but still there under the skin, waiting like an idea that hadn’t decided what language to use yet.

When they reached the unit, the door was half open. The lock lay in two neat halves on the concrete. No light. No sound.

Angelo motioned her back. He went first. The smell met them before sight did—burnt oil and something older, the scent of a candle snuffed by breath.

Rector was still in the chair. The rope around his wrists hadn’t moved. His head had.

It was tilted back as if he were watching a ceiling that wasn’t there. His mouth was open. Inside it, carved into the soft pink roof, was the mark—the circle, the hook, the three slashes—done in blood or something that had learned the art of imitation.

Claudia stepped closer. The air thickened. The ink on Angelo’s arm rose in gooseflesh.

The ledger in her bag trembled once, subtle as a shiver. She didn’t need to open it to know a new page had written itself.

“Page fifty-four,” she said.

Angelo looked down at Rector. “Inheritance paid.”

The city outside sighed through the cracks in the wall, and the sound wasn’t wind. It was breath

Chapter 16— The Scriptorium

Morning didn't arrive so much as bleed through the blinds. Claudia hadn't slept. The ledger lay open on the table, its pages curling at the edges as if warmed from within. Even when she closed it, heat ghosted the covers like breath on glass.

Angelo stood by the window. He hadn't turned on the light. Outside, the street looked ordinary, but the fog carried patterns that refused to settle—circles, hooks, lines drawn and erased by invisible chalk.

"You ever been underground?" he asked.

"Basements, archives, parking garages. Why?"

"There's a place under Pier Twelve. Looks like a church that forgot its prayers. Dominguez used it once for storage. If there's a hand writing this book, it's there."

She slid the ledger into the fireproof bag. The air cooled, but not enough. "We're not bringing it."

"It'll bring itself," he said. "Things that want witnesses always do."

They drove south. The city aged beneath the tires—glass to brick, brick to stone, stone to water-eaten wood. The truck's headlights carved faces from mist and erased them. By the river, the wind tasted like iron filings and old pennies.

Pier Twelve waited like a rumor. Rusted gates sagged over the entrance, stamped deep with the sigil—curve, hook, three slashes—as if the metal had been taught a letter it couldn't unlearn. Angelo cut the chain. The sound carried too far for so small an act.

Inside, a stone staircase pitched steep into dark. Cold ran ahead of them. Claudia felt it between her teeth. Her palm stung; the faint mark at the base of her thumb brightened under the skin like a coal acknowledging oxygen.

“Last chance to call this a bad idea,” he said.

“I did,” she said. “Then we came anyway.”

He grinned without humor. “Usual.”

They descended.

The stairs opened into a nave the size of an argument with God. Benches stood in rows, petrified by salt. Candles had burned themselves into wax fossils. Symbols layered the walls in patient hands; generations of the same mark, corrected and perfected, until the stone looked tattooed.

“This is the scriptorium,” Angelo said. “A library for debts.”

“Whose debts.”

“Everyone’s who matters.”

Something breathed. Not wind. Pages.

On a dais, a book the size of a suitcase rested in a cradle of stone, bound in dark leather too supple to be new and too proud to be human. Chains held it like jewelry holds a throat. As they stepped closer, the links pulsed once, a slow light that didn’t illuminate anything so much as admit there was something to see.

Claudia reached and met resistance a foot above the cover. Air thickened, the way water does when you push your hand through a lake. The ledger in her bag trembled. Pages riffled themselves and settled on a blank sheet that wasn’t blank at all; pressure-writing surfaced where the lamp’s angle found it: VALE, CLAUDIA — entry pending.

“Don’t touch,” Angelo said, catching her wrist.

“It knows me,” she said. “It always did.”

She flattened her palm over the invisible weight and pressed. The air yielded like scar tissue. Her hand met leather. Heat climbed her arm to the shoulder and sat there, heavy and satisfied.

The chains popped one by one with the polite clicks of a lock that enjoyed its job. The cover lifted a fraction and shadows spilled out—not darkness, not smoke; annotations. Writing in the shape of people and coats and old decisions, flowing off the page to take up their places in the pews.

Angelo drew the pistol. The shadows didn't flinch. They looked at him the way bored jurors look at a new attorney.

Words rose from the book like steam, gathered, fell back as ink. A line wrote itself across the top of the open page in a hand that wasn't hers and yet wore her rhythm like a stolen coat: You opened it. Now write it back.

"What does that mean," Angelo asked, voice low.

"That the writer owes the ledger, not the other way," she said, and something in her chest tilted toward terror and chose focus instead.

"Claudia." He angled his chin toward the pews.

Shapes sat there now—men in robes, women in dresses a century out of fashion, a judge in a threadbare black coat, a nurse with a folded cap, a boy whose skin showed through where his cheeks should have been. Each bore the sigil somewhere—woven into a cuff, stitched where a pocket might go, burned into the hollow of a throat. None had mouths. Their words came from just above where one should be, as if removed surgically and replaced with obligation.

One stood. Sound rustled from the hole where a voice should live. "Sentence of Forever," it said, and the title didn't sound like poetry here. It sounded like policy. "Signed in blood, sealed in sin. Welcome home, Vale."

Angelo lifted the pistol. Claudia set her hand on the barrel and pushed it down. "Bullets are punctuation," she said. "They won't change the grammar."

"You sure?"

"No." She stepped to the dais anyway. "But I know a contract when I see one."

The page turned. Images bled up through the fibers: a child at a kitchen table, a man with a bottle, the edge of a courtroom door. Her history reduced to a neat column of transactions. Under each event, a number. Under the numbers, a second hand wrote in Latin: debitum, debitum, debitum.

"You've been keeping books on me since before I could read," she said.

Ink swirled and drew two lines beneath her name as if underlining a conclusion. Linea peccati. Sanguis debitum. Line of sin. Blood debt.

"You want me to pay."

The page didn't nod. It didn't have to. The pews leaned in.

Angelo took a step toward the cradle. "We walk. We burn it from up top. Call the river. Call the city. Call—"

"We tried fire," Claudia said. "Fire pays attention to itself. This pays attention to everything else."

He looked at the book as a man looks at a bomb he doesn't have the code for. "What does it want."

"The same thing every ledger wants," she said. "Balance."

She placed her palm on the margin. Not touching the words; touching the space where words could be. Heat warmed her skin without burning. The mark beneath her thumb pulsed in time with a heartbeat not her own.

“Claudia—”

“I’m not signing,” she said. “I’m auditing.”

She spoke low, the way she did when she wanted jurors to lean in. “If sin leaves signatures, then signatures can be forged. If debts are tallied, tallies can be corrected. Show the entries you hid.”

The book made a sound like paper choosing sides. Columns thickened, thinned, rewrote themselves. Names rose. Her father’s among them, and her mother’s in a smaller hand that still refused apology. Angelo’s too—his entries older, written in two inks, the darker bleeding through, the newer laid over it like a bandage.

“What did they take from you,” she asked the page softly.

Ink tremored. The pews shifted. For a second the chamber smelled like rosemary and hospital—cleansing and endings.

Angelo circled, looking for exits that weren’t carved into stone. “We can’t win a debate with a book.”

“It’s not a debate,” she said. “It’s an audit trail.”

She traced an inch above the paper where her line item read: witness intimidation (indirect). The pressure-writing rose: COMPULSION. She angled the light from her phone. A palimpsest surfaced—older entries beneath the new. Protection sworn. Debt transferred.

“To me,” she whispered. “He moved his debt.”

“Who.”

“My father.” She tasted the word like rust. “He didn’t pay. He pawned.”

The book answered without letters. The chains twitched. The shadows in the pews stood as one. Not attack—attention.

“Fine,” Claudia said. “Then I return the pawn. I don’t pay his debt. I pay mine.”

She cut her palm with the pocket knife she kept for oranges, small and clean. Angelo swore—too late to stop the sting—and reached for her. She caught his wrist and held it away.

“Don’t,” she said. “Not this.”

She pressed the blood to the margin beside her name. The drop sank like a signature. The book heated, then cooled, then drank. The pews exhaled. Somewhere deep in the stone, water moved.

“Terms,” she said.

A line wrote itself in tidy English as if obliged to be courteous: Payment in kind. Service rendered. Sentence ongoing.

“Meaning?” Angelo asked.

“Meaning I don’t die for him,” she said. “I work for me.”

He laughed, a small, unbelieving burst. “You just negotiated with a demon ledger.”

“I negotiate for a living.” She swallowed. “And I’m not finished.”

She angled the book toward him. The ink on his shoulder answered, rising in gooseflesh. Under ANGELO — collection, enforcement another hand had written, in faint, careful letters: Hunter class. Sanctified annulled.

“What did you do,” she asked, almost tender.

“Once?” He shrugged without looking at the page. “I hunted the people who hunted witches. I was good at it until someone better wrote a different story on me.”

“You were sanctified,” she said. “And then they crossed it out.”

"Sanctified makes a man stupid."

"No," she said. "Sanctified makes a man dangerous to the wrong book."

The pews rustled, as if the room disapproved of editorializing.

Something deeper moved—a pressure change that felt like weather and felt like attention and felt like a door choosing which way it wanted to be. Beneath the dais, the stone grated softly. A seam revealed itself, square and mean.

"A vault," Angelo said.

"No," Claudia said. "A witness box."

They pried it open. Inside lay objects arranged with the neatness of ritual: a judge's gavel worn smooth as worry beads; a rosary strung with teeth; a ledger far smaller than the dais-book, bound in blue cloth; a brass scale with one pan heavier than sense allowed; a photograph of a courthouse that never existed in this city.

Claudia lifted the blue-book. It shivered and opened to the middle. There, in a neat church hand:
VALE LINE — covenant registered: Mothers to daughters; debt transferable by blood; collectors must present sign and countersign.

Beneath it, older ink: Claudia — pending.

"Countersign," she said to the shadows. "You brought your mark. Here's mine." She raised her palm. The faint red sigil flared under the skin like an ember getting air. "I acknowledge the line. I sever transfer."

The dais-book hissed. The blue-book warmed in her hands until the cloth smoked but didn't burn. Letters rewrote: transfer voided; direct assessment resumed.

"To me," Claudia said into the hush. "Only me."

The pews stood. The judge-shadow stepped forward, gavel raised. Angelo moved between them on instinct. The gavel fell—onto his shoulder, not hard, but with the weight of a stamp. The ink at his shoulder flared bright, then rearranged, thorn-curves bending into the hook-and-circle.

He hissed and caught himself before he swore in church.

"Language," Claudia murmured, and if she'd been a different person she would have smiled.

Cracks snaked through the ceiling. Dust sifted down in a neat gray snow. The river pressed its face against the foundation and said it would like to come in.

"Time to leave," Angelo said.

"Almost." She leaned over the dais-book and spoke in the measured cadence that had forced more than one courtroom to listen past its boredom. "By your own entries, debt without consent is theft. Return what was moved without signature. Wipe the father from the daughter's balance."

Silence. Then, the smallest movement of ink: Partial.

"Good enough for a Tuesday," she said, and slammed the cover shut.

The chains snapped back around the book with a clatter that sounded like applause from enemies. The pew-shadows elongated, reaching. The river made up its mind.

They ran.

Water punched through the seam. Cold rose up their shins in a breath. Angelo took the stairs two at a time, then three, dragging her when the stone chose slipperiness over courtesy. Claudia hugged the blue-book to her chest. The ledger in her bag vibrated until her teeth ached.

A shape flowed beside them along the wall—no mouth, the suggestion of a robe, the brand bright and eager. It kept pace as if interested in the sport of it. Angelo fired once, a punctuation shot. The echo came back with a laugh in it.

“Up,” he said. “Up up up.”

They burst into daylight. The river flung mist in their faces like a scold. Behind them, the pier exhaled and settled, not collapsed, but changed, as if the city had decided the room now existed on another floor. They didn’t stop moving until the truck’s doors thunked shut and the engine agreed to be loyal. Angelo drove without looking at the speedometer. Claudia stared at her hands until the red under-sigil dimmed to a memory of heat.

“Are you hurt,” he asked finally.

“Only in ways that won’t show.”

“Those are the expensive ones.”

She opened the blue-book in her lap. New lines had written themselves during their sprint, tidy and prim even when terrified: Sentence of Forever — claimant acknowledged; countersign incomplete; collector identified.

“Collector,” she said. “Who.”

A line inked itself in answer, slow as a grin: Angelo.

He didn’t look over. His scar tugged, humorless. “Should’ve seen that coming.”

“Don’t make jokes you intend to be true,” she said.

“Don’t make sentences you intend to serve,” he said back, and somehow that qualified as a kind of promise.

They parked three blocks from the apartment and walked the rest, not from paranoia but habit. On the second landing, the old woman’s door stood open again. The TV murmured a courtroom show pretending to be justice. She lifted two fingers and drew the hook-and-circle in the air, absent, like scratching an itch.

Claudia paused. “Do you know what that means.”

The woman blinked owlishly. “Means the post is watched,” she said, as if reciting a proverb learned from a grandmother who’d never been young. “Means don’t lie to the wall.”

“Thank you,” Claudia said, and meant it.

Inside, the apartment had the careful quiet of a place waiting for bad news. Claudia set the blue-book on the table beside the ledger. The two volumes trembled toward each other and then behaved.

She washed the thin cut on her palm and taped it closed. The bandage looked almost ceremonial. Angelo’s shoulder showed a new bloom where the gavel had found him—ink redrawn, thorn into hook. It would scar clever if she let it. She didn’t intend to.

“We rest?” he asked.

“We plan.”

“Same thing for people like us.”

She angled the lamp. The ledger’s margin revealed fresh pressure-writing under her name: service begins. Under his: collector—stay.

“Stay,” she read. “That’s not a threat. That’s a job description.”
“You offering benefits?”

“Dental,” she said, deadpan. “And vengeance.”

He laughed once, genuine, and short. The kind that exists because a person decides to be human in defiance of a room’s preferences.

Claudia wrote in the blue-book’s blank space with a pen that had signed ordinary contracts yesterday: Audit initiated. Transfers voided without consent. Identify witches' ledger keepers. Identify annulment of sanctified.

The page accepted the ink like it had been starving for ink that smelled like truth instead of smoke.

Outside, the fog thinned. Morning finally arrived the right way, not bleeding but arriving. The city cleared its throat and pretended to be ordinary for the breakfast crowd. Claudia didn't believe it, which made her fond of it.

"Next," she said. "We find who runs the accounts upstairs and downstairs. We find who cut your sanctified. We find why the book wants me to write it back."

"And Rector?"

"We make him say who sent the call," she said. "And we make him say it twice."

Angelo nodded. He scratched the margin of the blue-book with a fingernail. The mark under his skin answered with a small heat that admitted their conspiracy.

They sat in the quiet, planning like prayer—names, places, levers. The books waited, breathing. The city listened with its ear to the wall.

On the drive for supplies, the city began to keep time with them. Streetlights blinked in threes—on, on, off—hook, hook, slashes. A flock of starlings tore the sky into a circle and closed it like a fist. A man outside the bodega asked the price of lemons and, when Claudia said "debitum" under her breath just to test the air, his pupils swallowed his irises for one slow blink; then he was ordinary again, complaining about sour fruit.

Back upstairs, she washed the thin cut in her palm. The water didn't bead; it gathered into five precise drops that sat without running. Each drop trembled, bulged, and wrote a name on her skin in water—HELENA, M., R. VALE, ETIENNE, R.—before vanishing. She recognized none of them and all of them. The last bead formed a small hooked circle, then split into three slashes and slid down the drain as if satisfied with its penmanship.

“Report?” Angelo called from the doorway, eyes on the hall like the building might decide to relocate.

“Family reunion,” she said, drying her hands. “Guest list keeps updating.”

He touched his shoulder where the gavel had stamped him. The ink stung, then settled, a dog deciding to behave.

That night—what passed for night—the ledger’s heat dimmed just enough for human sleep to trick her. She dozed in the chair. The blue-book lay open on her lap like a cat that had selected her. The apartment’s small sounds braided into something almost kind.

Dream took her as a professional courtesy and then reneged. She stood in a courtroom whose walls were salt and bone. A horned judge weighed hearts on a brass scale that didn’t understand mercy as a unit. The gallery buzzed with robed silhouettes and men in suits with their mouths erased. Her mother sat in the front row, younger than Claudia had ever seen her, hands folded as if prayer still had jurisdiction. Angelo stood at counsel table with a blade where a pen should be. Claudia’s own briefcase opened to reveal not files but contracts written in her handwriting, every signature hers in a hundred inks.

Write us clean, counselor, the judge whispered, though his mouth didn’t move. When he banged the gavel, it struck not wood but the mark on Angelo’s shoulder; the sound ran up Claudia’s bones like a tuning fork. The gallery chanted, her name backward, syllables lapping like tide: A-idualC, A-idualC, a lullaby from people who didn’t sleep.

She woke hard, breath sharp, the room obediently itself again. The blue-book’s page held new, faint impressions as if her sleeping wrist had been a stylus: audit continues; countersign sought. On her forearm, just below the elbow’s inner bend, pale words had been etched like the memory of ink: Sentence ongoing. She scrubbed at them. They faded—not disappeared, only shy.

“Report,” Angelo said again, softer this time.

“They asked for a miracle,” she said, looking at the ghost-text. “I offered accounting.”

He nodded, as if that were the correct liturgy. “We’ll need names for your water-trick.”

“We’ll need a witch who remembers why names matter,” she said. “And someone upstairs who cuts sanctified without getting their hands burned.”

They planned until the sky let in a seam of honest daylight. The books hummed like chill metal. The city listened with its ear to the wall.

Somewhere under Pier Twelve, chains re-fastened themselves around a book that had learned a new signature and wasn’t sure whether to be pleased. The water level rose a finger’s breadth, and drowned voices finished Claudia’s name backward as if signing off.

Chapter 17 — The Collector's Trial

The storage lot crouched behind the river like a row of teeth. By the time Angelo rolled the truck inside, the fog had grown heavy enough to muffle sound. The unit's door hung half open, swaying in its track. Claudia tasted metal in the air—the flavor of wet coins and lightning waiting for somewhere to land.

Rector sat where they'd left him, but he wasn't the same man. The ropes still crossed his chest, yet his veins traced dark through the skin, thin cords of ink pulsing to a rhythm she could almost hear. A halo of burnt dust ringed the concrete under the chair.

"Don't step in it," Angelo said.

"Why?"

He toed the edge with his boot. The ash hissed, recoiled, then stilled. "Because it's listening."

Claudia circled wide, heels clicking in slow verdicts. Rector's eyes tracked her—too wide, too dry. The pupils flickered from black to a color no language had bothered naming.

"Morning, counselor," he rasped. "You brought the book."

"You made the call." She set the ledger bag on the table between them. The air thickened immediately, as though paper carried its own gravity.

"I called because I wanted to see if you'd answer," he said, voice splitting on the plural: we'd answer. "Most people don't. You should have ignored us."

"I've spent my life not ignoring things that scare other people," she said. "Tell me who 'we' is."

Rector's smile cracked. "Names have fees."

"Bill me."

The concrete beneath his chair trembled once, like the building had cleared its throat. The mark carved into the roof of his mouth glowed faintly when he spoke.

"We are what happens when the ink dries," he said. "You think you write verdicts. You only copy ours."

Claudia leaned forward until her reflection caught in his eyes—two small shards of her staring back from something deeper. "And who gave you the right to collect?"

"The same judge who gave you the right to defend," he said, and then laughed until it turned into a cough that left black flecks on his sleeve.

Angelo moved behind him. "You're leaking."

"Paying," Rector said. "Every word costs."

Claudia slid a photograph across the table—Dominguez's signature, the symbol hidden in the flourish. "You recognize this."
He nodded once, slow. "Page forty-seven. Inked in blood that wasn't his."

"What does it buy?"

"Time." He looked up at her. "You're almost out."

The ledger in the bag thumped, one soft heartbeat. Angelo's hand went to the gun automatically; Claudia raised a palm to stop him. The mark under her skin answered with heat.

She unzipped the bag. The ledger opened by itself, pages riffing until one settled mid-book. Fresh ink glistened.

RECTOR, H. — recalled for audit. DEBT OUTSTANDING.
COLLECTOR: ANGELO R. WITNESS: CLAUDIA VALE.

"Guess I'm the paperwork," Angelo muttered.

Rector's head jerked toward him. "You were sanctified once," he said. "Now you're just collateral."

Angelo didn't flinch. "You talk a lot for collateral damage."

"Shoot me," Rector whispered. "It won't change the math."

Claudia crouched until she was level with him. "I don't need you alive," she said, "but I do need you honest. Who wrote the first line of this ledger?"

His jaw twitched. "Mother Glass."

The name filled the room like perfume—sweet, metallic, familiar in a way memory couldn't explain. The lights flickered twice, then steadied at half strength. Shadows lengthened, uninvited.

"Where do we find her?" Claudia asked.

"She finds the ones who owe," Rector said. "That's you now."

He closed his eyes. His chest sagged. For a moment she thought he'd fallen asleep, but the mark on his throat began to move, carving new shapes in the skin from the inside. Angelo stepped forward; Claudia raised a hand again.

The wound opened without blood—only light, thin and white as candle flame. The beam twisted upward, painting a circle in the damp air, then hardened into glass. On the far side of that impossible window, a woman stood watching them.

She wore a pale coat. Her hands were ink-stained. Candlelight fluttered behind her though there were no candles. Her face was long, her eyes reflecting the room exactly as it was—three people, two books, one decision.

"Mother Glass," Claudia said.

The woman smiled, and the glass between them rippled. "Counselor Vale. You've been writing in my margins." The woman in the glass did not step forward so much as allow the world to decide she already had. A shiver went through the concrete. The circle of light turned inside out; then there she was, standing on the warehouse floor as if she had always belonged to it.

Her coat was the color of smoke before rain. Ink stains bloomed on the cuffs, old and layered like fossils. When she moved, her reflection lagged half a heartbeat behind. Every surface caught her twice—one version pale and calm, the other blurred and burning at the edges.

"Mother Glass," Claudia said again, the name tasting like clean cuts. "You're real."

"Reality is a bookkeeping error," the witch replied. Her voice carried no echo; the room absorbed it greedily. "And I am excellent at corrections."

Angelo kept his gun trained on the floor. "You walk through mirrors now?"

"I never stopped. You're the ones who built walls and called them safe."

She glanced at the ropes around Rector. They untied themselves. He slumped forward, mouth slack, the glow fading from his veins.

"Dead?" Claudia asked.

"Balanced," Mother Glass said. "Debts don't die, they convert."

The ledger on the table flipped a page by itself. A faint breath of parchment brushed Claudia's cheek.

"You've been writing in my margins," the witch said. "Bold, for someone who hasn't paid her filing fees."

"I'm here for answers, not invoices."

Mother Glass smiled, showing small, even teeth. "Every question is an invoice."

The mirror-light behind her stretched until it framed the entire room. The air thickened; sound slowed. Angelo's voice came out half a second late.

"What is this?"

"A deposition," the witch said. "You wanted to interrogate. I prefer proper venues."

The warehouse dissolved around them like dust in water. In its place stood a courtroom built from reflection: pews of glass, a floor that showed the underside of their shoes, chandeliers made of suspended drops of mercury. Claudia's breath fogged the air and the fog became handwriting that immediately erased itself.

She looked down. Her reflection stood independently, a shade half a gesture behind. When she raised her hand, the double hesitated, then wrote invisible symbols in the air before catching up.

Mother Glass stepped to the judge's dais. "Proceed, Counselor Vale. The court recognizes your obsession with fairness."

"I want to know what the ledger is."

"It is the sum of intention. Every oath, every bargain. When mortals stopped fearing gods, they invented contracts. We simply kept the minutes."

"And why me?"
The witch tilted her head. "Because you still believe words can save anyone."

Claudia's pulse kicked hard. The mark on her palm warmed, pulsing in rhythm with her heart. "And you want me to write it back."

"I want you to decide whether the world deserves to keep its signatures."

The mirrors around them flexed; images surfaced—faces of people Claudia had defended, won for, lost for. Some alive, some not. Each face had the sigil glowing faintly on its brow.

"You made these marks," the witch said. "Every verdict leaves a scar somewhere. Look closely."

Claudia turned, scanning the endless gallery. "You're saying I damned them?"

"I'm saying you made them legible."

Angelo reached for her shoulder. His reflection did not. The ghost-copy stayed frozen, mouth open in a silent warning.

"Something's wrong with the mirrors," he said.

"Nothing's wrong," Mother Glass murmured. "They're honest."

The reflected Angelo began to move on his own, drawing his pistol. Claudia's mirror-self mirrored her hesitation exactly one breath too late. When Mother Glass spoke again, her voice came from both versions at once.

"This is how contracts work," she said. "Each side thinks the other is reflection."

The gunshot cracked. The sound looped twice before stopping, leaving a thread of smoke curling backward into the barrel.

The bullet hung in midair, turning slowly. In its mirrored surface Claudia saw her own eye, and within it the witch's.

"Lesson one," Mother Glass said. "Intent precedes cause."

The bullet dropped. The warehouse returned, shuddering like a dream remembered too fast. Rector's body was gone. Only the ropes remained, knotted into the sigil.

Claudia steadied herself on the table. "You call this teaching?"

"I call it disclosure," the witch said. "Next comes testimony." The room exhaled and became glass again.

A judge's bench unfolded from a single pane as if a lake had learned carpentry. Pew after pew rippled up from the floor, their surfaces catching all the wrong reflections—faces seated where no bodies sat, shadows of verdicts long since handed down. The ceiling arched into a dome of mirror that showed not the chamber but a starless sky with a thin crescent cut into it like the hook of the sigil.

Angelo shifted three degrees to cover Claudia and the bench in one sightline. His reflection lagged, then broke position altogether, drifting like a second guard who didn't agree with the plan.

"Court is in session," Mother Glass said. She did not sit; she stood at a modest table under the bench. "Style of cause: The Ledger versus Claudia Vale, with attached party Angelo R. under collection."
"I'm not a party," Angelo said.

"Collectors are always parties," Mother Glass replied. "They just prefer different music."

A figure mounted the bench. He wore no face—only a smooth blank, like glass backed in smoke. When he lifted the gavel, the gavel was also a scale. Two pans hung from the handle by chains that didn't quite touch the air; they trembled as if someone had spoken inside them.

"Announce the charge," the judge said, and the sound arrived as text first, then voice, as if language itself had paperwork to file.

Mother Glass held up a page that had never been paper: a rectangle of polished silver etched with lines that moved when you looked at them. "Charge: Interference with succession and unauthorized audit of covenant VALE-LINEA."

Claudia stepped forward. The mark on her palm heated, a small honest sun. "Response: The covenant was executed without informed consent and perpetuated by fraud across generations. I assert audit under right of injured party."

“Basis?” the judge asked.

She lifted the blue-book from her bag. Its cloth binding misted like breath. “Registered clause: transfers voidable without countersign; debtor may demand proof of consideration. No consideration was offered to me. Only cost.”

The scale tilted a hair in her favor. Angelo exhaled, the sound of a man verifying a bridge would hold at least one more step.

Bailiffs emerged from the far doors—silhouettes wearing robes that remembered human shoulders. Their hands were quills; their fingers flicked ink. Where they walked, the floor signed the path beneath them with small strokes.

“Witnesses,” Mother Glass said, and the pews obliged. Faces surfaced across the panes—men, women, a child with freckles like scored glass, a nurse in a neat cap, a boy with a crew cut and eyes like wet stone. Each bore the hook-and-circle badge somewhere near the throat. None had mouths, but when they turned, language moved in the little hollows where breath begins.

Claudia felt the courtroom part of herself straighten her spine and nod to a judge who could not see it. “For the record,” she said, “I am counsel pro se.”

“Noted,” the judge said. “The court expects you to object to yourself within reason.”

Mother Glass smiled. “Proceed.”

Claudia set the blue-book on the table and let its weight declare itself. “Your Honor, the ledger claims a debt called Sentence of Forever owed by the Vale line. Exhibit A establishes my father transferred his balance without my consent.”

Ink surfaced on the bench in the shape of a paragraph, then crossed itself out and wrote again, faster. The judge’s blank face did not move;

the room moved around it, accepting its decisions like weather accepts barometric pressure.

"Show harm," the judge said.

The mark at Claudia's wrist burned, then cooled. She held it up. The faint letters sentence ongoing glimmered beneath her skin, shy as bruises in morning light. "Physical inscription without consent. Surveillance of my person and practice. Coercion of associates." She inclined her head toward Angelo. "Alteration of a collector's sanctified status to force alignment."

Angelo's shoulder answered, warmth at the ink. He didn't touch it; he watched the doors.

"Testimony," Mother Glass said, and a pane in the first pew brightened. Her mother sat there, younger than any photograph Claudia possessed, hair pulled back, gaze steady as if she'd been practicing for this trial in another life.

"Name," Claudia said, and the answer arrived as ripples through the glass: MARIA VALE.

"Did you consent to covenant?"

The ripples stuttered, then drew a single slash: NO.

"Who presented the terms?"

A new ripple: THEM. The word stretched, broke into three not-quite words that ate their own tails: COLLECTOR—WITCH—PRIEST.

"And did you sign?" Claudia asked.

The glass showed hands—their hands—knuckles white around a pen that became a quill that became a thorn that became the hook. Then it showed empty hands and a cradle; then it showed Claudia's face as an infant, mouth open with the sincere outrage of the newly alive.

I signed for you, the pane seemed to say without saying. I picked the lesser oath and still it ate us.

Angelo's breath thickened once; he kept it under control. The scale tilted another grain toward Claudia.

"The court accepts this as harm," the judge said. "But harm is common coin. Show defect."

Claudia had already turned the blue-book to the page that had bothered her on waking. She angled it to the bench. Pressure-writing surfaced: countersign incomplete; collector identified: ANGELO. Beneath, almost invisible, older letters: sanctified annulled for cause: insubordination; scope: mercy.

She looked at Angelo. He shrugged a fraction. The admission cost him nothing because the fact had already charged his life.

"The defect is motive," she said. "A collector who refused to deliver a debtor was punished by erasure of sanctified. The ledger enforces obedience, not balance."

A murmur crossed the pews—a sound like a hundred pens scratching at once, restless for more paper.

Mother Glass shifted. "Careful, Counselor. Balance is a sacred word in this court."

"Sacred words need better arguments," Claudia said. She faced the judge. "Your Honor, I move to stay execution of Sentence of Forever pending audit, with prejudice against further transfer."

The bailiffs' quill-hands tensed. The door behind Angelo sighed open without opening. He sighted the distance and adjusted his stance by a half-foot.

"On what security," the judge asked.

"My service," Claudia said.

Angelo's head turned an inch. She did not look at him.

"And the collector?" the judge said.

"He stays," Mother Glass answered before either of them could. "He was born to collect."

"No," Claudia said, her voice the knife edge she saved for juries who thought they could nap through a closing. "He chooses to stand. There's a difference."

The mirror dome blackened as if an eclipse had been told to hurry. The first bailiff stepped off the line of his reflection and reached for Angelo with a quill-hand that pinched like forceps. Angelo fired once; the bullet struck glass, sank, and wrote a star that refused to heal. The bailiff staggered but did not fall. Ink slopped from his wrist and pooled into letters that wriggled across the floor: OBSTRUCTING COLLECTION.

"Claudia," Angelo said, not loudly.

She stepped between him and the bench, palms forward, the half-healed cut radiating heat that did not invite. "You don't get to use him as a tool on my case."

The judge's gavel lifted. "Sentence stands until stayed. Payment is due."

Claudia felt the decision like weather turning bone-deep. She breathed once. Her father's voice crept up the back stairs of her memory to knock; she did not let him in.

"Then here is my clause," she said. She spoke as if dictating into an old machine that had never once misheard her. "Payment postponed until audit complete. Audit to include all transfers and all erasures of sanctified performed to coerce collection. Witness present. Collector to remain independent until audit resolved."

The dome groaned. The pew-panes shivered, each showing her face saying those words in endless rooms where endless Claudias had never before been allowed to change anything. The scale rose a thumb's width in her favor, then stopped, the other pan pulling back with a stubborn grace.

"Denied," the judge said, and the word rolled like a marble across tile.

"Appeal," Claudia said immediately.

"To whom," the judge asked.

Claudia lifted her marked palm and set it against the bench. The heat met her hand like a lover who both forgives and does not. "To the city," she said. "To the court that taught you to exist. The one with grates that breathe and tags that watch. This ledger claims to be the minutes of our oaths. Then let the city answer whether it consents."

Mother Glass went very still. "That is not procedure."
"Procedure changes when a courtroom remembers it sits on a street."

For a heartbeat nothing. Then the chandeliers—mercury drops—began to fall, one by one, not shattering but ringing, each with the exact pitch of the crosswalk beeps outside the courthouse at Third and Leyden. Far away and right here, simultaneously, a bus sighed. Steam rose from imagined grates inside the glass, imitating the real.

The city answered in three motions: the circle, the hook, the slashes, repeating along the rims of every pane until the room looked tattooed with consent or disobedience—Claudia could not afford to decide which. The judge's scale trembled. In the far pew, her mother's hands lifted and laced, not in prayer—never again—but in readiness.

"Appeal recognized," the judge said, and every word cost him the kind of effort language hides. "Stay granted pending audit. Collector independent."

The bailiffs recoiled, quill-hands dripping punctuation that coughed in the dust.

"Conditions," Mother Glass said softly, not to help and not to hinder, only to be exact. "The debtor works."

Claudia nodded once. “I always do.”

The dome cracked. The first line ran from east to west like a bad idea committed to. Another fracture crossed it. The bench shed glitter. The room’s reflections started disagreeing with their sources, looking left when the bodies looked right, smiling when the mouths did not.

“Time to leave,” Angelo said, as if remarking on weather.

The nearest bailiff lunged. Angelo met him with the kind of violence you only ever see performed by someone who has given it up before. Two movements: a strike at the wrist to break the quill-hand, a twist at the elbow to convince the arm to forget its job. Glass squealed. The bailiff folded like paperwork abandoned in the rain.

Claudia grabbed the blue-book; the ledger leapt into her other hand as if it had been called by a bell. She felt for the mark on her wrist and it found her first, hot and faithful.

“Mother Glass,” she said, turning. “Why me.”

The witch stood under the cracking dome, face lit by the shattering shine. Ink stains on her cuffs made constellations. “Because you know the difference between guilt and debt,” she said, and her smile, for the first time, warmed. “And because you do not confuse mercy with permission.”

The pane behind Mother Glass blew inward. Wind the color of the river rushed the room. The witch stepped into it as if stepping past a threshold she herself had drawn.

“Counselor,” she added, last thing, “a mirror is a clause made visible. Do not break the wrong one.”

She was gone. The bench sloughed into ripples. The pews flattened. The dome fell in quiet, continuous ribbons that did not cut. The world chose warehouse again.

Rector's chair lay on its side. The ash circle had rearranged into the sigil but miscopied—the hook too long, the slashes four, wrong as an off-by-one verdict. The mistake made Claudia's teeth ache.

Angelo steadied her with a hand on her elbow. "Stay granted," he said, as if reminding himself the words were real enough to stand on.

The ledger warmed twice. Fresh ink wrote along the bottom edge of the page in tidy, prim script: Audit initiated. Collector status: independent. Oversight: City.

Claudia lifted the book; it lifted her right back, the way a tool chooses its hand.

From outside, the fog horned. Light bled under the unit door in three pulses: on, on, off. The city knocking.

"Let's go," she said.

"Through the front?" Angelo asked.

"Through the clause we didn't break," she answered, and when she pushed the door, the night opened like an affidavit that had finally remembered its addendum.

They stepped out into damp air that smelled like iron filings and lemons from the bodega three neighborhoods ago. Above them, a flock of starlings wrote a circle and a hook

Chapter 18 — Ash and Ink

The door closed behind them with the sound of a stamp sealing wax.

Light slid down the walls in slow drips until it gathered on the far side of the room—a shallow pool of mirror that pulsed like a vein under glass. Shelves leaned inward, their books humming in the same key as the city outside. The air smelled of candle smoke and the faint sweetness of iron.

Angelo stayed near the threshold, one hand on the frame, the other hovering near his weapon. The mirror on the opposite wall breathed, expanding and contracting with a rhythm that wasn't human.

Claudia stepped forward until her reflection met her halfway. The twin behind the glass did not mimic her exactly; its movements came a fraction early, as if it were predicting her.

"Contract mirror," Helena had said. "It remembers every clause ever broken."

Claudia touched the surface. The glass accepted her finger like water too dense to ripple. Words rose beneath her touch—fine, hair-thin, endless.

"VALE LINE COVENANT — GENERATIONAL — SEVEN WITNESSES IN ATTENDANCE."

Seven. The number tasted like a verdict.

"Angelo," she said. "Get the blue-book."

He set it beside her on a narrow table. Its pages fluttered, eager. The mark on her wrist burned once, then steadied, a pulse finding its pair. From the mirror, the reflection of her wound glowed brighter than the real one.

"Name them," she said to the glass.

Ink bled through the surface as if from behind the world.

SILENCE / FLESH / COIN / FIRE / BREATH / TIME / WORD

The letters carved themselves into the air before sinking again.

“The witnesses,” she whispered. “Every contract needs them.”

Angelo’s reflection turned its head first. The real Angelo frowned. “What happens if one’s missing?”

“Then the agreement unravels,” she said. “Or rewrites itself to find a substitute.”

A ripple ran through the mirror. Seven silhouettes stepped out in outline only—white fire shaped like people.

Helena’s voice reached them from the other side of the door, muffled but clear. “If it starts listing clauses, don’t argue. It’s reciting precedent.”

The mirror whispered, seven voices braided:

‘Silence holds confession. Flesh holds price. Coin holds choice. Fire holds memory. Breath holds promise. Time holds consequence. Word holds law.’

Claudia felt the air shift around her, heavy as testimony. The reflection of Angelo’s scar shone gold, then black, then gold again.

“Which one are we dealing with now?” he asked.

“All of them,” she said. “The covenant’s reassembling itself.”

The blue-book’s paper quivered; lines of ink grew upward, spelling a new heading:

AUDIT CLAUSE INITIATED BY CLAUDIA VALE.
SEVEN WITNESSES CALLED TO REVIEW.

The mirror deepened, showing a table ringed by the seven luminous forms. In the center lay a single quill suspended over nothing.

"Counselor," said a voice that might have belonged to all of them. "You have written without permission. State your intent."

Claudia straightened. "To correct fraud. To balance what was taken from my line."

"And what do you offer in return?"

"Truth," she said.

The mirror laughed—not loud, not cruel, but knowing. "Truth is coin without mint. Useless unless accepted."

"Then take proof," she said, holding up the blue-book. Her blood from the earlier cut had dried dark along the margin. "This is what you made of us."

The mirror brightened. One of the figures—Flesh—leaned forward, a ripple of muscle and shadow. Its voice came like paper tearing: "Blood is old currency. We prefer narrative."

"Then listen," Claudia said. And she told them. About her father's transfer, the Dominguez file, the scriptorium, the audit. Each word came out clean; the mirror recorded them in light.

When she finished, the air cooled. The seven forms shifted in deliberation.

Finally the figure called Silence raised a hand. Its motion erased all sound for a breath, then returned it. "Your claim is registered. But witnesses require countersign. Produce it."

Claudia glanced at Angelo. "We don't have one."

"You do," Silence said. "You brought him."

Angelo's hand tightened on the pistol. "I'm not signing with blood again."

The figure of Word answered, voice edged with static: "Not blood. Breath."
It extended a thin filament of light toward him. Angelo looked to Claudia once—she nodded—and exhaled. The filament inhaled in return, glowing brighter until it wrapped his shoulder. The gavel mark flared gold, then settled.

"Collector reaffirmed," the voices said together. "Audit proceeding."

The mirror rippled outward; text scrolled across its surface like wind over water. Helena burst through the door, breathless. "It's summoning the docket—you need to anchor it or it'll pull you in."

"How?" Claudia asked.

"Name it," Helena said. "Give the covenant its title before it gives itself one."

Claudia stepped closer, every word heavy with knowing. "Sentence of Forever."

The mirror froze. The reflection of her face multiplied—seven, fourteen, hundreds—each mouthing the title back at her.

Then the glass cracked. Once. Twice. Seven times.

From each fracture spilled a different color of light—white, crimson, silver, green, blue, amber, violet. The seven witnesses dissolved into smoke, but their voices stayed:

'The audit stands. The witnesses will be found. The debtor writes.'

The light withdrew into the mirror until only her reflection remained—one heartbeat ahead, one heartbeat behind.

Angelo holstered his weapon slowly. "That went well."

Helena rubbed the bridge of her nose. “You just filed a case against theology.”

Claudia closed the blue-book. “Then let’s win it.” Cracks webbed the mirror like veins made of light. Each fissure glowed its own color—white, crimson, silver, green, blue, amber, violet—seven cuts, seven promises. The hum that followed felt larger than the room; it vibrated up through the soles of their boots and out through their teeth.

Helena whispered, “It’s dividing the record. Each color’s a domain.”

The largest crack flared crimson. A breath of heat rolled through, smelling of copper and new blood. From it stepped a shape that was mostly shadow, mostly muscle—a man’s outline stitched together with gold thread that never held the same line twice. When he spoke, the air thickened.

“I am Flesh,” the voice said, layered, intimate. “You have invoked what you cannot return.”

Claudia met the shape’s eyeless stare. “I invoked an audit. That includes the body.”

Flesh tilted its head, amused. “Audits carve as easily as knives.”

Angelo moved between them without meaning to. The scar on his shoulder burned gold. Flesh’s gaze—or whatever counted as gaze—followed the light, curious. “A sanctified collector. Half redeemed, half stolen.” A low laugh. “They made you out of both of us.”

“Stay back,” Angelo said.
Flesh smiled wider. “You couldn’t afford me.”

The crimson light winked out. Where Flesh had stood, a single flake of gold skin fell to the floor and melted into a faint sigil.

Before anyone spoke, a second crack pulsed white. The sound in the room collapsed—no hum, no breathing, no heartbeat. Silence entered like fog. It wore nothing and everything; its edges dissolved into the absence it carried.

Claudia felt her throat tighten. She couldn't hear her own pulse. The mark on her wrist dimmed, trying not to be rude. Silence drifted forward until it shared her reflection. A thousand words balanced unsaid between them.

When it finally spoke, its voice was thought rather than sound: The audit cannot proceed in noise.

Images flared in Claudia's mind—courtrooms paused mid-verdict, streets emptied, a city holding its breath. She understood: to find Silence, one had to follow what wasn't spoken.

Then Silence touched her chest, a feather of cold. Her next inhale came back as echo, carrying a single syllable not her own: "Seek."

The white crack sealed. Sound returned, brutal and ordinary. The lights flickered; one bulb popped in protest.

Helena steadied herself against the shelves. "Two called. Five remain."

Claudia's hand trembled. Across her palm, the sigil had changed shape, the circle now nested inside the hook. Around it, faint new letters bled through the skin: SILENCE / FLESH / LOCATED.

Angelo looked from her hand to the mirror. "You're a map now."

"An index," she said, voice rough. "Every name I find, the mark updates."

He nodded once. "Then let's start the search." The mirror's surface shivered, then rearranged itself into a circle within a square—the old sigil for arbitration.
Light pooled at their feet. The remaining five cracks breathed, one after another, as if the glass were trying on different hearts.

Amber came first. It pulsed once, twice, and the air tasted of burnt coin and warm brass.

"Coin," Helena murmured. "Commerce made covenant."

A figure stepped out of the amber fissure. It wasn't a person so much as a ledger given spine and voice: scales in one hand, quill in the other, face hidden behind a veil of numbers cascading down like rain. When it turned toward Claudia, she heard the sound of cash registers, old and new, from every life she'd ever argued about in court.

"I am Coin," the voice said, precise as arithmetic. "You audit value. Do you understand what value costs?"

"Usually," Claudia answered. "Sometimes I win."

Coin's laughter was like change shaken in a glass jar. "Value is the name you give to the things you still want to lose yourself for. When you stop wanting, we stop counting."

It reached toward her—its fingers lines of gold penwork—but stopped short of her skin.
"In your blood," Coin said, "is a credit opened and never closed. Settle it before the balance decides for you."
Then it stepped backward and folded into itself, vanishing with a clink that echoed far longer than sound should.

Next came blue—fire without smoke. The temperature rose, and the scent of candle wax caught between breath and throat. The crack flared, split wide, and Fire arrived.

She—no, it—looked like every flame Claudia had ever seen: courtroom votive, motel lighter, the halo that had crowned the scriptorium ceiling. Human only by outline, every inch of it shimmered. Where the face should be, tongues of flame formed a mouth that spoke in exhalations.

"I remember," Fire said. "Everything you tried to burn."

Claudia swallowed. "Some of it needed to go."

"And yet," Fire said, "here it is."

A flicker; images burned through the air—her father's ledger, her own trial briefings, every guilty plea she'd crafted to save the unsavable.

The heat pressed against her eyes until tears welled and evaporated before they could fall.

Angelo stepped closer, halo-glow matching flame. “You done?”

Fire inclined its head toward him. “Sanctified light. We used to work together.”

“Not anymore,” he said.

“Until the next ignition,” Fire replied, and with that the heat dropped, the flame dimmed, and the crack sealed itself with a hiss like a match dying in rain.

Helena exhaled, smoke curling from her lips though she hadn’t lit anything. “That’s three found. Four still on the docket.”

“Which means we’re halfway to a case,” Claudia said, voice steadying on professional instinct.

The mirror, as if amused, rippled and projected images into the air—seven shapes of the city. Each glow marked a point: the cathedral-turned-data-center, a courthouse basement, a derelict foundry near the river, the clock tower downtown, and one circle drawn exactly over their building.

“Their domains,” Helena whispered. “They’re manifesting through the city grid.”

Claudia traced the lights with her finger. “Flesh in the foundry, Silence in the courthouse vaults, Coin downtown, Fire near the river—”

“Breath, Time, Word,” Angelo finished. “Not yet awake.”

The mirror pulsed once more, acknowledging comprehension. Across Claudia’s wrist, new script formed, cool rather than hot this time: COIN / FIRE / PENDING.

She looked up at the cracked glass. “We’ll find the rest.”

The mirror's reflection of her leaned forward a fraction. When it spoke, its voice was hers, but steadier, older.
"You will find what is willing to be found. The rest will summon you."

Then the mirror went still. The cracks dulled to faint threads of light, humming at the edge of hearing.

Helena stepped back, brushing dust from her palms. "That's all it'll give today. Mirrors get tired of being oracles."

Claudia nodded, closing the blue-book. "Then we take the hint."

She and Angelo turned for the door. As they did, the mirror flashed one last time. Their reflections stayed behind, watching them leave, mouths moving in perfect unison.

Helena called after them. "When you start chasing Witnesses, keep your receipts. Every miracle comes with a return policy."

Claudia smiled without showing teeth. "Lawyers understand returns."

They stepped into the hallway. The bell over the shop's front door cleared its throat again, politely registering their exit. Outside, the street had gone quiet, traffic paused at green lights as if the city were thinking.

Angelo tilted his head toward the horizon. "Which witness first?"

"Silence," she said. "We start where no one else is talking."

The city exhaled, a low sigh of wind through alleys and vents—agreement, or warning, it didn't matter.

They walked toward the courthouse.

Chapter 19 — The Seven Witnesses

The courthouse looked wrong in daylight.
Its columns had always been smug marble—white, dependable, self-important—but now they had the hue of teeth left too long in a mouth that lied for a living. The flags above the steps hung limp, even though the wind kept trying to move them.

Angelo parked two streets away, and they walked the rest. The air felt padded, like the city had lined its lungs with cotton. No dogs barked. No horns. Even their footsteps landed like apologies.

"Silence likes ceremony," Claudia said. "We're about to give it a parade."

They climbed the steps. The brass door handles were cold enough to sting.
Inside, motion detectors blinked red and refused to beep. The ceiling lights burned steady and soundless. A clerk at the security station looked up from a newspaper that had stopped halfway through turning a page. His lips moved; no sound followed. When he blinked, dust rose from his eyes like fine gray confetti.

The echo of her own breathing vanished two strides past the metal detector.

Angelo mouthed you good?
She nodded. Her pulse made a drum where sound used to be.

They passed the gallery—rows of wooden benches waiting for cases that would never be called. Paper files lay open on tables, the text smudged as if embarrassed to be caught speaking. On the far wall, the bronze state seal had grown a hairline crack in the shape of a hook and circle.

At the clerk's desk, a stack of transcripts shifted. One slid off, landing face-up. The header read:

STATE V. UNKNOWN — VERDICT SEALED BY ORDER OF SILENCE.

Her throat tightened. She turned the page. The entire transcript was blank except for the judge's signature: an elegant loop identical to the sigil burned into her palm.

The air cooled. Letters began to rise on the parchment—white against white—words visible only in absence.
"Do you still believe the law makes a sound when no one listens?"

Claudia laid her hand on the page. The mark on her wrist pulsed once, answering. The next line surfaced:
"Then listen wrong."

She closed her eyes. The courthouse spoke—not with words, but with remembered noises: gavels, heels, sobs, the rustle of a jury standing. Every sound she had ever heard in rooms like this folded inward, compressing into a single heartbeat. Then even that stopped.

When she opened her eyes, the courtroom doors had unlatched themselves.

Angelo gestured, after you.

Inside, the benches were full. Figures made of dust and expectation sat in neat rows. They faced the judge's bench, where Silence waited, translucent and immense, the shape of a human built from air pressure. Where its mouth should have been, the faint shimmer of a speaker's cone vibrated without sound.
Claudia stepped forward, every motion deliberate. She felt like she was walking on verdicts.

Silence raised a hand. Words formed in light above it:

YOU CAME.

She nodded. "You summoned."

YOU OWE.

“I’m auditing.”

THE AUDITOR MAKES NOISE.

Her voice died in her throat. She tried again; nothing. The rule had begun.

Silence tilted its head. PAY.

She understood: to speak, she would have to give something. She tore a scrap from the blue-book and pricked her thumb, pressing the blood to the page. Words reappeared, her handwriting alive again.

I give you one voice, borrowed, for one truth owed.

The shimmer pulsed—agreement.

Sound slammed back into the room.

Angelo staggered, clutching his ears. “Jesus—”

“Careful,” she warned. “Names are invoices.”

Silence folded its non-arms. The dust-jury turned its heads in unison. On the judge’s bench, a fresh groove burned through the wood, carving the same sigil they’d found under Pier Twelve.

Angelo pointed. “They’ve been running infernal trials in here.”

“Not just here,” Claudia said. “Everywhere justice stopped listening.”

She reached for the gavel. The handle was hot. Beneath it lay a slip of parchment, sealed with wax that smelled like lemon and ash. She broke it.

RECORD OF WITNESS ONE — SILENCE LOCATED.
BALANCE: STABLE.
AWAITING FLESH.

The words sank into the wood and disappeared.

The light dimmed; the dust-jury dissolved into air.

Angelo rubbed his temples. “That’s it?”
Claudia stared at the empty bench. “No. It’s a summons. Flesh is next.”

A sound—wet, faint—came from the hallway. The walls trembled as if breathing.
They turned toward the doors, and the silence outside wasn’t empty anymore. It pulsed with the slow, deliberate thud of a heart that wasn’t theirs.

“Foundry,” she said. “That’s where Flesh is nesting.”

Angelo checked the gun, habit more than hope. “Then we move.”

They walked out of the courthouse and into a city that had just remembered how to make noise. The first thing it said was thunder.
The foundry hunched on the river’s elbow like a rusted knuckle. Half its roof had fallen in years ago; gulls nested in the ribs. The gate hung by one hinge. Something had dragged a trail through the dust inside—wide, sinuous, wet in places where nothing should be wet.

Heat met them at the door, not furnace-hot, but human, the temperature of a crowded elevator. Claudia’s skin prickled. Angelo swept left, then right. The hum of the city dulled to a slower music—breathing measured by machines that no longer existed.

A catwalk cut the room in thirds. Beneath it, smelter pits gaped like dark mouths. A single arc lamp buzzed on a chain, swinging though there was no wind. It lit the trail to a steel table the size of a bed.

“Stay behind me,” Angelo said.

“Not my style,” she said, and kept pace.

The light brightened, and the shape on the table resolved: a human outline drawn in stitches. No body. Just thick black thread crisscrossing empty air, holding nothing into a person. The thread pulsed, then slackened, then tightened again, syncing to a heartbeat she could feel in her teeth.

"Claudia Vale," said a voice that came from everywhere skin would be. "You brought your gold dog."

Angelo's jaw worked. "Try a different tone."

A laugh shook the catwalk. Thread-lines quivered. "Collector. Sanctified. Half unmade, half forgiven. The body remembers both."

Claudia stepped closer. "Flesh."

"Debt auditor," it replied, amused. "Solicitor of miracles. You came to balance a book no rib could carry."

The stitched outline sat upright without disturbing the thread. Where its face should have been, knotwork thickened into the suggestion of eyes. It cocked its head like a man deciding whether to be kind.

"You took my line," Claudia said. "You priced us."

"We priced everyone," Flesh said. "The soul is theory. Meat is ledger."

"Then name the price."

"Simple." The thread-body swung its legs off the table and stood. "Pain for knowledge."

"No," Angelo said.

"Yes," Flesh said, with the even confidence of a specialist describing a routine procedure. "Law understands exchange. The more it hurts, the truer it is."

Claudia set the blue-book on a crate. "Marked down to a tolerable truth. I give you an old pain for a new answer."

Flesh's stitched eyes curved. "Bargaining is a muscle you stretch too well, Counselor. Which pain."

She reached for memory and chose one that had already been turned into a story out of self-defense: a night on a kitchen floor, the bottle, the chair, the line of sin spoken like a bedtime curse. She opened the door to it the width of a fingernail. The thread-body leaned in as if smelling steam.

“Acceptable,” it said, delighted. “Ask.”

“Who spoke the first clause of our covenant?”

“Your mother,” Flesh said, without hesitation. “But she did not choose the words. Word did.”

The room tilted. Angelo’s hand closed on her elbow and kept the tilt from turning to fall.

“Next,” Flesh said cheerfully. “Pain for payment. One more answer.”

“Terms first,” Claudia said, throat dry. “No scars. No marks. Pain returns to me, not to anyone who ever loved me.”

Flesh looked pleased at the precision. “Signed. Ask.”

“How do we reverse the sanctified annulment on him?” She didn’t look at Angelo when she said it.

“Sanctified is not permission,” Flesh said. “It’s alignment. To reverse an annulment, you make the ledger admit it punished him for mercy instead of justice. Find the case. Find the person he refused to deliver.”

Angelo’s mouth thinned. “I know the face,” he said quietly. “I never learned her name.”

Claudia nodded once. “We’ll learn it.”

The stitched body clapped its threaded hands with a papery sound. “Paid in full,” it said, and reached toward Claudia’s sternum with two fingers of nothing.

The pain came like a clean blade through old fabric—sharp, then gone—but what it cut free left the room colder. Her breath hitched once. Angelo took half a step he didn't mean to. She caught his hand and squeezed before he did something expensive.

"Receipt," she said, voice level.

Flesh's fingers traced a quick series of motions in the air. A glyph hung there, gold for a breath, then burned itself onto the blue-book's margin as a tidy notation: FLESH – PAID / ANSWERS: WORD SPOKE / CASE OF MERCY.

"Two more items," Flesh said, indulgent. "A bonus for style."

"I don't want your generosity," Claudia said.

"It isn't generosity," Flesh replied. "It's alignment. First: the one called Coin has already priced your future and found it unprofitable for everyone else. Beware gifts. Second: your city is learning to bleed slower. That buys you hours, not days."

The thread-face tilted past her toward the catwalk. "And third—"

Angelo turned on instinct. The stitches above lit up with footfalls that weren't there, a man-shaped vacancy crossing shadow.

Rector.

No, not Rector—what wore him. He had a mouth again, and it had too many teeth for one man's decisions. He moved wrong, as if the ligaments in his knees had been drafted into a different army.

"Hello, auditors," Rector said pleasantly. "We missed court."

"Back on your feet fast," Angelo said.

"Bodies are rentals," Rector said. "Paperwork is forever."

Flesh made a small sound of annoyance. "Collectors," it said to Rector. "Always breaking retainer agreements."

“Change of venue,” Rector said, and reached for the chain of the arc lamp.

Claudia didn’t think. She palmed the blue-book, shoved it at Angelo, and moved. By the time Rector yanked the chain, she was inside the lamp’s circle, heat on her face. The chain came down like a bell rope; the lamp swung in a bright arc. Angelo grabbed it mid-swing and ripped it free, sparks copying fire.

Rector laughed, not with his lungs. “Audit or no audit, the clock runs.” He tilted his head. “Balance won’t wait.”

Flesh stepped between them with lazy grace. Thread fingers unfolded into a net. They brushed Rector’s chest and found something worth holding. He jerked, brightness pin holed behind his eyes.

“Apologies,” Flesh told Claudia. “House rules.”

Rector blinked hard, then went still. He looked at Angelo, and for a breath the human looked back out of the borrowed face. “Find her,” he said, just once, voice his. “The one you saved.”

Then the borrowed teeth smiled. “See you at the river.”

He stepped backward into shadow and unraveled like bad sewing.

Angelo lowered the ruined lamp. His breathing had edges. Gold light beat once under his skin, then went silent.

Claudia turned to Flesh. “We’re done.”

“Until the next pain,” Flesh said, satisfied. It lay back on the table and came apart—threads slackening into a loose tangle that the air blew gently into a pile. The heat in the room dropped to ordinary.

They stood in the foundry’s echo, soot powdering their shoes, the blue-book warm against Claudia’s palm. On the margin, fresh writing inked itself with bureaucratic calm:

WITNESS – FLESH: CLEARED.
TASKS: IDENTIFY “MERCY CASE.” PURSUE WORD.

Angelo unbuttoned his sleeve and examined the bruise at his shoulder. The thorn-curve had begun to glow thinly again, a seam of gold under the black. It looked like sunrise arguing with night.

“Who is she?” Claudia asked.

“The woman I didn’t deliver,” he said. “I hid her. A long time back. They took my sanctified for it.”

“Then we get her name,” Claudia said. “And make the ledger say it out loud.”

He nodded. The nod meant: whatever it costs.

They stepped out into weather that had settled on rain. The city had found its sounds again—tires hissing, crosswalks ticking, some kid testing a trumpet three floors up and missing the note by a mile. Across the river, a low orange smear began to pulse—by the old ferry docks, where the city stored its mistakes.

“Fire,” Angelo said.

“Let’s put it out.”

They headed for the truck. As they passed the gate, a strip of flaking paint curled from the chain-link and fell. Underneath, the rust had written a tidy sentence in negative space, as if the metal had decided to keep minutes:

COIN AWAITS WHERE WORD WAS SPOKEN FIRST.

Claudia looked at the clock tower rising over downtown. It had been the first city hall before it became a bell, then a view, then a ruin tourists liked. On its face, the hands were moving too slow. Time’s domain taking notes.

“We’re being scheduled,” she said.

"We'll keep our own calendar," Angelo said.

The rain agreed to be ordinary for five more minutes. They used them well.

—

Next, the city's riverfront will flare into a tribunal of flames, and Fire will test Claudia's memory against what she tried to burn. From there, Coin and Word begin to close their jaws—an escalation that tightens the noose on the "mercy case" and pushes Angelo's sanctified toward gold. They followed the smell before they saw the light.
Down at the docks the air had that scorched-copper tang of a transformer burning, and the mist glowed faint orange even when the streetlamps blinked out. A freight sign clanged once and then stayed still, its metal too hot for wind.

Fire was waiting in plain sight.

Every window in the derelict ferry terminal shone from within, yet the glass didn't melt. The light pulsed in a slow rhythm, three beats—on, on, off—like the city's own breath.

Angelo parked crooked and left the engine running. "Feels like an ambush."

"It's a witness," Claudia said. "Ambush is just testimony with bad manners."

They stepped inside. Heat rose from the tiles in waves that distorted the world into ripples. Old posters for river tours curled on the walls, faces of smiling couples blackened at the edges. At the far end, the ticket counter was a hearth; paper burned without ash. Behind it stood the woman of flame they had seen in the mirror.

Fire wore a human outline tonight—female, mid-thirties, the kind of beauty that comes from absolute conviction. Her hair wove itself from embers; her eyes were candle wicks that never blinked.

“Counselor Vale,” she said, every syllable a spark. “You’ve brought your collector to the river. He used to work here.”

Angelo’s knuckles whitened. “I was never on your payroll.”

“You burned a man once,” Fire said. “You thought it was mercy.”

Claudia moved between them. “We’re not here for confession.”

Fire smiled. “That’s why you’ll get one anyway.”

Flames licked up the columns. The room filled with images drawn in heat: a courthouse at night, a body carried down marble steps, a prayer cut short. Angelo saw himself younger, sword instead of gun, light instead of logic. The body in his arms shifted to smoke.

“That’s enough,” Claudia said, voice low. “He’s paid.”

“Not to me,” Fire said. “The audit requests evidence of motive. You can’t balance without seeing what you burned.”

Claudia’s mark flared through her sleeve. She stepped forward until the heat lifted her hair from her shoulders. “Then show me mine.”

Fire’s head tilted. “Brave. Unwise.”

The room inverted. She stood in her own memory—the night she burned the Dominguez file. Paper in the sink, lighter in her hand, the smell of lemon cleaner and guilt. The flame whispered then exactly as it did now: this won’t erase anything.

“I know,” she said aloud. “But it kept me human long enough to fight you.”

The memory collapsed. They were back in the terminal. The flame-woman looked pleased, like a teacher grading a stubborn pupil.

“Truth confirmed,” Fire said. “You remember why balance hurts. Keep that; it will make you dangerous.”

She turned to Angelo. “And you—stop carrying light like a weapon. It burns paperwork.”
He almost smiled. “I’ll switch to ink.”

The laughter that followed rattled the rafters. Sparks rained down and died midair. Fire’s outline thinned to a filament.

“Record this,” she said, and pointed a burning finger at Claudia. “Word will try to draft you. When it does, choose verbs over nouns. Verbs move; nouns bind.”

The flame winked out. The heat faded. On the counter, a single line of soot wrote itself before drifting away:

FIRE — CLEARED. NEXT : COIN.

The blue-book in Claudia’s hand warmed, new ink scrolling across the margin:
Witness Three complete. Audit in progress. Balance unstable.

Outside, rain hissed against the roof. Steam lifted, forming a brief circle-and-hook before wind tore it apart.

Angelo exhaled. “Three down.”

“Four,” she said, already turning toward the river road. “The city just changed its currency.”

He followed her gaze. Across the water, the old financial district glimmered gold—every window reflecting the same spinning symbol, a coin turning in slow, impossible gravity. The next Witness was awake.
Downtown had always looked holy at night: glass spires glowing like votive candles, the hum of servers in their basements pretending to be prayer.
Now the light was wrong. Too even. Too gold. Every window carried the same reflection—a single coin turning end over end, never landing.

Traffic had stopped itself. Cars sat at perfect angles, engines idling in polite synchrony. On every dashboard lay a dollar bill folded into the shape of a hook and circle.

Angelo killed the headlights a block from the old exchange building. "Coin likes pageantry," he said. "All this feels like an offering."

"It's an audit," Claudia said. "Everything's inventory until proven otherwise."

They stepped into air that smelled of ozone and perfume—wealth's aftertaste. The revolving door at the lobby spun though no one touched it. Inside, the marble floor rippled with faint light like a pool of molten metal trying to remember liquidity.

A voice echoed from everywhere and nowhere at once:
WELCOME, CLAUDIA VALE. YOUR BALANCE HAS EARNED INTEREST.

She flinched; the words vibrated inside her molars. On the far wall, the ticker board scrolled not numbers but names—every client she'd ever defended, every plea bargain, every dollar that bought someone's second chance.

Angelo drew the pistol out of habit. The muzzle gleamed gold before dulling back to black.

"Put that away," she said. "Violence depreciates."

A laugh followed, the rustle of silk and coins dropped in a fountain. From behind the teller cages stepped the witness.
Coin wore a suit that wasn't tailored so much as built—seams soldered, buttons hammered from aureate script. Its face was a mask of mirrored bronze; its eyes spun like dials.
"Value incarnate," Claudia said softly.

Coin bowed. "Profit personified if you prefer poetry. You've been circulating my currency. I've come to audit the auditor."

The marble under her shoes warmed; circles of light appeared with every step she took toward it, shrinking, calculating. She stopped an arm's length away. "I'm here for records, not dividends."

"Everything is a dividend," Coin said. "Even mercy pays out eventually."

It lifted a hand. Gold dust spilled from its fingers and arranged itself midair into a set of scales. On one pan rested a heart-shaped ember, on the other, a fountain pen.

"Which weighs more?" Coin asked.

"Depends who's paying," she said.

"Exactly." It gestured, and the scales vanished. "Your father sold his compassion wholesale. Your line's stock rose. Congratulations; you're solvent."

"I'm indebted," she corrected.

"Semantics," Coin purred. "All law is."

Angelo stepped forward. "She doesn't owe you."

Coin tilted its bronze head. "Everyone owes me. Even you, collector. You chose compassion once—an unapproved expense. I covered it. With interest."

Gold light crawled up Angelo's wrist like a bracelet tightening. He grunted; the mark on his shoulder flared, caught between gold and black. Claudia placed her hand over the spreading light, palm against skin. "You don't get to repossess him," she said.

The air trembled. Coin considered. "Balance then. A trade. You surrender potential profit—your future verdicts—and I release him."

"What happens if I decline?"

"Then his sanctified returns early. Entirely. He stops being a man and becomes an asset."

Angelo's eyes met hers, steady. "Don't you dare."

She didn't. Instead she smiled—thin, legal. "Offer withdrawn. Counterproposal: I show you what happens when value defaults."

Coin's mask rippled. "Demonstrate."

She opened the blue-book to the latest page, the ink still wet from Fire's signature. Her own blood gleamed in the margin. "Here's my collateral."

The pages rustled; lines multiplied. Every case she had ever argued appeared, each with a new notation: profit realized = 0. The word zero repeated until the ledger screamed in gold.

Coin staggered. "You falsify balance?"

"I correct it," she said. "The ledger's been cooking its books for generations. You're welcome to audit my math."

Light bled from its seams. "You erase value itself."

"Only the kind that eats people," she said.

Coin laughed once, a sharp chime that broke windows on the mezzanine. "Very well, Counselor Vale. Your audit stands." It removed a single coin from its pocket, silver on one face, gold on the other. "Call when you wish to buy time."

It flipped the coin toward her. She caught it; it was weightless.

"Payment in advance?" she asked.

"A warning," Coin said. "When Time arrives, show her that."

The witness stepped backward into its own reflection. The gold light drained from the room, leaving only the building's ordinary fluorescence. The ticker board froze on a single line of text:

COIN — CLEARED. INTEREST SUSPENDED.

The blue-book closed itself. The margin read:

Witness Four complete. Proceed to Breath.

Angelo flexed his hand; the gold bruising faded to gray. “That was expensive,” he said.

“Not yet,” she answered. “We’ll see the invoice later.”

They stepped outside. The city had gone quiet again, holding its breath—literally. Fog hung low, unmoving, as if waiting for permission to inhale.

Angelo looked up. “That’s our next one.”

Claudia pocketed the silver-and-gold coin. “Then let’s go teach Breath how to breathe.” By dawn the city had turned blue.
Not sky-blue, not morning—blood-without-oxygen blue. Steam froze half-risen from grates, a million suspended exhalations. Sirens wheezed once and stayed there, tone held mid-note. Even the pigeons sat with beaks open, throats working soundlessly.

Helena’s voice crackled through the radio once before dying: “Hospitals full—no pulse, no death. Find Breath.”

They drove until they reached the river hospital district, a row of brick buildings built when medicine still believed in prayer. The parking lot overflowed with motionless orderlies. Each chest lifted once every minute, air going in but never out.

Inside smelled like mint, antiseptic, and fear. IV bags bulged, never draining. Monitors traced perfect flat lines—life held between inhale and exhale. In every room a shadow hovered near the ceiling, rising, and falling as if to remind them what rhythm used to mean.

At the far ward, the air thickened to velvet. A nurse stood at the window, her breath visible but looping back into her mouth. She turned as they entered. Her eyes were the soft gray of smoke; her pupils dilated with every word she didn’t say.

“Counselor Vale,” she whispered, voice folded into itself. “Collector. We’ve been expecting your testimony.”

Her body blurred; her outline filled with light. The windowpanes fogged. When she inhaled, the curtains drew inward; when she exhaled, they didn't move at all.

"Breath," Claudia said.

The nurse-shape smiled. "The one that makes all others possible. You've been talking too much."

Claudia felt her lungs stutter. "Occupational hazard."

"Silence was your first witness," Breath said. "She asked me to see whether you remembered to listen."

Angelo steadied her arm. "She's killing the air."

"Borrowing it," Breath said. "There's a difference."

The blue-book fluttered open on its own. Its pages turned to blankness so white it hurt. Words began to appear, written in condensation.

CLAIM: HUMANS ABUSE RESOURCE: OXYGEN. PENALTY: SUSPENSION.

Claudia forced a breath. It felt borrowed. "Overruled," she said, though the word came out smaller than she liked. "We appeal under necessity. You suffocate the innocent to punish the guilty."

"Innocent?" Breath's head tilted. "Every lie is air wasted."

"Then I'll pay," Claudia said. "Take mine. Let them breathe."

Angelo grabbed her shoulder. "Don't you—"

She touched his wrist. "Rule two. Don't sign what isn't yours."

Breath studied her a moment longer, then drew in a slow, enormous inhale. The air around Claudia rushed out of her lungs, out of her skin. Vision went gray at the edges. In the roaring quiet she saw something vast: the city's skyline bending as if bowing, windows fogging in unison, a pulse beating under asphalt.

Then, softer than a verdict whispered across chambers, Breath spoke inside her head. This is what you guard when you argue—air between hearts. Do not forget what it costs.

She collapsed against Angelo's chest, the borrowed air rushing back. Breath stepped closer, her outline human again. "Audit acknowledged," she said. "Next time, bring offerings that breathe."

The witness faded. Every monitor in the ward jumped once, a bright green arc, and people all over the floor gasped awake.

Claudia bent double, coughing, laughing, alive. Angelo steadied her. "That counts as a win?"

"Appeal granted," she rasped. "Interest pending."

The blue-book's margin steamed, then dried.
WITNESS – BREATH CLEARED. CITY STABILIZING. NEXT: TIME.

Outside, clocks began to tick again—but out of order. Noon struck twice, once backward. A second hand spun counter to the first.

Angelo frowned. "Looks like the next witness already showed up."

Claudia wiped her mouth, tasted blood and smoke. "Then we'd better get to court before the past starts arguing." The city was wrong again, but in a new key.
Every stoplight pulsed through its cycle too fast, then too slow; traffic moved in fits of déjà vu. Pedestrians stepped off curbs and reappeared back on them, shaking their heads as if they'd forgotten what they meant to do. The air itself had begun to rewind.

Angelo pulled to the side of the courthouse square. The clock tower above them chimed once, twice, then once again in reverse, the sound unrolling like tape played backward.

“Feels like vertigo,” he muttered. “Every breath’s recycled.”

“Time’s filing appeals,” Claudia said. “Every minute wants a rehearing.”

Inside, the courthouse archives had become a labyrinth. Case boxes multiplied like cells, files stacked and restacked by unseen clerks. The air smelled of dust and ozone, and the hum of fluorescent lights was now a low chant: objection overruled, objection sustained.

The main hall’s portrait gallery shimmered. Judges and attorneys moved within their frames, repeating the same gestures on a loop—gavel raised, gavel lowered, mouths forming verdicts that never landed.

“Every verdict ever spoken here,” Claudia said softly, “is replaying itself.”

“Then we find the one that started it.”

A doorway opened that hadn’t existed a heartbeat before. Down the hall, an elevator waited with its doors ajar, light inside flickering between gold and blue.

They stepped in. The panel listed no floors—only dates. 1993, 1957, 1881, 2034. Claudia pressed 2034. The button lit and the elevator began to fall upward.

The doors opened onto the same hall—but older. The marble was new, the air heavy with varnish. Lawyers in nineteenth-century suits passed by, flickering like film projections. Each carried a folder stamped with the same emblem: the hook and circle.

“Trial of Origin,” Claudia murmured. “The first case.”

Time waited for them in the courtroom beyond.

She looked nothing like the others. She wore a judge’s robe so long it pooled into mist. Her face was young and ancient in the same breath; her hair moved like an hourglass, grains flowing from crown to collar. The gavel in her hand ticked instead of thudded.

“Counselor Vale,” Time said, voice layered—past, present, future together. “You stand in your own precedent.”

Claudia bowed her head a fraction. “We’re auditing the covenant. I need the record of the ‘mercy case.’”

Time smiled with no warmth. “The one your collector refused to close.”

The clock-hands on her sleeves spun faster. “He gave me that moment. I kept it for interest. You want her name, you pay the delay.”

“How?” Claudia asked.

“Every second you’ve ever wasted—bring them to account.”

Claudia’s mark burned; memories blurred—moments of hesitation, words unsaid, seconds spent staring at ceilings. Each one peeled from her skin as a spark. Time caught them in her gavel, weighing them like coins.

“Acceptable,” she said. “Her name was Marisol Reyes. The mercy case. You’ll find her where speech begins.”

“Word,” Claudia whispered.

Time nodded. “And hurry. You’ve already done this once.”

“What?”

But the question came out late; the courtroom had already shifted. The walls flickered between centuries—gaslight to neon to darkness. Angelo grabbed her wrist. “We’re slipping.”

“Not yet,” she said, fighting the vertigo. “Time—grant stay of execution for the city. It’s still breathing.”

Time tapped her gavel once. The motion froze the world mid-collapse. "Stay granted," she said. "For one turn of the hourglass. After that, all debts mature."

Then she reversed the gavel. The tick became a tock, and they were falling again—down through years, through rulings, through every appeal ever filed.

They hit the present with a thud that rattled the lights. The elevator doors opened onto an empty hall, everything back to now. The blue-book trembled in Claudia's hands.

New script crawled across the margin:

WITNESS – TIME CLEARED. MERCY CASE: MARISOL REYES. NEXT: WORD.

Angelo's pulse still stuttered against his throat. "She said we've done this before."

Claudia looked up at the portraits. In one of them, a woman in a dark suit stared back—her own face, older by a few years, gavel in hand. "I think we lost the first trial," she said.

Angelo holstered his gun. "Then let's appeal."

Outside, the clock tower struck once—backward—and every speaker in the city crackled with a single syllable, half-heard, half-felt:

Word. The city spoke first.

A whisper came through every intercom, billboard, phone screen and passing mouth. Letters peeled off street signs, fluttered upward like startled birds, and re-formed midair into new words that dissolved as quickly as they read: WITNESS ARRIVES.

By the time they reached the old courthouse steps the sound had become a vibration, a bass note that rattled fillings and bones alike. The doors opened inward on their own. Inside, language dripped down the walls—sentences melting into punctuation, punctuation into breath.

Angelo's gun hummed, safety clicking off without his finger. "Feels like we're standing inside a throat," he said.

Claudia stepped onto the marble floor. Each heel print left behind a phrase: I am, I was, I will be. The air smelled of ink and ozone.

"Word," she said.

Light bent. The room folded itself into a spiral of text, paragraphs running along the pillars like vines. From the center stepped the last Witness: a figure made entirely of shifting letters, each character a different alphabet, every language that had ever lied to tell the truth.

"You are the final clause," Word said. "The author who forgot she wrote."

Claudia's voice trembled. "You bound my line."

"You bound yourselves," Word corrected. "Humans begged for definitions. We granted grammar. You used it to cage mercy."

Angelo lifted the pistol. "Back away from her."

Word smiled with all the warmth of an illuminated manuscript. "A bullet is a sentence with bad syntax."

The gun clicked—then spoke instead of firing. Bang came out as an actual word, glowing for a moment before collapsing into ash.

Claudia held up the blue-book. "I came for amendment."

Word tilted its head. "And offer?"

"Revision. Free will reinstated, all debts negotiable."

"Revisions require editors," Word said. "Become mine."
The letters around them closed in, wrapping the walls. Clauses began to circle her ankles, tugging upward—if, therefore, whereas. The smell of paper burning from the inside out filled her lungs.

She remembered Mother Glass's warning: a mirror is a clause made visible. Do not break the wrong one.

Claudia drew the coin had given her—the silver-and-gold disc—and held it up. "Two sides. Value and void. I choose the margin between them."

Word's body flickered, letters stuttering. "Define margin."

"The place sentences go when they're rewritten." She flipped the coin. It landed on edge, spinning, light pouring from its rim. Every clause binding her froze mid-verb.

"Clause suspended," she said. "By authority of the author who remembers."

The spiral shook. Word's shape blurred. Its voice fractured into dialects and then into a single human tone—hers.

"Claudia Vale," it said, softly now. "Do you understand what it means to author?"

"Yes." She stepped forward until her reflection overlapped with its dissolving form. "It means responsibility for everything that follows."

She pressed her hand to its chest of text. The mark on her wrist blazed white, searing through ink and language. Word's body exploded outward into pages—millions of them—each one blank. The wind they made roared through the courthouse, carrying a single echo:

Sentence adjourned.

When silence returned, the room was only a room again—dust, benches, ordinary air. Angelo lowered the useless gun. Claudia sagged against the wall, breath catching.

"You killed it?" he asked.

"No." She looked at the single blank page left in her hand. "I edited it."

The blue-book opened by itself. On the final page, neat type appeared:

WITNESS – WORD CLEARED. AUDIT COMPLETE.
SENTENCE OF FOREVER: REVISED.
AUTHOR OF RECORD: CLAUDIA VALE.

Angelo exhaled a laugh that sounded half like relief. “So… we win?”

“For now.” She folded the blank page into the blue-book. “Revisions always need proofreading.”

Outside, the sky rippled, words reforming into clouds, then dissolving. The city drew a slow, careful breath—the kind you take before speaking again for the first time.

Chapter 20 — The Archive

The building had been empty for twenty years.
At least that was what the city records said.
Claudia stood across the street staring at the dark windows while the wind pushed damp air off the river and into the narrow lane. The brass plaque beside the entrance was green with age.
Municipal Records Annex.
Closed indefinitely.
Angelo shut the truck door beside her.
"You sure this is it?" he asked.
Claudia held up the photograph they had pulled from the ledger earlier. The faded image showed the same stone facade, the same arch over the door, the same carved scales of justice above the frame.
Only the photo had been taken when the building was still alive.
Lights glowing.
People walking in and out.
Now it looked like something the city had deliberately forgotten.
"The address matches," she said.
Angelo studied the street.
Empty.
No cars.
No foot traffic.
Just the dull buzz of a streetlamp struggling to stay lit.
He exhaled slowly.
"I don't like it."
"You don't like anything about this case."

"That's because every time we get closer to an answer, someone ends up dead."
Claudia slipped the photograph back into her coat pocket.
"Then let's try not to be those people."
Angelo gave her a look that said *that's not how this works*.
But he followed her across the street anyway.
The front door opened easier than it should have.
The hinges groaned softly as Angelo pushed it inward.
Cold air spilled out.
Not outside cold.
Still air.
The kind that belonged to sealed rooms and forgotten spaces.
Claudia stepped inside first.
Her shoes echoed against marble.
The lobby was bigger than she expected.
Dust lay across the floor in undisturbed sheets. Tall cabinets lined the walls where old public records must have once been kept. Their glass doors were clouded with grime.
Angelo shut the door behind them.
The street noise vanished instantly.
Too instantly.
He clicked on his flashlight.
The beam cut through the darkness and revealed a staircase descending at the far end of the room.
"Records annex," he muttered. "Which means the real stuff is downstairs."
Claudia had already noticed.
The ledger in her bag felt heavier.
Not physically.
Something else.
Like a magnet pulling toward a buried piece of iron.
"That way," she said quietly.
Angelo noticed the tone.
"You feel it too."
She didn't answer.
She was already moving toward the stairs.
The air grew colder as they descended.
Not damp.
Not moldy.

Just old.
The smell of paper and leather thickened with every step.
Angelo swept the flashlight beam across the walls.
Stone.
No windows.
No modern wiring.
“This place is older than the city records say,” he murmured.
Claudia reached the bottom step.
Then she stopped.
The room beyond stretched farther than the light could reach.
Shelves.
Hundreds of them.
Not books.
Ledgers.
Rows and rows of thick volumes bound in dark leather.
Some looked ancient.
Some looked only a few decades old.
All arranged in perfect order.
Angelo stepped beside her.
“Well,” he said quietly.
“That’s not suspicious at all.”
Claudia walked forward slowly.
Her fingers hovered over the nearest shelf.
The leather spines were stamped with dates.

1874.
1875.
1876.
1877.

Every decade.
Every year.
Recorded.
“Municipal records,” Angelo guessed.
Claudia pulled one free.
Dust lifted into the flashlight beam.
She opened the cover.
Inside were names.
Thousands of them.
Columns of handwriting.
Dates.
Symbols.

Her breath slowed.
"This isn't city paperwork."
Angelo leaned over her shoulder.
"What is it then?"
Claudia ran her finger down the page.
Each entry followed the same structure.
Name.
Date.
A small mark beside it.
A circle.
A hook.
Three slashes.
The same symbol they had been chasing since the beginning.
"This is the ledger," she whispered.
Angelo frowned.
"You mean copies?"
"No."
She turned another page.
More names.
More symbols.
Different handwriting.
Different ink.
Different centuries.
"This is the archive."
They moved deeper between the shelves.
The beam of Angelo's flashlight revealed ledger after ledger.
Some so old the leather had cracked.
Some so new the ink still looked sharp.
Claudia opened another.
Same format.
Same symbol.
"Every case," she said slowly.
"Every contract."
Angelo stiffened slightly.
"You're assuming those are contracts."
Claudia turned the book toward him.
"Look."
One entry read:
Rector, Daniel — Witness
Below it:

Collection — fulfilled
Angelo exhaled sharply.
"Well."
"That's… comforting."
Claudia flipped another page.
Names she didn't recognize.
Cities.
Dates stretching back centuries.
"Someone has been keeping track of this system for a very long time."
Angelo scanned the shelves again.
"How long?"
Claudia reached for another volume.
The leather crumbled slightly under her fingers as she opened it.
The first entry inside was dated:
1813.
She closed the book slowly.
"Long enough."
They walked deeper into the archive.
The flashlight beam flickered across the shelves.
Claudia felt something tightening in her chest.
The deeper they went, the stronger the feeling became.
Like walking toward the center of something.
Then she stopped.
Her hand froze halfway to another ledger.
Angelo noticed instantly.
"What?"
Claudia didn't answer.
She had opened the book already.
The page stared back at her.
One entry.
Only one.
Written decades ago.
Vale, Robert
Her father's name.
The air in the room shifted.
Angelo saw the color leave her face.
"Claudia."
She kept staring.
The entry continued.
Witness.

Confirmed.
Below it was the same symbol.
Hook.
Circle.
Three slashes.
Angelo's voice softened.
"You didn't know."
"No."
She closed the book carefully.
Her hands were shaking now.
"For years I thought he was just a drunk who ruined our family."
Angelo didn't interrupt.
Claudia looked around the endless shelves.
"He wasn't hiding from people."
Her voice dropped to a whisper.
"He was hiding from this."
The room had grown quieter.
Too quiet.
Angelo's flashlight flickered once.
Then steadied.
Claudia noticed something strange.
Symbols.
Faint scratches along the wooden shelves.
The same mark.
Hook.
Circle.
Three slashes.
Everywhere.
She turned slowly.
"Angelo."
He followed her gaze.
"…yeah."
"This place isn't abandoned."
"No."
His voice was tight now.
"It's maintained."
Claudia frowned.
"By who?"
Angelo didn't answer.
Instead he turned the flashlight toward the center of the room.

There was a desk there.
Old wood.
Ink bottle.
A pen.
And an open ledger.
Fresh ink glistened on the page.
Claudia stepped closer.
The words were still drying.
She read them slowly.
Vale, Claudia
Witness — confirmed.
Below it another line had begun.
The ink was still forming.
Angelo leaned closer.
Neither of them touched the book.
The final line finished writing itself.
Collector — pending.
Silence swallowed the room.
Angelo exhaled slowly.
"Well."
"That can't be good."
Claudia stared at the page.
The ink shimmered slightly under the flashlight beam.
As if acknowledging her.
For the first time since this investigation began, Claudia Vale realized something terrifying.
She hadn't discovered the system.
The system had discovered her.
And somewhere in the city…
Someone had just been assigned to collect.
Claudia didn't touch the page.
She didn't need to.
The ink was still wet.
Angelo leaned closer, the beam of his flashlight tightening on the words.
"Tell me that wasn't there before."
"It wasn't."
The air in the archive shifted.
Not wind.
Not movement.

Just a pressure change that made the room feel suddenly smaller.
Claudia slowly closed the ledger.
The sound echoed through the shelves.
For a moment nothing happened.
Then somewhere deeper in the archive…
a page turned.
Not in the book she held.
Somewhere else.
A dry, deliberate sound.
Paper sliding across paper.
Angelo swung the flashlight toward the darkness.
Rows of shelves stared back at them.
Still.
Silent.
Claudia swallowed.
"Did you hear—"
Another page turned.
Farther away this time.
Like someone moving through the aisles.
Angelo's voice dropped.
"We're not alone."
Claudia looked down at the ledger in her hands.
The symbol on the page seemed darker now.
Waiting.
Somewhere in the darkness another page flipped.
Then another.
Then another.
One after another.
Hundreds of pages turning in distant shelves.
Like the archive itself was waking up.
Claudia grabbed Angelo's arm.
"Time to go."
He didn't argue.
As they hurried back toward the stairs, the sound followed them.
Pages turning.
Ink scratching.
Names being written.
Behind them, deep in the archive, a new ledger slid slowly open.
And a fresh line began to write itself.

Chapter 21 — The Word That Burns

The pages were still turning when they ran.

Claudia didn't remember grabbing the ledger. She only knew it was in her hands as Angelo shoved the archive door open and the two of them burst into the alley behind the courthouse, lungs burning, footsteps too loud in the wet dark.

Behind them, somewhere under stone and iron and the civilized lies of the city, the archive kept waking.

Page after page.

Name after name.

Ink scratching in the dark like tiny bones learning to walk.

Cold air hit Claudia's face. She bent forward, one hand braced against her knee, the ledger clutched against her ribs. Rain drifted down in a thin mist, silver under the streetlamp.

For a moment neither of them spoke.

The city looked normal.

That was the first insult.

A bus groaned through the intersection at the mouth of the alley. A traffic signal changed from yellow to red. A couple under a shared umbrella hurried past the courthouse steps without looking up. Somewhere farther off, a siren rose and fell.

Normal.

As if the world had not just opened its throat beneath their feet.

Angelo took the ledger from her carefully, like it might burn him if he touched the wrong place. His chest rose and fell hard under his shirt. Water darkened the scar at his collar.

"What the hell did we just open?" he said.

Claudia straightened slowly, forcing air back into her lungs.

"I don't think we opened it," she said. "I think we interrupted it."

He looked toward the courthouse.

His whole body sharpened.

"Claudia."

She turned.

Smoke was rising from the upper windows.

At first it looked like fog trapped under the eaves. Then one pane burst outward with a crack like a rifle shot, and orange light rolled through the opening.

Flame.

Not a little fire. Not an accident with wiring. A hungry interior blaze lighting old stone from the inside out.

The courthouse burned like something had finally remembered what it was built on.

Sirens screamed louder now, converging from three different directions. The couple under the umbrella had stopped in the street. Someone shouted. Another person began running toward the corner with a phone already in hand.

Claudia stared at the flames with the stunned stillness of a witness being sworn in.

"That's not coincidence," she said.

"No."

Angelo's voice had gone flat in the way it did when fear got sharpened into function.

He shoved the ledger back at her.

"We don't stay here."

He caught her by the wrist and pulled her down the alley.

They moved fast, not running full out, just hard enough to look like people with a destination instead of people fleeing an impossible fire. By the time they hit the next block, the courthouse bells had begun ringing. Not because anyone was pulling them. Because heat does strange things to metal. Because the city liked drama. Because God, if He was watching, had a rotten sense of timing.

They cut across two side streets and made it to the truck with the smoke already climbing higher over downtown. Angelo unlocked the doors. Claudia slid in, clutching the ledger bag against her stomach. He started the engine before his own door was even fully shut.

The truck lunged from the curb.

For three blocks they said nothing.

The windshield wipers beat a steady rhythm. Rain smeared the city into light and shadow. Claudia kept seeing the book in the archive, chained and breathing, and the line that had lifted itself across the page in wet black script:

You opened it. Now write it back.

Her hand ached where she'd cut it.

The mark under her skin pulsed once.

Then again.

She looked down.

The faint hooked circle near the base of her thumb glowed like heat trapped in a bruise.

"You're doing that thing again," Angelo said.

"What thing."

"Bleeding panic in total silence."

She almost smiled.

"It's more dignified than screaming."

"Debatable."

He took the next turn too fast. The truck's tires hissed over wet pavement.

The city outside had changed.
Not dramatically at first.
Just enough.
A black symbol painted fresh on a retaining wall.
Then another on the side of a laundromat.
Then one scratched into the back of a stop sign, deep enough to show silver under the red paint.
Circle.
Hook.
Three slashes.
Claudia sat up straighter.
"Slow down."
Angelo did.
Neither of them spoke as the truck rolled past a bus stop where the sigil had been traced into condensation from the inside. Past a closed deli with the same mark painted across the metal shutter. Past a church wall where it was burned, not painted, into the brick itself.
The city was being tagged in real time.
Not by kids.
Not by gangs.
By the system.
"They know," Claudia said.
"Yeah."
He didn't ask who *they* were. He was past that now.
Two blocks later they saw smoke rising from another building.
Not downtown this time.
Closer to the river.
A narrow records annex, city-owned, mostly overflow storage and paper trails no one thought about until they needed them. Black smoke pushed from the top floor in thick deliberate ribbons.

Another symbol above the door.
Another correction.
Claudia felt something cold settle into place inside her.
"The archive isn't just recording names."
"No."
"It's moving."
Angelo nodded once.
"Looks like it's cleaning house."
He drove in silence after that.
Every light they hit seemed to hold a beat too long before changing. Every person on the sidewalk felt watchful. Twice Claudia caught people staring at the truck with blank, inward faces, like they were listening to instructions no one else could hear.
By the time they reached the apartment, she felt like the whole city had tilted half a degree toward them.
Angelo parked. Killed the engine. Stayed motionless for one long second.
"You want to tell me we're imagining this?" he asked.
"No."
"Good."
They climbed the stairs in damp silence.
On the second landing, the old woman's door stood open three inches. Blue television light flickered through the crack. As they passed, she spoke without looking at them.
"They don't usually mark this many walls at once."
Claudia stopped.
Angelo did too, a half-step behind her.
"Who doesn't?" Claudia asked.
The old woman turned her head slowly. Her face was a soft geography of age, but her eyes were clear enough to be unnerving.

“The Watchers,” she said. “The ones who paint before collection.” Her gaze dropped to Claudia’s hand. “Yours is warm.”

The mark answered with a sharp sting.

“What does that mean,” Claudia asked.

The old woman smiled faintly.

“It means they’ve started reading you properly.”

Then she turned back to her television, where a silent judge hammered a silent gavel into static.

Angelo unlocked the apartment and got them inside fast. He locked the deadbolt. Set the chain. Checked the windows. Checked them again.

Claudia stood in the middle of the room with the ledger bag still clutched to her chest and suddenly didn’t know what to do with her own body. Sit. Pace. Throw up. Pray. None of it felt specific enough.

The apartment was exactly the same as when they had left. The same narrow couch. The same table. The same ugly lamp by the bed. The same chipped mug in the sink.

And all of it felt thinner now.

As if reality had stretched just enough for something else to slip through.

Angelo tossed his jacket over a chair.

“You’re shaking.”

Claudia looked down.

He was right.

Her hands trembled around the ledger strap.

“It’s adrenaline.”

“It’s not just adrenaline.”

His voice was gentle enough to be dangerous.

She laughed once, sharp and humorless.

“Well, don’t stop me if I decide to have a breakdown. It seems earned.”

Angelo stepped closer.

"Claudia."

She looked up.

He was close enough now that she could see the damp caught in the dark line of his lashes. Smoke still clung faintly to him from the courthouse fire. His face was tired in a way that made him look less guarded, more human, and for some reason that made everything worse.

"My father knew," she said. "He knew enough to run. To drink. To rot in it. And I spent years thinking he was weak." Her throat tightened. "What if he was just scared."

Angelo didn't answer immediately.

Then: "He probably was."

The simplicity of it struck harder than comfort would have. No excuse. No redemption. Just fact.

Claudia set the ledger on the table, finally letting it leave her hands, and pressed her palms against her eyes.

"I don't know what I'm supposed to do with that."

"You don't have to do anything with it tonight."

That undid her more than it should have.

She lowered her hands.

He was still there. Still close. Not touching.

For a long moment neither of them moved.

Outside, sirens rose and fell across the city. Somewhere a helicopter beat the rain into a different kind of noise. Something large shattered in the distance.

Inside, the room narrowed to the space between them.

"You can still walk away," she said quietly.

Angelo actually looked offended.

"From you?"

"From this."

"Same answer."

His hand lifted as if he meant to touch her face. Hesitated. Then brushed a strand of hair away from her cheek with a gentleness that felt almost cruel after everything else the night had been.

"You think I stayed this long by accident?" he asked.

Claudia's pulse jumped.

The mark in her hand burned.

The city screamed outside.

And still the only thing she could think about was the heat of his fingers near her face.

"You should stop doing that," she said softly.

"Doing what."

"Acting like you're not worried."

A shadow of a smile crossed his mouth.

"That's the trick."

"And when the trick stops working?"

His hand slid to her waist.

"Then I stop pretending."

The room went still.

Claudia kissed him.

There was nothing careful about it.

No testing. No uncertainty.

One moment they were standing there full of smoke and fear and too much truth. The next her hands were fisted in the front of his shirt and Angelo was kissing her back like restraint had finally become a physical burden he was allowed to put down.

Her back met the wall with a soft thud.

His mouth was rough, hungry, almost angry with wanting. Claudia gasped against him, and his hand tightened at her waist as though he'd been waiting weeks for permission to hold her exactly this close.

Maybe he had.

The kiss deepened.

Everything they'd held back—every brush of tension in a hallway, every argument that had burned too hot, every time one of them had almost said something and chosen silence instead—crashed together between them.

Outside, the city kept burning.

Inside, it narrowed to heat.

Angelo pulled back just enough to look at her. His breathing was unsteady now. His eyes were darker.

"Tell me to stop," he said.

Claudia slid her hand behind his neck and pulled him back down.

That was his answer.

He kissed her harder.

His hands moved over her sides, up her back, learning her body with the kind of focus men usually reserved for weapons or prayer. Claudia felt herself come apart under the pressure of it—fear melting into something hotter, something with less language and more truth.

He lifted her as if she weighed nothing.

She wrapped her legs around his waist on instinct, and he carried her the few steps to the couch, never fully breaking the kiss.

They landed hard enough to shift the cushions.

A stack of papers slid from the armrest to the floor. Neither of them noticed.

Angelo's forehead came to rest against hers for one breathless second.

"This is terrible timing," he murmured.

Claudia laughed against his mouth, half wrecked already. "Everything about us has terrible timing."

His thumb brushed her cheek.

"You're trouble."

"You stayed."
"Yeah."
"Then stop complaining."
He laughed then—low, rough, brief—and kissed her again.
The room softened at the edges after that.
Not because the world gentled. It didn't. Sirens still haunted the streets. Smoke still climbed somewhere beyond the river. The ledger still sat on the table like a heart waiting to decide who it belonged to.
But for a little while, they let the rest of it go.
Claudia let herself feel the weight of his body, the steadiness of his hands, the strange relief of being held by someone who knew exactly how dangerous the world was and had stayed anyway. Angelo let his control slip inch by inch until it wasn't control anymore, just honesty—raw, physical, undeniable.
The city could keep its ledgers.
For that stretch of time, they belonged only to each other.
Later, the room had gone quiet again.
The lamp by the couch threw a soft amber pool across the floor. Rain ticked against the window. Somewhere below, a siren receded into distance.
Claudia lay with her head against Angelo's chest, the blanket tangled around both of them. His fingers moved lazily up and down her arm like he was proving to himself that she was still there.
Neither of them had spoken in several minutes.
It didn't feel awkward.
It felt like the first honest silence of the night.
"You're staring at the ceiling like it owes you money," she said finally.
Angelo huffed a quiet laugh.
"Just thinking."

"That's dangerous."
"Usually."
She lifted her head enough to look at him.
"Do you regret it?"
His hand stilled for half a beat.
Then resumed.
"No."
She watched his face in the low light.
"Good."
He looked down at her.
"Do you?"
Claudia's answer came easier than she expected.
"No."
His mouth softened into the smallest hint of a smile.
"Good."
She touched the scar near his collarbone lightly.
"You still haven't told me how you got this."
He glanced down at her fingers, then away.
"Wrong job. Wrong night."
"That sounds suspiciously like a non-answer."
"It is."
She sighed and let her head fall back to his chest.
Outside, another siren began.
Neither of them moved.
Then—
Scratch.
Claudia went still.
Angelo felt it immediately.
"What."
She sat up.
The sound came again.
Soft.
Dry.

Careful.
A pen writing on paper.
The ledger bag sat on the table where she had left it.
Closed. Motionless. Harmless in the way a snake looked harmless before the strike.
Scratch.
Angelo rose first, reaching automatically for the pistol on the side table.
"Stay behind me."
"That has never once stopped me."
"I know. Humor me."
They crossed the room slowly.
The sound stopped the second they reached the table.
That made it worse.
Claudia stared at the bag.
Angelo stared at the bag.
For one ridiculous second she thought: *maybe if we leave it closed, it stays hypothetical.*
Then she unzipped it.
The ledger lay inside.
Open.
The pen rested across the page.
Wet ink shone under the lamp.
Two new lines had been added beneath the last entry.
Witness — confirmed.
Collector — pending.
Below them, fresh and darker than the rest:
Contact — established.
Claudia felt all the warmth leave her body.
Angelo leaned in.
"Contact with who?"
The pen twitched.
Neither of them touched it.

The tip lowered to the page and began moving.
Slowly. Deliberately.
Vale — Claudia.
Then beneath it:
Collection window — opened.
The mark in her palm ignited hard enough to make her hiss.
Angelo's hand closed around her wrist before she even realized she'd moved.
The pen kept writing.
Resistance — anticipated.
He gave a short, humorless laugh.
"Well. At least it knows us."
Claudia closed the ledger hard enough to make the pen jump.
"No more tonight."
"You sure that matters?"
"No." She met his eyes. "But I'm tired of letting it speak first."
He studied her for a long second, then nodded once.
She slid the ledger back into the bag and pulled the zipper shut.
The room settled.
Not safely. Just temporarily.
Angelo leaned against the table.
"You realize what that means."
"That the system expects a fight."
"Yeah."
She crossed her arms.
"Then we give it one."
Outside, another distant boom rolled through the city.
Closer than the earlier ones.
The windows rattled.
Smoke drifted higher over the skyline.

Claudia walked to the window.

From up here she could see thin columns of firelight reflecting in wet rooftops. Not everywhere. Not random. Controlled strikes. Corrective ones.

The city wasn't simply burning.

It was being balanced.

Angelo came to stand beside her.

"Get any sleep," he said, "because tomorrow is going to be worse."

Claudia looked at the reflection of the two of them in the glass.

Tired. Rumpled. Bound now by more than the case.

"You always this optimistic?"

"Only when things are actively on fire."

She almost smiled.

Behind them, from inside the sealed bag—

A page turned.

Then another.

Claudia didn't move.

Neither did Angelo.

The sound stopped.

After a long moment, he said quietly, "Tell me that's not writing again."

"It's writing again."

They both kept staring out at the city anyway.

Because some terrors were easier to face reflected in glass.

Dawn came slowly.

Gray first.

Then silver.

Then the pale color of a bruise beginning to heal.

Claudia woke on the couch under the blanket, alone except for the sound of rain easing off at last.

Angelo sat at the table with the bag in front of him, arms folded, eyes on it as though he'd spent the whole night making sure it didn't crawl away.

"You didn't sleep," she said.

He didn't look over.

"No."

"How bad."

A pause.

Then: "Pretty bad."

She sat up too fast and winced.

Angelo finally turned toward her.

The look on his face was enough.

He slid the ledger bag across the table.

Claudia opened it.

The ledger was on a new page now.

Fresh ink dried at the bottom.

Not her name.

His.

Angelo — collector candidate.

And beneath it:

Evaluation — underway.

The room went hollow.

Claudia stared at the page until the letters blurred.

Then she closed the book slowly.

Angelo leaned back in the chair and gave the kind of laugh a man gives when the universe tells a joke he doesn't enjoy.

"Well," he said.

Claudia looked up at him.

The city outside kept smoking.

The archive had noticed them.

The collectors had been deployed.

And now the system had started writing both of them into the account.

She slipped the ledger back into the bag and stood.
“Get your jacket.”
Angelo’s brow lifted.
“Where are we going.”
Claudia picked up the bag, the weight of it now something personal.
“To find out who built this thing,” she said.
“And then?”
She looked at the fading firelight still haunting the skyline.
“Then we make it regret learning our names.”
Outside, the city breathed in smoke and morning and waited to see who would write the next line.

Chapter 22— The Debt Walks

Morning didn't arrive so much as settle over the city like ash.

From the apartment window the skyline looked bruised. Smoke drifted from several buildings across downtown, thin gray ribbons rising into a sky that hadn't decided whether to rain again.

Claudia stood with her arms folded, watching it.

The fires were too precise.

Not random destruction.

Records buildings.

Court annexes.

One church archive.

Every place that stored names.

Behind her, the apartment creaked quietly as Angelo leaned back in the kitchen chair.

"You're doing the thing again," he said.

Claudia didn't turn.

"What thing."

"The one where you stare at a city like you're about to cross-examine it."

She exhaled slowly.

"If the ledger is correcting debts," she said, "those fires aren't accidents."

"No," Angelo replied.

"They're erasing records."

He watched the skyline for a moment.

"Or rewriting them."

That possibility hung heavier in the air.

Claudia finally turned from the window and walked back toward the table where the ledger sat inside its bag.

It felt heavier this morning.

Not physically.

Something else.
The new entry from the night before still burned in her mind.
Angelo — collector candidate.
Evaluation — underway.
The system had begun moving pieces.
And one of those pieces was the man sitting ten feet away from her.
Angelo noticed her staring.
"You keep looking at me like I'm about to sprout horns."
"You might."
"Fair."
He rolled his shoulder slightly.
The mark there—faint, dark, almost like a bruise shaped into the hooked sigil—had deepened overnight.
The archive hadn't simply written his name.
It had started claiming him.
"Does it hurt?" she asked.
He shrugged.
"Like a sunburn that learned patience."
"That's not comforting."
"Wasn't meant to be."
Claudia stepped closer and brushed her fingers lightly across the mark.
Heat pulsed beneath her touch.
Alive.
Angelo inhaled slightly.
Not pain.
Something deeper.
Claudia withdrew her hand slowly.
"It's tethering you," she said.
"Yeah," Angelo replied. "That was my guess too."
"You're too calm about it."

He leaned forward slightly.
"I spent ten years killing people who worked for systems worse than this."
"That's not comforting either."
"No," he admitted.
"But it means I know one thing."
"What."
"Everything built on rules can be broken."
Claudia looked at the ledger bag again.
"You think this thing has rules."
"I think it runs on them."
She sighed and sat beside him on the couch.
Outside the city continued waking—car doors, footsteps, traffic slowly building.
Normal sounds.
Claudia hated how normal everything felt.
"I thought this was about my father," she said quietly.
"It was."
"But it isn't anymore."
"No."
She leaned forward.
"The system is expanding the line."
"To you."
"Yes."
"And now something after you."
Silence followed.
Claudia stared at the floor.
Angelo leaned back into the couch cushions.
"Well," he said finally.
"That's cheerful."
She shot him a look.
"You're not taking this seriously."
"I'm taking it extremely seriously."

“You don’t look like it.”
“That’s because panic doesn’t solve math.”
He gestured toward the ledger bag.
“That thing runs on accounting.”
Claudia frowned.
“You think it's predictable.”
“I think it's structured.”
“Same difference.”
“No,” Angelo said.
“Structured means we can break it.”
Claudia studied him.
“Have I ever mentioned how irritatingly optimistic you are about supernatural death systems?”
He shrugged.
“Comes with experience.”
“With what.”
“Killing people who thought they ran the world.”
She stared at him.
“That sounds like a story.”
“It is.”
“You’re not telling it.”
“Not today.”
Claudia sighed and leaned back.
For several minutes the apartment fell quiet.
Then Angelo reached over and took her hand.
His thumb brushed slowly across the mark in her palm.
The heat softened.
“You’re thinking too far ahead,” he said.
“I have to.”
“Not right now.”
“If the ledger is rewriting bloodlines—”
“Claudia.”
His voice stopped her.

She looked up.
“The city’s on fire,” he said.
“We’re marked by a supernatural bookkeeping system.”
“And someone out there is probably already being sent to collect.”
She waited.
“And you’re still trying to solve it before breakfast.”
Her laugh was quiet and exhausted.
“You say that like it's unreasonable.”
“It is.”
His fingers tightened around her hand.
“For five minutes,” he said, “stop fighting the universe.”
“That’s terrible advice.”
“Probably.”
“But you’re going to listen.”
She shook her head.
“You’re very confident.”
“Yeah.”
“Why.”
“Because I know what happens if you don’t slow down.”
“And what’s that.”
“You burn out before the system even gets a chance to kill you.”
That answer stole the argument from her.
He pulled her closer gently.
Claudia leaned into him without thinking.
Her head rested against his shoulder.
His arm wrapped around her.
Outside the sky brightened to pale gray.
Morning had arrived.
“You ever notice,” Angelo said quietly, “that the quiet moments are the ones people remember.”
Claudia frowned.

"What quiet moments."

"The ones right before everything changes."

She looked up at him.

"You're not helping the anxiety problem."

He smiled faintly.

"Just telling the truth."

She studied his face.

The scar near his collarbone.

The tired eyes.

The stubborn calm that refused to leave him even now.

"You know," she said slowly, "if you do end up becoming a collector…"

Angelo groaned.

"…you're going to be a very annoying one."

He laughed quietly.

"Yeah."

"You'll argue with the system."

"Absolutely."

"You'll try to negotiate with it."

"Definitely."

"And you'll lose."

He tilted his head.

"Maybe."

Claudia traced the scar on his chest lightly.

"You're not supposed to die in this story."

Angelo's eyes softened.

"Funny thing about stories."

"What."

"They rarely ask our permission."

The mark on his shoulder pulsed.

Both of them felt it.

Then—

Scratch.

Claudia froze.

The sound came again.

Soft.

Dry.

Ink on paper.

The ledger bag shifted slightly on the table.

Angelo reached for the pistol.

"Stay behind me."

"That has never once stopped me."

"Humor me."

They approached the table slowly.

Claudia unzipped the bag.

The ledger lay open.

Fresh ink glistened across the page.

Two lines had been added.

Witness — confirmed.

Collector — pending.

Another line began writing itself.

Slow.

Deliberate.

Contact — established.

Angelo frowned.

"Contact with who?"

The pen moved again.

Vale — Claudia.

The mark in her palm burned sharply.

Claudia inhaled.

Angelo grabbed her wrist.

"What does that mean."

She forced the words out.

"It means the system isn't just watching us."

"What is it doing."

Claudia stared at the final word forming.

Inheritance.

Silence swallowed the room.

The system had made its decision.

Angelo leaned back slowly.

“Well,” he said.

“That can’t be good.”

Claudia closed the book carefully.

“You realize what that means.”

“Yeah.”

“You’re part of the system now.”

He shrugged lightly.

“I was already involved.”

“Not like this.”

“No.”

He glanced down at the mark on his shoulder.

The hooked sigil had darkened.

Alive.

Claudia felt fear for him for the first time.

Real fear.

“Angelo,” she said quietly.

He looked at her.

“If the ledger made you a collector…”

“…then sooner or later it’s going to ask me to collect something.”

She nodded slowly.

“And if the next name it writes is mine?”

The room went still.

Angelo didn’t answer immediately.

He walked to the window and looked out at the smoke rising across the city.

When he finally spoke, his voice was calm.

“Then the system picked the wrong man.”

Claudia watched him.

And for the first time since the archive opened…
she believed him.
Outside the city burned quietly.
And somewhere beneath it all—
the ledger continued writing.

Chapter 23— Affidavit of Sin

The first sign came just after dusk.
Claudia felt it before she saw anything.
The mark in her palm burned.
Not the dull warmth it had carried all day.
This was sharper. Alive. Like something under the skin had suddenly remembered it belonged to fire.
She stopped halfway across the apartment floor.
Angelo looked up from the table where he had been watching the ledger like a man watching a loaded weapon.
"What is it?"
Claudia opened her hand.
The faint hooked symbol beneath the skin glowed faintly red.
"It's starting."
Outside, the sky had turned the color of old iron. Storm clouds rolled low over the city, swallowing what little evening light remained.
The ledger lay open.
Neither of them had touched it.
The pen beside it lifted.
Angelo stood slowly.
The mark on his shoulder answered hers with a pulse of heat.
For a moment they simply looked at each other.
They both understood.
The system had moved again.
Claudia stepped toward the table.
The page was blank.
Waiting.
Angelo watched the empty space with quiet dread.

"That's worse than when it writes."
"Yes," Claudia said.
The pen lowered.
Ink spread slowly across the page.
Each letter deliberate.
Unavoidable.
Collection — authorized.
Claudia felt the air leave her lungs.
Angelo didn't react.
He was watching the next line form.
Collector — Angelo.
The room went silent.
The words looked final.
Claudia slammed the book closed.
"No."
Angelo looked at her calmly.
"Claudia—"
"I'm not letting that thing turn you into its executioner."
"I don't think it's asking."
"I don't care."
The ledger shuddered inside the bag.
Then the apartment went quiet.
Not normal quiet.
The kind of quiet that falls when something is listening.
Angelo's eyes lifted toward the door.
"Claudia."
She followed his gaze.
The hallway outside had gone silent.
No footsteps.
No voices.
The city noise had faded like someone turning down a dial.
Then the door handle moved.
Slowly.

Claudia felt her heart slam against her ribs.
The deadbolt held.
For a moment.
Then the metal twisted.
Wood cracked.
The door bent inward.
The handle turned again.
Angelo stepped in front of her.
"Stay behind me."
"You already tried that once."
"Humor me."
The doorframe splintered.
The door swung inward.
Three figures stepped into the apartment.
They looked human the way shadows sometimes look human when they move across a wall.
Tall.
Still.
Their coats hung strangely, like fabric draped over something not entirely shaped like a person.
Each of them bore the sigil somewhere.
Burned into skin.
Carved into bone.
Stitched into cloth.
Collectors.
The air around them felt colder.
Wrong.
The first one spoke.
Its voice sounded like paper tearing.
"Collection confirmed."
The ledger behind Claudia shuddered violently.
Angelo raised the pistol.
"Well," he muttered.

"Guess that answers the question."
The collector stepped forward.
Angelo fired.
The gunshot exploded through the apartment.
The bullet struck the collector square in the chest.
The figure staggered.
For a moment Claudia thought—
Then the wound closed.
Like ink drying on paper.
Angelo fired again.
And again.
Three shots.
Three wounds.
Three disappearances.
"Right," he muttered.
"That would've been too easy."
The second collector moved.
Fast.
Angelo slammed into it before it reached Claudia.
The impact drove both of them into the wall.
Plaster cracked.
Wood splintered.
Claudia stumbled backward as the third collector advanced.
The ledger flew open.
Pages whipping violently.
Ink splattering across the paper.
Names writing themselves faster than she could read.
Angelo drove his elbow into the collector's throat.
It barely reacted.
The second one grabbed him.
The mark on Angelo's shoulder ignited.
Red light burned through his shirt.
Claudia saw it.

"Angelo!"
He tore free and slammed one of the collectors into the doorframe.
The wood shattered.
"Run!" he shouted.
"I'm not leaving you!"
The third collector reached her.
Claudia grabbed the lamp from the table and swung.
The ceramic base shattered against its head.
The collector didn't even blink.
It grabbed her wrist.
The mark in her palm exploded with heat.
The collector froze.
For one second.
That second saved her.
Angelo tackled it from behind.
All three of them crashed across the apartment floor.
Furniture overturned.
Glass shattered.
Angelo fought like a man who understood exactly what was happening.
He drove one collector into the wall.
Kicked another across the room.
The pistol fired again.
None of it mattered.
They kept coming.
Relentless.
The ledger stopped flipping.
The pen lifted.
A new line began writing.
Claudia saw it through blurred vision.
Collector — active.
Angelo slammed one of the figures against the wall again.

It grabbed his arm.
The mark on his shoulder burned brighter.
Brighter.
Claudia saw the moment he understood.
The system had already made its decision.
He looked at her.
Something in his expression softened.
"Claudia—"
The collector's hand pierced his chest.
Not violently.
Almost gently.
Like a pen entering paper.
Angelo gasped.
The room froze.
Claudia screamed.
The collectors stepped back.
Their work was finished.
The ledger snapped shut.
One of the collectors spoke again.
"Debt balanced."
Then they were gone.
The apartment fell silent.
Claudia dropped to her knees beside Angelo.
Blood soaked through his shirt.
Her hands pressed desperately against the wound.
"Stay with me."
"Claudia—"
"Don't you dare."
Her voice broke.
"You don't get to die."
Angelo smiled faintly.
"Funny thing about stories."
"Stop saying that!"

"They don't ask permission."
Her tears fell onto his face.
"I can fix this."
He coughed softly.
"No."
"You're not leaving me."
His hand found hers weakly.
"You were never going to be alone."
She shook her head violently.
"Yes I am."
"No."
His eyes drifted toward the ledger.
It had opened again.
Another line forming.
Vale line — continuation confirmed.
Angelo saw it too.
His smile softened.
"Looks like the story keeps going."
Claudia's breath trembled.
"I don't want it without you."
"You'll have more than me."
She frowned.
"What do you mean?"
Angelo glanced down toward her stomach.
Just for a moment.
Then back to her.
Understanding hit slowly.
Her breath caught.
The ledger turned another page.
Ink forming again.
Next entry — pending.
Angelo's hand trembled in hers.
"You're stronger than this city," he whispered.

“I’m not.”
“You are.”
His grip loosened.
“Tell them… I fought.”
“You did.”
“Tell them… I chose you.”
Her voice shattered.
“I will.”
Angelo exhaled slowly.
His fingers slipped from hers.
And the room went still.
Claudia stayed there beside him for a long time.
The city outside began moving again.
Traffic.
Voices.
Life continuing.
Eventually she looked at the ledger.
The final page glowed faintly.
And somewhere in the future—
a child had already been written into the story.
A child the system would one day regret allowing to exist.
Claudia closed the ledger.
And the story waited.
.

About the Author

Bel Hayes writes stories born from shadow and stitched with hope. Married to her best friend and mom to two wild-hearted boys, she fills her days with love, laughter, and just a little chaos — courtesy of two snakes, a baby tortoise, and two loyal dogs.

Having survived her own darkness, Bel channels those scars into her work, crafting tales that remind readers that light can still bloom in the ruins. When she isn't writing, she's hosting exchange students, dancing in the kitchen, dreaming up her next story about love that refuses to die.

www.ingramcontent.com/pod-product-compliance
Lightning Source LLC
LaVergne TN
LVHW020705110826
845149LV00012B/2115

9798993518107